The Gentleman an... ...ogue

Bonnie Dee & Summer Devon

ISBN 978-1-48393-921-6

Chapter One

April 6, 1813

It was a hanging offense if he got caught. Jem knew that. But he also knew he could get half a crown for the act and sleep with a full belly tonight. Now he just had to decide if the gent in the fancy waistcoat was a real customer or a troublemaker setting him up to take a fall. Another glance at the expensive carriage waiting on the street convinced him the dark-haired man was the former. A beak wouldn't get that elaborate in his attempt to set up a whore. He might approach him in a tavern or on the street and whisper a furtive request, but wouldn't hire a rich man's carriage to complete the ruse. Would he?

Jem looked into the man's eyes, trying to read them, but it was a dark night. The fog rose along with the stench from the rubbish in the alleys and crept out to claim the London streets. A man could hardly see his own hand, let alone a stranger's face, in the swirling gray.

"Will you take a ride?" the man asked again. Street slang decoded the words to mean the cove wasn't just seeking fast relief. This wouldn't be a quick tour around a couple of streets and back again. The man wanted a full ride.

Jem decided he'd give it to him. He shrugged. "Cold night. Aye, I'll take a ride with you."

The gentry cove nodded and gestured for Jem to go first into the carriage. He climbed the step and slid across the seat, breathing in the delicious aroma of leather, tobacco, and wealth. He'd wished for shelter from the frigid wind, and it appeared his wish had been granted for now. No fool, he'd take a little warmth while he could get it.

He looked out the small window at the street he knew so well—or what he could see of it through the fog and the night. The buildings looked different from this high perch, more squalid and decrepit than he'd realized. His heart beat faster; Jem was both excited and nervous at the prospect of an evening spent somewhere better. Sure, it was only for a few hours and only because this man wanted to bugger his rear. But for a few fleeting moments he'd be out of this hell and in a warm place. Maybe even a plush hotel room.

Jem studied his temporary employer as the man climbed into the carriage and sat across from him. It was as dark as the inside of a slut's cunny, but Jem could make out a few details of the man's face and figure. He was of medium height and build, not too old, but no youth either. His dark hair was cut short and brushed straight back from his high forehead. The style wasn't the high pompadour currently in fashion for society fops, nor was his cravat so elaborate that it forced his chin up. In fact, if Jem had to guess the man's status or profession, he might have said the clergy from the plainness of his dress.

"What's your name?" The low voice floated to him in the intimate darkness of the carriage like a seductive caress. Jem's cock hardened in his breeches. Tonight would be no chore at all. He'd enjoy being fucked for his supper.

"You call me whatever you like" was his stock answer.

There was a long pause before the man spoke again. "I'd *like* to know your name."

"Jem." He didn't ask for the man's name. It wasn't his place. Jem patted the seat beside him. "Do you want to come over here? I can make it a pleasant ride to wherever you're taking me."

The movement of the man's head shaking was almost indiscernible in the shadow. "No. I'd prefer…to take some time and learn a little about you."

"Fair enough." Jem bobbed his chin. "I'm a working lad. Live in Southwark, will probably die here. I've tried my hand at a number of different business ventures and found my current occupation the most lucrative."

He grinned, enjoying the sound of his own voice. He loved to mimic the swells' speech and mannerisms—his way of taunting them and showing his disdain.

"How old are you?" was the next question.

Knowing most customers liked to at least pretend they were plowing virgin territory, Jem subtracted half a dozen years from his age. "Thirteen."

His host chuckled softly, clearly not fooled into thinking week-old haddock was freshly caught. "Is that so?"

"All right. Fifteen," Jem lied again. Nineteen wasn't nearly as attractive to prospective customers. "But those extra years bring experience from which you'll greatly benefit, sir."

Another breathless laugh. Not actual amusement, and Jem wondered what the man's problem was that he had to talk and laugh instead of getting straight to work. To the good part.

"What's funny, then, sir?" Jem didn't like the frisson of fear that ghostly laugh gave him.

"Nothing at all, I expect." The voice was soft yet clipped, the voice of authority. The dark figure in the corner shifted. The gent added, almost silently, "I am quite glad one of us has some experience."

Jem wanted to laugh, make a ribald comment, but he wouldn't because he wasn't supposed to have heard.

The carriage jolted, and he grabbed for a hold. He was thrown toward the other man, knocked against the hard warmth of him. The gentleman grabbed him easily and hauled him upright, then almost threw Jem back onto the seat—away from his corner. A swell though he was—no doubt about that—the man had some muscle on him, and he moved fast for one who'd been drinking. For the instant he'd been against him, Jem dragged in a lungful of air and caught the scent of brandy.

"Didn't mean to launch myself at you, sir. Not unless invited," he said and waited for the man's laugh, which didn't come.

Jem wondered if he should mention money now or suggest the man might be hungry, because he sure as hell was gutfoundered and wouldn't mind stopping for a bite. He wasn't fool enough to bring up the matter. It was up to the gentleman to set their course. Jem repressed a sigh.

"Have you ever been out of London?"

Not a moment of his life, but why did the gent care? What was his game? "Naturally I got the country estate," Jem said. "Hunting, shooting, and what have you, all the livelong day. Cows," he added. "Sheep."

"Jem." The voice was softer than ever. "Is that short for Jeremy?"

Fine, there wouldn't be jesting, and a well-developed sense of self-preservation told Jem to stick to the truth as much as possible. "Naw. Just Jem." No last names shared between men like them.

Near the middle of the night, rumbling through the streets muffled in fog, the dark interior of the carriage—anything might happen. They slowed. Over the thud of the horses' hooves and rumble of the wheels, Jem heard his own breathing coming fast. And he felt the slight rise of fear in his gut. He was no coward, but something about the unknown, very still gentleman in the corner of the carriage touched nerves in the most unlikely places. For instance, his cock was growing even harder.

The peculiar etiquette of the situation said he shouldn't ask, but he did anyway. "Where're we off to, then, sir?" He was pleased by his attempt at cheery nonchalance.

"My home. We're nearly there."

Not married, then. Or the cat was away and the mouse was playing. Only this was no mouse. The carriage stopped, the door opened, and for the first time, Jem saw the coachman. His smile froze. "Gawd," he whispered.

The devil had been driving them. A huge, hulking devil with a great scar down his face. Two great scars. Part of an ear was gone. Jem had seen plenty of mangled and scarred souls in his time—who hadn't?—but this one would have sent the children running and screaming even before he'd lost chunks of his face. He loomed over them.

"Badgeman." Jem's host ignored Jem as he spoke to the coachman. "Take my…guest round to the kitchen. I think it best that he bathe. Some of Jonathan's clothes will fit him, I believe."

The devil driver grunted and stood back. The gent stepped out. He nodded at the hideous coachman. Their faces were easy to make out by the oil lantern. They wore the same grim expression. Blank. Dark. Jem could read nothing warm or good in those two.

Jem swallowed hard and wondered if this was the moment he jumped out and ran to freedom. But curiosity, an empty stomach, and the knowledge that he carried a handy little knife kept him still. And desire. Don't forget that, he mocked himself. He'd been in a state of semiarousal since getting into the big rattling carriage.

Before he could slide out of the carriage, the driver ordered "wait." The door slammed shut. Jem clutched the knife and sat forward in the dark. He didn't have to wait long. The carriage lurched. The horses walked forward for less than thirty seconds.

When the door opened again, the monster stood outside, haloed by fog, his boots and the bottom of his long black greatcoat surrounded by the stuff so he looked as if he were rising from the swirling smoke of hell.

Jem tucked away the blade and stepped out as if he were royalty exiting a coach in front of a cheering crowd. He had an unfortunate method for facing fear: annoy whoever provoked it. At the moment it felt as if he had no choice. "Mr. Badger," he drawled and bowed.

"Badgeman," the man rumbled. "Come, then." He turned on his heel and strode toward a door.

Jem looked the building up and down. Large, granite, imposing. And this was the servants' entrance. "So, Badger." He did a passable imitation of cheeriness. "How many men have you two lured into this den of yers? Regular activity, is it? Once a week you two go out, pick up an unsuspecting young cove, and bathe him?"

The groom turned and stared at him. "Never before."

Jem believed him. Poor Badger fretted over his employer for good reason, then. "Ah, that's why you're worried? You're the monster, not me. I ain't out to harm your master."

"Worried about you?" For the first time something like a smile twisted the man's face. Only one side. The other side of his mouth was cut by a scar that ran from his cheek to his chin. The cut must have hit something that made it impossible to smile.

"Then you always look like you lost your best friend? You and your master?"

The single eyebrow went up. Badgeman didn't move for a moment, and then he said, "Badajoz. 'Tis the anniversary."

"Oh." Jem had no idea who or what a Badajoz was, although the word sounded familiar. "Anniversaries are the devil, ain't they? Hardly bear it when that date rolls round again. All them bad memories. Or do I mean good ones?"

"Shut it," Badgeman said without heat. "Wait out here." He went inside the building, and Jem leaned against the wall. He shoved his trembling hands into his tattered waistcoat pockets.

Softly, so none of the neighbor houses could hear, he began to whistle a bawdy song. Quality didn't usually bring a man like him home. Didn't want to shit where they lived, so to speak. It was a dangerous proposition to let a street lad in. The servants might gossip about what their master was up to, or the dirty rascal might nick the best silver. Lord Muckety-muck was either a naive fool or confident that Jem wouldn't dare cross him.

A chill breeze cut through his coat, and Jem hunched his shoulders, shivering. One more minute; that's all he'd give, and then he was leaving, even though it meant hoofing it all the way back to Crowder Street.

The back door opened, and the mountain filling its frame beckoned him. "Come in. Your bath's ready."

Jem made a show of sniffing himself. "What, am I a little too rank for his lordship?"

"In here." The Badger directed him through the entryway to the kitchen. A fire burned low on the hearth, and a copper tub filled with steaming water stood before it. Jem had never had more than a quick scrub in a basin of water in his entire life, unless one counted an occasional swim in the Thames on a hot summer's day.

He stared at the water, then at the coachman or manservant, whichever he was. "You want me to get in that?"

The big man had taken off his coat and wore only his shirtsleeves and braces. He folded his arms over his chest. "Strip."

"With you watchin'? Are you gonna scrub me too, while the master looks on? I'd have to charge extra for that."

It was like talking to a rock. The man showed no expression. "Take off your clothes, and wash yourself. There's soap and a rag on the stand by the tub and a towel to dry off with after."

Jem considered for a moment, but just then, the wind rattled the windowpane, and he knew he didn't want to go back out into the cold just yet. He'd see how this played out and hope he didn't find himself later with his throat cut, dead in an alley. He shrugged off his coat, let it drop to the floor, and began to unbutton his shirt.

Old Badger gazed off into space, not watching him. He was there to guard the silver, no doubt. Wise decision.

Jem took off his shoes and breeches, and when he was completely naked, he padded across the cold flagstones to the bath and tested it with one hand. The water was deliciously warm. He glanced over his shoulder at the servant, but the man was still giving him privacy by ignoring him completely.

Gingerly Jem stepped over the edge of the tub, and his leg sank into the water. He paused for a moment, almost afraid to take his other foot off the floor. But he couldn't hang there forever, so he took the plunge.

As he sank into the water, the level rose until he was covered nearly to his neck. Once he'd adjusted to the heat and the odd sensation of floating, he found it heavenly. He reached for the flannel, wet it, and rubbed it over the soap. He scrubbed his face and rinsed it with a quick dip, the suds stinging his eyes. Then he washed the rest of his body leisurely, resuming his whistling as he soaped and splashed.

"The hair too. Master don't want your fleas hopping through his house."

Jem kept his mouth shut for once and did as he was told, submerging his head completely underwater and scrubbing his hair with the soap. Wasn't his place to argue if his customer wanted him clean, and truth to tell, the bath wasn't so bad. The heated water relaxed his muscles till they felt like jelly and warmed him to his very bones.

"Hurry along now," Badger urged as the water grew colder.

Jem reluctantly rose, toweled off his torso, then stepped out of the water, leaving a puddle on the floor, and dried his legs. He slung the towel around his hips and stared at Badgeman. "Now what?"

"Clothes are there. Put 'em on."

Jem picked up the trousers from the pile on the wooden chair. They were smooth broadcloth, finer than any fabric that had ever touched his body. The shirt was soft linen, white and as clean as snow before chimney soot got mixed up in it. So he was playing a role, then, maybe the part of someone Lord Fancy had loved and lost, which would explain all the talk about anniversaries. He'd give the gentleman his money's worth, put on his best impression of gentry, talk high-class, and pretend the bath had washed the stink of the gutter from him.

When Jem had dressed from his skin out, including slipping his feet into high, buckled shoes that were a bit too tight, he turned to Badgeman and drawled in a nasal tone, "Very well, then. I'm ready to meet his lordship. Lead on, sirrah."

ఌ

Alan sank deep into the cushions of the wing chair that faced the fireplace in his study. The room had become his lair, his den from which he rarely emerged these days. He'd brooded here so much, he was losing his muscle tone, the fit shape from years of riding that had served him well on the battlefield. Soon he'd be nothing more than a lumpish, nearly middle-aged man perched on this chair like a gargoyle, slowly drinking himself to death.

Enough dwelling on a future he had no interest in facing. Tonight's venture to Southwark was part of it. He'd decided to allow himself one last bit of pleasure. The youth standing outside the tavern had caught his eye, but mostly his ear with his joyful laughter. Christ, how could anyone living in the hellish stew of Southwark sound so damned happy?

Alan had drifted closer, intrigued. That was when the rest of his senses had been engaged. The lad was handsome, with a smooth, clear-skinned face framed by dirty, disheveled brown hair. His bone structure was strong, with a firm chin, sharp jaw, straight nose, and high cheekbones. But the feature that truly riveted Alan was the young man's eyes, so wide and blue. Even in the dim light from the smudged windows of the pub, Alan could see their pale clarity. They were as guileless as a child's, yet perversely knowing. He'd wanted to take the lad's hand and pull him off the street, take him away someplace and bathe in that joyful laughter.

The youth, Jem, had turned from the friend to whom he was speaking and focused on Alan.

“Good evening, sir. Cold night, eh?”

From there he'd turned the conversation to “What's yer pleasure?” and Alan had found himself offering a ride. This was the young man he wanted to share his bed with. Just once. Just tonight on the anniversary of the horror of Badajoz, the day the siege ended. The boy would be gone before morning, and if he was strong enough to go through with it, so would Alan.

The erection he'd sported on the ride home in the carriage had flagged while he waited for his guest to get cleaned up and dressed. Now he was half regretting his decision to bring the lad home at all. Hell, he should pay Jem the half crown or whatever it was he owed him and have Badgeman take him back where he'd come from.

But a soft rap on the door of the study set his cock raging again. It rose like a saluting soldier at the very thought of seeing the handsome young man again.

Badgeman opened the door and stepped inside. “Your guest, sir.”

Jem followed him into the study and stood looking around while Badgeman discreetly disappeared.

Alan caught his breath. The man was more handsome than ever. His hair, wet from the bath, was slicked back and held in a small queue at the nape. Jonathan's clothes fit him quite well, if a little short at the cuffs and ankles. Jem hadn't attempted to knot the cravat, and Alan saw the piece of fabric peeking out from his jacket pocket. How familiar the jacket was. He remembered his brother wearing it often, as it was one of his favorites. Hell, they should've buried him in it instead of the suit his aunt had chosen.

Suddenly Alan could hardly bear to look at the young man standing before him. What had he been thinking of, having him dress in his dead brother's old clothes?

“What a fine establishment you have here. Very impressive.”

Jem's attempt at a cultured accent wasn't half bad but so exaggerated, it almost made Alan smile. He gestured to the chair across from him. “Please sit.”

“Don't mind if I do.”

He perched on the edge of the seat, forearms on his knees, and gazed at Alan. The firelight flickered, sending light and shadow dancing over his beautiful face. His blue eyes shone as luminous as stars. Alan swallowed. He couldn't tear his own away from that sapphire gaze.

“So, now you've got me all cleaned up and presentable, what are you going to do with me?” His voice was huskier, deeper than before. The sound of it tugged on Alan's cock like an invisible thread. His stomach flipped, and his erection grew harder.

“Would you like a drink?” Suddenly as nervous as an unbroken colt, Alan rose from his chair and went to the sideboard to pour a goblet of brandy from the decanter. He resisted the urge to down a shot and refill before carrying the glass over to his guest.

Those astonishing blue eyes gazed up at Alan, and he could barely breathe. His hand shook slightly as he offered the glass to the handsome young man who hardly looked the part of a whore.

Cleaned up and clothed in Jonathan's castoffs, he could've been a student home on holiday from university...or with those soulful, innocent eyes, an angel. Then he opened his mouth, and the illusion of innocence vanished.

"What you got for me beneath them trousers?" Jem set the brandy on a nearby table and reached to brush the back of his hand against the bulge in Alan's trousers.

He gasped and jerked away as a bolt of lightning shot through his crotch from the casual touch. Alan could easily count the number of times he'd surrendered to his need for a sex partner. This wasn't something he indulged in regularly, and even though he'd brought the lad home for this purpose, he couldn't help his shock and his shame.

"What? You don't like to be touched?" Jem lowered his lids. His seductive look made Alan's stomach flip. "Maybe you'd rather watch till you get a little more used to me, eh?"

With that, he reached for the front of his shirt and unbuttoned it, revealing no underlinen, only his smooth, muscled chest. He trailed his hand from his collarbone over his chest, then down his taut abdomen to the fly of his trousers, which he then began to unfasten. Before Alan could summon enough saliva in his dry mouth to form words like "No. Not here. Wait. I'm not ready," the young man already had his erect cock out of his pants. It thrust, hard and proud, from the nest of brown hair between his thighs. Jem stroked its length while focusing his gaze on Alan. He ran his tongue over his lips, making them glisten, and gasped softly as he pumped his dick with his fist.

Alan couldn't drag his gaze from the thick column and the purple head protruding from its foreskin. From the torn knuckles of

Jem's fist, it looked as if he'd been in a fight recently, which suggested he was more than a pretty face. He knew how to handle himself and to survive in one of London's grittiest slums.

Guilt washed over Alan. It was wrong to take the body this young man sold through necessity, but he couldn't resist now if he tried. He wanted to touch him so badly—to feel his smooth, clean skin, smell his hair, taste his cock. He wanted to fill him and to be filled, to spend the night curled into the warmth of another body. He *needed* to experience the union with another human being, which he'd denied himself for so long.

Once. Just once more. Maybe God will forgive me.

He took one step forward and another, then knelt in front of the chair while setting his glass on the floor. Jem slid his hand down his cock to the base and tilted it toward him like an offering.

Alan's breath sounded harsh to his own ears as he leaned in and rested his hand on one of Jem's hard thighs. A single pearl beaded on the dark head of the other man's cock. It seemed to fill his vision as he bent closer. Alan slipped his tongue from between his lips and tasted it—that one perfect drop, musky, salty, satisfying.

The young man sighed. "That's good. Now take me inside."

Alan obliged, happy to obey his command. He sucked the head then the entire length of that sturdy cock into his mouth, feeling the smoothness of velvet skin against his tongue. The tip hit the back of his throat, and he nearly gagged before pulling back.

"Wrap your hand around it like so." Jem continued to tutor as if he were the master and Alan the novice—which was right. For all his youth, the lad probably had years more experience doing this than Alan did, and he seemed to instinctively understand his client didn't want to take the lead. It was a relief to surrender control and just feel the sensations as they washed over him.

A hand settled on his head and petted him, stroking his hair. “Feels so good. Didn't expect this tonight.” His voice was rough. He gave a little grunt as Alan's teeth scraped the underside of his shaft.

“Now look at me,” he commanded as imperiously as a prince. “Look up. Don't be ashamed 'cause you like cocks. Lots o' coves do, you know. More than you'd think.”

It was harder than Alan expected, but he'd led troops into battle against overwhelming odds; he could surely meet and hold a street boy's gaze. He looked up the lightly haired stomach and ridged abdomen to the muscled chest, a half crescent of brown nipple peeking out on either side of the open white shirt. He studied the corded muscles of Jem's neck, his strong chin and sensuous lips, his jutting nose, and at last, his translucent eyes, all without breaking his rhythm. As Alan sucked and pumped with his fist, he registered the pleasure in the younger man's eyes.

The hand resting softly on his head suddenly clutched his hair and twisted, pulling his head away. “Stop now. Don't want me to come too soon, do you?” Jem gasped.

But Alan did want him to come. He wanted to see his face transported in ecstasy and watch his cock erupt, semen spilling over his fist and spurting onto Jem's belly. Alan's cock was as hard as the walking stick with the gold lion knob which still gathered dust in the umbrella stand in the front hall, but there'd be plenty of time for his own relief later. Right now he was desperate to see Jem come.

"Go ahead," he murmured low. "I want to see it." Alan encircled his girth and began to pump harder, drawing his hand over the head with each stroke.

Jem groaned and thrust his hips. He clutched the wide arms of the chair and let his head roll against the back. His pale throat was exposed. Alan could see the pulse jumping in its hollow. Jem's lips were parted, damp, pink. His long lashes lay against his cheeks, so beautiful. Alan rubbed his erection against the other man's leg while he continued to massage him to climax.

"Gawd," Jem grunted, and his body bowed up off the chair as his seed spurted from his cock and landed halfway up his chest. Alan groaned and thrust harder against his leg, too many layers of fabric keeping his cock from the touch it sought.

Collapsing back into his seat, the young man opened his eyes. He stared down at Alan with eyes hazy with desire and so dilated they appeared more black than blue.

"Thank you very much, sir. You're most kind." Jem smiled at his own mimicry of upper-crust tones. "Now you must let me return the favor. I insist."

Alan rose abruptly, his throbbing cock scraping painfully against the fabric of his drawers. "I want you, now. In my bed."

"As you wish, sir. I'm at your command."

Chapter Two

The fire had been banked low in Alan's room, so it was slightly cool, the way he liked it for sleeping—not that he slept much. And tonight he was hot enough without an external source of heat. Simply looking at Jem, his cocky strut as he preceded Alan into the bedroom and the impish glance he cast over his shoulder, was enough to make Alan's body burn.

"Nice set o' rooms you got." Jem looked around the dimly lit chamber at the heavy oak furniture, the burgundy velvet draping the bed, and the thick carpet on the floor. He pointed to the map of the Iberian Peninsula, which hung over the mantel and was covered with markings. "You a military man? Thought you might be from the way you carry yourself."

Alan glanced at the map he studied every day, the battles marked, the troop movements noted, and then he turned his back on it. "I don't want to talk about that."

"Fair enough." Jem nodded. "There's more interesting things to do."

With that, he slipped his open shirt down his arms and let it drop to the floor. Alan caught his breath. The fading glow of the fire burnished his pale body, turning it golden. The muscles of his shoulders, arms, and chest were delineated by shadows that sculpted him and turned him into a living statue—almost too perfect to be real.

"More?" Jem didn't wait for a reply, but reached for the fly of his trousers. In a trice, he'd kicked off his shoes and stripped off the rest of his clothes.

Alan remained frozen, content to merely gaze at his body for the moment. Soon he'd be touching every bit of that handsome flesh, but anticipation was enough for now.

"Like what you see?" Jem's smile was smug, as if he knew he looked good and wasn't the least ashamed to be nude.

"You going to drink that?" He indicated the glass of brandy which Alan had carried upstairs with him. Jem had left his behind in the study, untouched. Now he crossed the room and took the goblet from Alan's hand to sip the amber liquid. His eyes widened at the taste. "Very nice. Better than gin."

The understatement startled a laugh from Alan. "Yes, it is." He accepted the glass back and took a large sip to settle his giddy nerves. Placing the brandy on the mantel, he turned to his naked guest once more.

Jem was about half a head shorter than him, so he had to look up to meet Alan's eyes. The young man studied his face, and for a moment, Alan thought he was going to lean in and kiss him. Instead Jem reached for the buttons on the front of Alan's shirt and began to unfasten them.

Alan stood silent, as compliant as a child being changed by its nursemaid, while the other man removed his shirt. Calloused palms slid over his bare shoulders and stroked his arms. They roamed across his chest, grazing his nipples and making him hiss with pleasure. Jem touched every inch of flesh as it was revealed, first with his hands, then with his mouth. His lips and tongue skated over the icy layer Alan had worn for so long and melted it. Skin tingling, heart pounding, and dark despair abated, Alan felt as energized as he had the minutes prior to combat, but with none of the anxious trepidation. Excitement filled him, and he clenched and released his fists by his sides while he submitted in restive stillness to Jem's exploration.

The young man traced the pale, jagged scar on his biceps with a light touch of his fingertips, then leaned to kiss it. He spent some time examining the larger gash on Alan's side, where a musket ball had taken a chunk of flesh. He carefully touched the horrible puckered scar before bending to kiss that wound too.

Alan bit down, clenching his jaw tight and blinking away the sudden stinging in his eyes. The emotions that simple act evoked were too powerful. He wanted to push Jem away, but just then, the lad moved lower, away from the scar.

His clever hands slipped down Alan's twitching stomach to his trousers and began their work there. Soon he'd stripped off his shoes, trousers, and drawers, leaving Alan standing naked and exposed in front of him.

Kneeling, Jem stroked his hands up Alan's legs from ankles to hips, making his legs tremble. He paused at the nearly healed scar on Alan's thigh—the wound which would've cost him his leg had the army surgeon, Schivvers, had his way. Jem kissed that awful red mark too before pressing his lips to Alan's hip bone.

He kissed and licked a path across his groin but navigated around the erect cock thrusting toward him. His teasing avoidance continued until Alan was nearly shaking with need.

At last his persecutor took his penis in hand, gripping it in a strong fist as he looked up into Alan's face. Jem guided the head slowly to his lips, stuck out his pink tongue, and flicked it over the flushed tip.

Alan groaned. He reached toward Jem's tousled brown hair, wanting to hold the man's head while he drove into his mouth. But he held back, digging his fingernails hard into his palms instead, afraid to take what he wanted. His hips, however, thrust of their own volition, reaching for what he still denied he needed.

The heat and wetness surrounding him, the hard sucking that threatened to draw the very life from him, and the steady rhythm of Jem's hand gliding up and down his shaft quickly brought Alan to the precipice. His pent desire would not allow him to hold out long, he knew, and he wanted more than Jem's mouth on his cock. Giving another groan, he pulled away.

The youth rose to face him and take his hand. "Come on, then." He pulled him toward the bed, drew back the counterpane, and lay on the mattress, bringing Alan down with him.

"How do you want it? Front, side, or back?" The husky voice was nearly enough to make Alan climax right then. To be asked that question so casually—as if buggery weren't a punishable crime by law, as if people wouldn't revile a man if he admitted to it, as if the act were perfectly normal—took his breath away.

He hadn't even known the front was possible. The few times he'd indulged his urge it had been standing up, a rushed grappling in an alley, and later, the back room of some tavern. "From behind" had been assumed. That's how he wanted it now. He wasn't ready to look into Jem's face while he fucked him.

Guessing his answer, Jem flipped over. Alan could barely swallow, his throat was so dry. He reached out a tentative hand and stroked the long stretch of the man's back from between his shoulder blades down to his softly rounded bum. His skin was velvety smooth despite a few light scars. How could this youth live the rough life he did and be so unblemished? And Alan didn't mean that in a purely physical way. There was a lightness, a sense of a soul untouched by the vagaries of life, that imbued Jem's very being. Cheerful. Buoyant. As if his terrible circumstances hadn't stolen his hope yet. What was his secret?

Alan stopped worrying about it as he indulged in exploring the young man's backside. He slipped a finger between the globes of his buttocks and traced the rim of the puckered hole there. His cock twitched with the desire to be buried inside it. The head was weeping drops, so ready to release Alan thought he might explode any second.

He reached for the drawer of the table by his bed, where he kept the oil he used when frigging himself on many a solitary night. He dropped a dollop of the slippery ointment in his palm and slid it down his shaft, gritting his teeth at even that slight friction. Moving onto his knees between the man's spread legs, he reached for Jem's bottom again and massaged his fingers into the tight opening between his cheeks.

He stretched and probed with one finger, then two. The other man raised his bum, pushing back onto his fingers and groaning in pleasure. "Deeper," he murmured.

Alan couldn't take another moment. He had to be inside. Guiding his slick cock to the widened opening, he pressed the tip inside then pushed, grunting as the resistant ring of muscle clenched around him.

"That's it, sir. Fuck me. Bugger me good," Jem growled.

The filthy words were like a riding crop to a horse's flank. Alan groaned and thrust harder, impaling himself deeply in the tight heat that surrounded him. The sound of the other man's quiet moan was another spur urging him on.

Pressing a hand between Jem's shoulder blades, he pinned him to the bed and pulled his cock from the sweet fire of his body before plunging in again. His groin slapped against the other man's rear, and sweat built between their heaving bodies as they clashed together, both striving toward ecstasy.

Alan angled his body lower, bracing himself against his hands, now on either side of Jem's shoulders. He wanted to feel the slide of flesh on flesh, his chest against the other man's back, softly curling brown hair mere inches from his face. Only a sliver of Jem's profile was visible to him, but he could see thick lashes resting against his cheek and the slight parting of his lips.

"Harder now," Jem urged. "Finish it."

Once more the whip nipped his flank, and Alan thrust deeper yet, surrounding himself in solid flesh. The friction of their two bodies created a nearly unbearable heat. He could no longer hold back the rolling thunder inside him. Like the approaching hoofbeats of an attacking army, the growing sensations pounded through his defenses and exploded in a powerful climax. He thrust once more, cried out, and orgasmed with a shudder.

Beneath him, Jem bucked and twisted, either trying to unseat him or experiencing a release of his own. Then both men lay still, breathing hard and meshed together like fighters winded from a long combat in which neither would yield.

Alan reveled in the feeling of the warm, sweating body fused to his own—the muscle and bone and coursing blood, the smell and taste and feel of another person in his arms. This nearness was what he'd craved for so long, and for a few precious moments, he was content, at peace.

But the dark creature dwelling deep within him rolled over and raised its monstrous head. Already his bliss was evaporating. It couldn't last. Jem wasn't his lover. He was merely a whore from the streets. Soon he'd be gone, and Alan would be alone with his ghosts.

Alan pulled himself apart from the other man and rolled onto his back. He was sticky and sweaty and felt filthy. What they'd done wasn't beautiful. It no longer felt like a revelation, but the dirty, animalistic act it was—unwholesome and impure.

He laid an arm over his eyes and wished the man sighing and stretching beside him would disappear so he could get on with the next part of his evening. This had been his last bit of pleasure on earth. Now let him inflict the last bit of pain and be done with it.

Chapter Three

His lordship appeared to have fallen asleep. Jem watched the man's unmoving form, one arm shielding his eyes, and wondered if he should poke him awake so he could get paid and get on his way. *Should've taken the money first.* And he would have if it'd been a regular job with the hand or the mouth in an alley. But since Lord Melancholy had been intent on having a full ride, the rules changed. It wasn't the thing to demand money up front when the customer wanted the illusion he was bedding a lover.

Maybe he wanted to have another go in a bit before he sent Jem away. If so, this could turn out to be a more lucrative night than anticipated. He simply had to be patient. But it grated on his nerves, not knowing how much he was being paid or when. Some of these rich gents could get suddenly stingy when the act was over, or even refuse to pay at all. Fucked if he'd let *that* happen. No way was he walking out of here empty-handed.

Jem glanced around the room, considering what he could easily nick if given the opportunity. His stomach grumbled. Too bad his lordship didn't keep a plate of biscuits in his bed chamber. The man could use some fattening up.

Jem examined the gent. His lean, concave belly rose and fell slowly enough he might be asleep, sprawled on the elegant bed. Not so elegant now that Jem had spilled on those fine sheets. He grinned remembering that pleasure. The lordship might be untutored in fucking, but he had passion enough to stir a dead man, and Jem wasn't close to dead—although if he didn't get some coins and eventually some food, he'd be flirting with the grave. That candlestick would fetch a few shillings, but it would show no matter where he tried to hide it on his person. Another grin at the thought of stuffing it down the front of his trousers. He padded over to the mantel. Nothing that would fit in his pockets. Besides, Badger would search him, no doubt about that.

Right then, the shillings he'd rightfully earned.

Still naked, he moved back to the bed and shuffled across the vast expanse on his hands and knees. Softer linen than any he'd touched in all his years, he thought, and he stopped for a moment to run a hand over the material. Maybe he could nick the counterpane as payment, although he'd be sad to part with it if he managed to smuggle it out of the place. Naw. He'd wake the gent, sweetly.

Jem stared down at the body, which seemed frozen stiff by some tension. If Jem leaned in to lick that delicious dip at the base of milord's throat, he'd likely get the man's hands wrapped around his neck and none too gently.

"Hoy," he whispered instead.

Nothing.

He reached out and prodded the man with a forefinger. Sure enough, the gent's hand flew to grab his finger. Fast and strong.

"Ow," Jem said, though he wasn't in pain.

"What do you want?" The man's voice was low, dangerous. He hadn't been sleeping after all—hadn't slept in some time if those shadows under his dark eyes meant anything.

Jem sat back on his heels. He could say "a sixpence at minimum, sir" and likely be on his way, but that would be too easy. This gentleman's hooded, bleak eyes challenged him to leave be, and that just made him want to prod some more. No matter how many times his mum had told him about curiosity and the cat, he never could get the lesson through his thick head.

"Why sir, what does any man want? A pot to piss in. Warmth in winter. Cool in summer." He waved a hand in a circle, as if conjuring the answer. "Laughs, of course. A hundred pounds a year. No, make it three thousand. Pray tell, what do *you* want?"

"Nothing."

"True enough, you want for nothing."

For a moment, a corner of the man's tight mouth twitched. Humor? Anger? "You mistake me, Jem. I crave nothing." No mistaking that tone. Jem heard bleak anguish. And the man confirmed it with a faint breath of the word "oblivion."

And somehow lying in this chamber finer than any Jem had ever beheld, a fire to take the chill from the air, probably more food than he could eat in a month, this man had allowed despair to seize him. What an arsehole.

Jem's breath stuttered with rage. He pushed close, one knee on the bed, and leaned over the man. Let the bigger, stronger attack. He drawled. "Ah, yes. Must be quite dull as can be, well fed, fine garments to wear. Heigh-ho with no fight left in you. Nothing to fight for, Lord Cowardly." He was so close at that moment, he could smell the brandy on the other man and the scent of sex and sweat. That mix, along with the surge of anger, set off the swirl of lust deep in his gut. Almost as strong as the hunger.

Give his lordship credit, he didn't so much as flinch or look away. "Do you think you know?" he whispered, and the vein in his temple showed, his well-formed mouth went thin. His nostrils flared. The impressive brow lowered. "You don't know shite, boy. Nothing."

Jem's good humor had returned. He rarely held anger long. A spark, a flash of rage, and it was gone. He moved back from the gent, gave him some breathing room. "Now here's a surprise, sir. You don't like being taunted." He plunked down on the edge of the bed, cool soft sheets against his bare bum, twisting sideways to hold the gent's gaze. "So I'll stop since I have a healthy respect for your ability to have me hanged, drawn and quartered, dipped in tar, and given the cut direct by all manner of good company. But you say I don't know shite? I do indeed know shite, although not the piles what you've waded through."

He examined the grim lord up and down and wished he could use his hands and mouth to explore. "You're a military man, and I'd give good odds those scars are signs of your hard service. Not that they make that body of yours any less toothsome, if you don't mind my saying so, sir."

The man's steady gaze shifted from Jem's face at last. Did the gent blush? Jem hoped so.

"But you're right enough, sir," Jem said. "I don't know what could bring a man—a gentleman, I should say—such as yourself to crave oblivion. Truth to tell, I can't imagine life could bring anyone to such a pass. I mean, there's always some promise, eh? Something ahead. The next friendly touch."

Here he didn't stop himself, briefly laying his palm on that powerful thigh, which was warm with a slight trace of rough hair. There might be a pucker of scars, but the flesh under his hand was so firm and sweet, his mouth watered.

When the man flinched, Jem moved his hand away but kept talking as if he hadn't noticed. "And if you're living like a hermit and hate humanity, well then, there's the next warm day to look forward to. Or the chance to see Bully Tate fall on his bum when he's preaching at the speaker's corner. So if I can't fadge the love of death, it's a lacking of imagination on my part. Sir."

"You're a stranger to despair?" The gentleman seemed to have released some of his own anger as well, and a flicker of curiosity lit his dark eyes.

"No, sir, not me. We're close acquaintances, me and Mr. Des Pair. On first name terms, you might say. But mostly it's when the promise of death, not life, is dangled in front of me that I meet up with the bastard."

The gentleman pulled himself up. He winced, and the lines on his face deepened, as if this look of pain was his habitual expression. He thrust the pillows against the massive bedstead and leaned back, lounging like a king. He moved without thinking, obviously used to sleeping on a heap of pillows. A bed of feathers and luxury, and a man couldn't look more grim.

"Jem," he whispered. And Jem wasn't sure if he'd actually said the word. Maybe he was imagining things. At that moment, his belly gave a loud protest, and he clapped a hand to it. "Beg your pardon, sir."

The man blinked, and a slow frown furrowed his brow. Confusion, not anger. "You're hungry?"

Jem didn't roll his eyes. "A bit." He winked. "Good thing you weren't asleep, or I mighta eaten you."

The gent didn't seem to catch the double meaning. Jem eyed the tidy limbs and good-sized cock displayed on the bed and wondered if he could get away with a demonstration. He abandoned the plan when the man slid across to the floor. Wrapping a sheet around his lean hips, he went to a bell pull. He hesitated, tossed his covering away, and reached for his drawers.

"Get dressed," he ordered.

Oh hell. "If you insist, sir." Jem swallowed his disappointment and then the pride that he couldn't afford. "But there is a matter of payment and—"

"Later. I'm ordering some food."

"Ah." For once Jem was at a loss for words.

He didn't have to go back out into the cold and scratch up a meal.

As he reached for his borrowed trousers, he was surprised to see his hand trembled. The gent pulled on his shirt, and the two of them silently dressed without meeting each other's eyes. The room reeked of sex, but they'd pretend nothing had occurred. Jem wanted to laugh. No, more than that, he wanted to make this man laugh, flat out roar with laughter. Those dry, humorless little chuckles didn't count. The cynical bastard would laugh before Jem was through.

The badger came to the summons. Jem didn't know much about a house like this, but he knew it was odd that a coachman would act as butler too. He'd wager neither man would bother to explain the arrangement.

"Evening, Badge," Jem said and, sure enough, was ignored. He leaned against the massive bedstead, his hands shoved in the pockets of his posh new jacket, watching the two men talk quietly at the door. Damned if the badger didn't give a salute and a funny half smile at something the gent said.

"What amused your badger?" Jem asked as the door closed.

"He's glad to fetch food."

"Worried you don't eat enough, I reckon. Right motherly sort. I can just see him wrapped in a holland apron, clucking at you, all dismayed you didn't finish up your nice porridge," Jem said and was pleased that the gent's mouth quirked up at that.

He indicated a table with two chairs set in the corner by the fireplace. A chessboard was on the table, set up with a game in progress. "We'll sit there."

"I'll move that, shall I?" Jem carefully lifted the board and froze when one of the pieces tumbled off.

"It doesn't matter." The gent pointed at the floor. "Dump it there."

Jem eyed the pieces as he set them carefully in the dark corner. Ivory, if he didn't miss his mark. Even one or two would fetch a nice price. He squatted over the board, his back to the gentleman, and slid a couple into this pocket, running his fingers over the smooth, polished surface. Lovely things.

Taking a seat across the empty table from his host, Jem folded his arms. He suddenly felt a bit awkward at the change in location. He knew what was expected of him in bed, but wasn't quite so sure what his client wanted from him now—more flirting and salacious remarks, or a weightier conversation.

His miserable lordship seemed equally ill at ease. He too had his arms crossed over his chest. Well, it was Jem's job to make sure the man had a good time—the better to earn a large tip—so he filled the silence.

"I see you're keeping track of the war." He indicated the map on the wall with pins marking cities and troop movements. "You home on leave or mustered out?"

For some reason, that question earned a bitter smile. "I'm finished with my military service."

"That's good, then." As Jem fished for something else to say, a light dawned on him. "Badajoz! I knew that name sounded familiar. It was a big battle, hey?"

The frown returned. "Not merely a battle. It was a place, a city full of people trying to live their lives."

"Your Badgeman said this was the anniversary."

He replied with a grunt. His morose expression was locked into place again, any hint of good humor extinguished.

"Must've been hell," Jem said, hesitant for once. "I heard there were lots of casualties."

"Yes."

"Sorry. A memory like that'd put anyone in a right foul mood."

Another grunt, and he shifted in his chair. "I'd prefer not to discuss the war," he warned for the second time.

"Of course." Jem couldn't stay seated any longer. He popped up and walked over to where the brandy had been abandoned. He took a long sip, felt the liquid sear his throat, and then carried the glass back to the table and offered it to his host.

"Here. Have a nip to keep the chill at bay." And it was growing chilly in the room as the fire smoldered lower.

The man drank deeply without grimacing at the potent brew. Jem guessed Lord Gloomy had been drinking long and hard since he'd been back from the war. He'd like to erase the sorrow from the man's face. Among his mates, Jem had always been the jester, the one who could get any sour scowler to smile.

"Is there a name I can call you, sir?" He made his voice soft and cajoling, weaving a spell of intimacy between them. "Just for tonight."

"Alan." He gave no title or last name, which was to be expected.

Jem nodded. "Alan. Lovely to meet you."

Silence wrapped around them like a silken cocoon holding them close together. Jem was caught by those mournful, dark brown eyes and found himself leaning inexorably toward the other man. In a moment their lips would touch.

A light tap on the door broke the spell. Jem jerked upright. Alan called, "Come in," and the door swung open.

Badgeman entered bearing a tray. The smell of hot tea and buttered toast assailed Jem, making his stomach turn and leap in excitement. His mouth watered, and he swept his tongue over his lips, watching avidly as the servant set the silver tray on the table. It was laden with cold meats, cheeses, toast, and a pile of dried fruit.

Jem took his seat, perched on the edge, as eager as a dog ready to perform tricks for a bone. He swallowed and laced his fingers together on his lap to keep from reaching out and grabbing food in both hands.

Badgeman poured a cup of tea for each of them. Jem's nostrils flared at the intoxicating scent.

"Anything else, sir?" the stone-faced giant asked.

"No, thank you, Badgeman."

Dismissed, the servant flicked one glance at Jem, which may or may not have contained a warning, before walking from the room.

"Help yourself," Alan urged.

Jem didn't wait for a second invitation. He dived into the meal, slapping together a sandwich of bread, meat, and cheese and taking a huge bite before his host even had a chance to nibble at one of the plums he'd selected. His stomach rumbled in greeting, welcoming the new addition to its domain. He wanted to display at least a modicum of good manners, but found it impossible. One half-chewed bite after another slipped down his gullet and landed with a satisfying thud in his empty stomach.

When he'd devoured the sandwich, he drank a deep draught of tea, then bit into a piece of dried fruit, the sweetly tart summer flavor of peach flowing into his mouth. He'd never had such a treat in his life. For a few moments, he forgot where he was, forgot about his client—forgot everything except his immediate needs. Only when he emerged sated from the fog of raging hunger did he remember his host. Jem wiped his mouth on the cuff of his sleeve and glanced sheepishly at Alan, who sat watching him with an unreadable expression on his face.

"Sorry, but it's been so long since I've had a bite, my navel was on speaking terms with my backbone."

A small smile curved the other man's lips. "I've been there myself while on campaign when rations were scarce."

"You look like you're halfway starved now," Jem said. "Could do with a bit of fattening up. Why don't you have more than fruit?" He assembled another sandwich with the crisp, buttered toast and cold cuts, and thrust it at Alan. "Here you go, sir. Eat. You must be nearly as hungry as I am from all the exercise."

He winked and jerked his head toward the bed. Alan might wish to pretend they hadn't had sex now that it was over, but Jem believed it wasn't healthy to deny who you were. He couldn't relieve the man's war memories, but accepting that he liked cock might go some way toward helping Lord Melancholy climb out of his black mood.

Alan accepted the sandwich in one long-fingered hand and began to eat, slowly at first, then nearly as ravening as Jem. He polished off the food and dabbed butter from his lips with a napkin.

Sitting back and sipping a second cup of tea, Jem watched him. "Nothing like a full stomach to perk up your mood, eh? That, a good fuck, and a good night's sleep. Downright restorative."

His comment earned another small smile but no reply. That made Jem more determined than ever to make the other man laugh.

"Do you believe in goblins, sir? I've an interesting tale to tell about a woman who met one. Miss Sally Purdy from Pritchett Street told me about her personal experience. Would you like to hear the story?"

Alan looked at him through the rising steam from his cup of tea and raised a brow. "Intriguing. Go on."

"Well, here's what happened, or so Miss Sally says. One morning she walked out her door and saw a little man in her garden. She snatched him up, saying, 'You're a goblin. I've caught you, and you owe me three wishes!'

"'Very well,' the wee man replied. 'What do you wish for?'

"Sally thought hard and replied, 'A big house to live in, a wardrobe full of fine clothes, and a table that will provide delicious food for the rest of me life.'

"'Aye, I'll grant your request, but to make your wishes come true, you have to spend the night having sex with me.'

"Old Spinster Sally hemmed and hawed but finally agreed, and that night, her maidenhead was taken at last. She and the man went at it all night long, and in the morning, she demanded her wishes be granted.

"'Tell me,' he said, 'how old are you?'

"'Thirty-five,' Sally admitted.

"'Och, lass! Thirty-five and ye still believe in goblins?' With that, the wee man scampered off."

A moment of utter silence followed the end of Jem's bawdy tale. He gazed at Alan with an expression as sober as a vicar on Sunday, waiting for him to get the joke.

Suddenly Alan began to laugh—one snort at first, followed by a chuckle warmer than the pot of tea.

Jem maintained his deadpan face and spun the tale further. "You shouldn't laugh, sir. Poor Sally was never the same after. Ruined, she was."

Alan laughed harder. Not quite the hilarity Jem had hoped for, but good enough for a start. His mission accomplished, Jem chose another slice of dried peach, popped it into his mouth, and bit down.

Chapter Four

Alan regarded the remarkable young man he'd brought home with him tonight. The lad was as refreshing as a tonic, with his sardonic wit and clever tongue. Sharing a late-evening snack with the whore he'd intended merely to fuck was not how he'd imagined the evening would end.

Then the man shifted, bent forward for another slice of cheese, and the candlelight glinted on something in his jacket pocket. No, *Jonathan's* jacket pocket. A bit of ivory. He knew that piece well. His grandfather had brought the set back from Italy.

The strongest emotion Alan had felt in months was restless self-pity, and so he almost welcomed the fury that surged through him. He got to his feet, walked around the table, and held out a hand that didn't tremble, thank God.

"Give them." He could barely force the words out.

For once Jem didn't speak. His smile vanished. He reached into his pocket, pulled out the chess pieces, and dropped them into Alan's hand. He rose and stood with feet apart and hands at his sides, as if waiting for the blow. By God, Alan was ready to give it. He grabbed the front of Jem's shirt and hauled him closer.

"You bastard. Why?" Then he felt like an idiot for asking. When a man picks up a rat from the street, he shouldn't be surprised when it bites him.

"Habit," Jem said after a moment. "Idiocy." He watched Alan's free hand, but still made no move to push away or defend himself.

Alan let go of the shirt and thrust his fist up and into Jem's stomach, but not as hard as he'd hoped, because the creature had thrown himself backward.

"Ain't gonna let you hurt me," Jem said, all traces of jolliness gone. "No matter I deserve it." He turned and walked toward the bed. Did he turn his back on Alan in scorn? Or perhaps a sign he knew Alan wouldn't attack from the rear?

Alan lunged. He managed to grab Jem by the back of the collar. But a second later, he gripped nothing but clothing.

Jem must have been unbuttoning the shirt as he walked away, because the coat fell to the ground, and the shirt tangled with the waistcoat dangled in Alan's hand.

Jem turned to face him. "I get my own stuff so as I don't leave here naked, sir. We part ways, and that's that." He crossed his arms over his pale chest. "I'm stupid, and I'm sorry, and that's a fact," he said matter-of-fact, no cozening in his manner.

"That easy?" The sense of betrayal still raged through Alan. He wanted blood.

"Not easy, sir. No." His voice broke. Of course the street rat regretted being caught. He'd lost more than a single payment for his whoring. He'd lost his chance with Alan.

That passing thought stopped Alan in his tracks. Chance? At what? Nothing. Nothing.

Yet oblivion had lost its appeal. He wanted to stay alive to beat the life out of the treacherous Jem.

He circled Jem, who pivoted on his heel, watching, wary. Alan had kept his attention on the man's hands. He made the mistake of looking up. Their eyes met and held.

Lust muddied his outrage. Both boiled in his gut. But lust meant Jem held power over Alan, and he would not allow such a thing. The charmer would not get away with stealing from him. He wouldn't let the man take his possessions or the uneasy peace he'd found when he'd decided to end his own life.

Cursing, Alan went for him again and grabbed his arms, hard, wiry flesh under his hands. Jem was a slippery fish, twisting and pulling. He'd obviously been grabbed before, and Alan had a flash of a life spent escaping from clutching hands. No sympathy, he warned himself. He'd treated the man well, fed him, and was rewarded with thievery.

Jem had escaped. His chest rose and fell fast, and he pushed his overlong hair from his eyes as he backed toward the door with cautious steps, like a man escaping a wild animal. Yes, thought Alan, I am an animal. He'd have to get the man before he escaped. But now Jem was against the dark wood of the door, reaching for the handle.

Alan threw himself at him, and they tumbled to the floor. Limbs entwined, scrabbling, grunting as Alan tried to get on top of him and hold him down, and... But suddenly he was on his back. The smaller, slighter man straddled his chest, knees holding his arms pinned. Good God. Alan had been trained to fight. He could kill a man with his bare hands and had more than once. Where had he gone wrong? He knew the answer, of course. He hadn't gouged Jem's eyes or thrust an elbow into his throat.

The rage at Jem had been exhilarating; he'd felt life pouring through him, but now the fury turned inward. His soft nature hadn't allowed him to escape the army and war with his spirit unscathed. And now again he'd proved he couldn't be ruthless enough to stop this undernourished rat from defeating him.

"Alan. Sir." Jem shifted. He held Alan's wrists with his hands now, and he peered down at him. "You still wanta kill me?"

Alan didn't bother to answer the wretch. He was too aware of the strong hands encircling his wrists, and it wasn't fear that touched him. He wanted those hands, with their scrapes and scars, to move down his arms.

"You look fair grim, sir. Get mad. Suits you better." The light bantering manner had returned. It only served to make Alan feel sick and foolish to think he'd fallen under the spell of the man.

Jem leaned close enough so Alan could smell the brandy and peach on his breath. "I shouldna done that. Stolen from you." So close, the moisture and heat of his mouth feathered Alan's skin just below his ear, and his body prickled with anticipation. Damn and blast, the arousal created shivers in his belly, hardening his cock.

"No, goddamn you, you shouldn't have." With a mighty heave, Alan threw Jem off, twisting hard to the side at the same moment. Jem flew and landed on his back. He missed the carpet, and his head made a loud *thwack* on the bare, polished wood floor.

Alan rose to his feet, ready for more, but the other man didn't move. Shit. Alan dropped to his knees. *No more death. Not Jem.*

Of course not. This was a sham. Alan shook his shoulder. "Come on, you bastard. Wake up."

He sat back on his heels and glanced around the room, searching for brandy, but the glass was empty. Damnation. He put his hand on Jem's bare shoulder, gently now. Stroking down to the tender skin of his inside arm. He couldn't trust the man, didn't think he could leave him alone in any room of the house, but he still desperately craved his touch.

"Come on, Jem. Open those eyes."

Lust didn't mean a blessed thing. He swallowed hard. He'd ignore the dismay he'd felt when Jem's head had hit the floor with a sickening thud, just as he'd ignore his relief when he saw Jem's eyelids flutter.

"Ow." The younger man groaned. "Aw, God's ballocks. I fucked myself royally, din' I?" No more imitating his betters.

Alan's chest expanded with his sigh. A dull pain lifted as he exhaled breath. "You're a fool," he said, and realized he still touched the man's arm.

"That I am, sir." He pushed himself to a sitting position and rubbed the side of his head.

Impatiently Alan moved his hand aside and checked for blood, but only felt the huge goose egg on the back of Jem's head. Alan bit back the automatic apology that rose to his lips. He had nothing to be sorry for. The whelp had tried to steal from him and had suffered the consequences. But Alan couldn't fight the urge to gently sift his fingers through the sandy brown hair and try to stroke away the pain. He paused with his hand cupping the side of Jem's head and once more stared into the younger man's wide blue eyes, so innocent-seeming.

"Will you let me go?"

"Well, I'm hardly going to call the constable, am I?" Alan took his hand away from the silken hair and the hard skull beneath, and as he did so, he suddenly felt bereft. This was the end of his evening. The lad would leave now, but not before Alan paid him his half crown anyway—such a meager amount for the extreme pleasure he'd given him. Alan realized he didn't want Jem to disappear back into the festering slum from which he'd come, never to be seen again.

He also realized that his plan to end his life didn't seem as inevitable as it had earlier that evening. The sex, the companionship, the laughter at Jem's silly joke, and even the anger over his thievery, had all conspired to make him think of something other than the necessity of blowing his brains out. Had life suddenly become a little less dire because of the thief sitting on his bedroom floor, cradling his head in both hands? He suspected that once Jem left him to silence again, morose inertia would settle over him once more. He didn't want to let go of this temporary distraction yet.

"Do you want to go?" he asked before his logical mind could pull the reins on the impulse.

"Pardon, sir?" Jem looked up, elbows on knees, hands still cupping either side of his head.

"Do you have another pressing engagement?"

The youth stared at him warily. "Why? What do I have to do to make up for the stealing?"

Alan waved a hand. "I'll forget that, provided you promise no such further behavior. Trust me, you wouldn't make it out of this house unscathed. Badgeman would see to it, if I didn't."

"What, then?" A frown still knit his finely arched brows. "You want another free fuck to make up for what I done?"

"I don't want a free anything. I'll still pay you what I owe for the evening's...entertainment, but it's late—very late—and I thought you might wish to sleep here tonight."

Jem's eyes widened again, and his brows rose as if Alan had asked him to climb naked on the roof and crow like a rooster. “Now there's an abrupt left turn. You've gone from trying to split me head open to asking me to stop the night. I don't often find myself flabbergasted, but you've left me speechless, sir. Absolutely speechless.”

“Not absolutely,” Alan said drily.

He had almost a lifetime of predictable, calm behavior, and in one evening he'd indulged in the most sinful of activities and displayed a range of volatile emotions he hadn't indulged in since his fourteenth year. That was the year he'd bounced between bleak despair and rage, when he'd understood his perverted taste could not be banished by icy baths or vigorous, exhausting exercise. At least as a lad he hadn't lost his mind. Tonight apparently he had.

Jem rose to his feet, wobbling and squinting. “Ugh.”

“Your head is still injured,” Alan said. “You should have the devil of a headache for a time, and someone should watch you, wake you on occasion.”

“Naw, no need to worry about my head. It's hard as a horseshoe. But if you care to wake me, I won't object.” Jem leered then simply grinned as if he laughed at himself.

Alan rubbed his cheek. “I'll ring for Badgeman to take the dishes away.”

He considered going to look for the ex-sergeant to explain privately that his guest would be staying the night, but he didn't want to leave Jem alone with all the tempting objects. The thief might hoist a window and toss some of the better pieces out into the garden to fetch later. And Alan didn't wish to explain a bloody thing to Badgeman even if the big man's concern was touching.

They'd been through so many corners of hell together… But no. Not tonight. No more ghosts of the past tonight.

He went to the bell while Jem silently pulled on his clothes again.

Badgeman appeared almost immediately, as if he'd been awaiting the summons.

"Take the dishes away, please," Alan said.

Badgeman glanced at Jem, silently asking if he should also escort him from the premises.

"That will be all," Alan said firmly. "I won't need you again tonight."

"Are you sure about that, sir?" The ex-sergeant added a bleak rumble of wordless disapproval. Loyal till death and beyond, he'd never be most householders' notion of the model servant.

"Yes," Alan said and thought *no.*

Badgeman bowed low, which he did only when thoroughly nettled with Alan. He lifted the tray. "Hungry, were you?" The tone made the question, directed at Jem, an accusation of gluttony.

"I was as well," Alan said.

"Ah." Badgeman paused, the tray in his hands. His eyes gleamed with pleasure, and his near-ruined mouth quirked up briefly. The big man was pleased.

The door closed behind him. "Do we remove our clothes again?" Jem's hands were already busy unbuttoning his waistcoat.

Alan's cock loved that idea and went into a full stand at the anticipation of Jem's smooth body. He shook his head. "We should be certain you're well enough…"

"Aha, you say that because you have something on your mind other than sleep, Lord Alan? See, where I come from, if you get a chance to be somewhere warm and private-like, where no one'll pinch your clothes, you shed them quick as you can. They last longer that way." He paused after he pulled the shirt over his head. "Not that these are mine. I know that, sir. Just that I love sleeping in the natural state."

Naked and with a semierection, Jem took a running jump and landed on the bed—then winced. "But it does appear I should move a bit more slowly." He lay back with a long sigh. "Oh, just about perfect." He turned his head to look at Alan. "Only thing missing is you."

The man had turned confident again. Cocky.

Alan had put on his boots. He sat on the edge of the bed to pull them off again. With his back to Jem, he cleared his throat and wondered what he could ask. That he should have such delicacy—scruples about prying into the young thief's life—amused him. "I have made it clear you don't have to provide anymore, uh, service, so I wonder if the fact that you appear willing to…to…"

"Act as catamite?" asked Jem. Alan couldn't see him, but he heard the laughter in his voice.

"Indeed. Do you enjoy the act?"

"Indeed," Jem drawled in a bad imitation of Alan, then hooted with laughter. "Oh, indeed, rather, yes, sir. I love it. Not always, mind you. Some fellows reek and make me fairly lose my dinner, what little I've et. And some…" He stopped.

Boots off, Alan stretched out on the bed fully dressed. He looked over at Jem. "Go on."

Jem's mobile mouth was thin. "Some loathe their own craving, and that means they gotta hate me—particularly once they've spent. I'm better now than when I was younger at spotting those poor creatures and at fighting them off when need be."

Alan recalled his own self-loathing after he'd reached his pleasure only a couple of hours earlier. Jem, the street whore, would call him a "poor creature."

"Do you know how many men you've, ah…"

Jem shook his head. "I don't talk of such a thing, begging your pardon, sir." He grabbed the counterpane and pulled it over his naked body. He gave another sigh and grinned. "Ahh, but I've never been with another who possessed such fine"—he paused to wiggle like an agile fish—"fine bedding as you, sir."

Alan wasn't going to give up the questions. He'd grown curious about Jem. "Do you usually steal from your customers?"

Jem didn't take offense. "If I get the opportunity and it won't cause a great hardship for either of us. Don't want to take a wallet from a vengeful man. I got no morals, I expect," he said as casually as if announcing he were out of salt.

"How did you know I wasn't vengeful?"

"You might well be." Jem yawned. "You might be waiting for me to fall asleep, and then you'll drag me to the docks and put me in His Majesty's navy. Or you might cut my throat."

"Too messy," Alan said.

"Aha, you *do* know how to make a joke, sir—or so I hope. Would it be poison, then? I'm so sleepy, might well be." He rubbed his chin, and the rasp was loud in the quiet, nearly dark room. "No, I know what 'tis."

Alan put his hands behind his head and crossed his ankles. "How will I kill you, Jem?"

"With kindness," came the sleepy answer. "Food, warmth, safe place to sleep. Kindness. Mm. And a body a man could..." But then his voice petered out to be replaced by his slow, deep breathing.

Alan hoisted himself onto an elbow and looked down at the sleeping Jem. Except for the faint shadow of stubble and his thin features, he could have been an innocent youth, although Alan expected he'd been a knowing, conniving sort since he first learned to speak.

As he considered Jem's face and wondered about the man's secrets, Alan realized he didn't detect his usual companion—empty misery. As if testing a sore tooth, he allowed his thoughts to veer into forbidden territory. He shut his eyes and envisioned bodies lying in ditches, the unending screams of horses and men, and later, the screams of women and children as the British invaded the city.

More memories he did not usually allow himself to see or feel flooded his mind, and he didn't fight the horror. Dragging a mangled Badgeman out of the pile of dead and dying. All those bodies of his men and boys, dead due to a general's stubbornness and folly. Coming home to find his family gone—father, mother, and brother as dead as soldiers killed in pointless battle. The nightmares he'd had while the medication for pain killed his spirit. He'd thrown off that yoke, but had been left a husk.

He wondered what Jem would say should he hear Alan's story. He might try to get Alan to laugh it off. He could tell an obscene, stupid jest. God above, and all Alan would want was his embrace. He wouldn't seek anything more lurid than the soothing presence of another person sharing his bed. Determined to ignore the steady thrum of lust, he stripped off his clothes and inched closer to the middle of the bed where Jem sprawled, lightly snoring—a rather pleasant, companionable sound. Alan tried to gain the illusion of comfort from the sleeping man's warmth.

His own behavior tonight had been erratic, crazy. It was lunacy to invite a prostitute and thief to spend the night in his house. Badgeman would probably be up all night, fearing his master's throat had been cut while he slept. But Alan was too sleepy and far too comfortable to care about how his actions might be construed or that he'd have to face reality in the morning. For now, he was content, at peace, and the comfort he gained from curling his body around the other man's was no illusion.

Chapter Five

Jem woke with sunlight in his eyes and a splitting headache that made him not want to open them. Not hungover, although his mouth was as dry as cotton. He slid his hands over the smooth sheet and the warm, hard body, and remembered where he was. A thrill of excitement woke him the rest of the way. This was an intriguing situation, something out of the ordinary, and who knew what the new day might bring?

He ungummed his eyes and gazed at the ceiling above him. No cracks, flaking plaster, or mold stains—he definitely wasn't in Southwark anymore. Reaching up, he rubbed the side of his head and felt a good-sized goose egg beneath his hair. No wonder his head ached. Of course it didn't help that Lord Nursemaid had woken him up several times during the night to make sure he was still alive. When Jem had groused, Alan had explained something about possible damage to the brain from the blow to his head and the need to make sure his pupils dilated properly. It was all nonsense, but Jem had bitten his tongue and submitted to having the other man peer into his eyes by candlelight—a small price to pay for a good, if not uninterrupted, night's sleep in a soft bed.

Jem stroked his hand over Alan's chest, combing the fine hairs between his fingers and touching the smooth skin underneath. He turned his aching head on the plump feather pillow and examined his sleeping companion, enjoying this chance to study him freely.

Lord Alan Bumbuggerer was a very handsome man when he wasn't scowling. His face was still severe, always would be with those deep grooves cutting either side of his mouth and the permanent frown lines between his brows. In sleep he appeared relaxed and peaceful at last. His lips were slack, breath whistling lightly between them. His jet-black hair, shot at the temples with a sprinkling of white, was a vivid contrast to the snowy white linen of the pillowcase. Thick eyelashes swept his cheeks. What secrets lay behind the shutters of his lids where his eyes moved restlessly back and forth?

Stubble darkened his jaw and chin, emphasizing the stark angularity of his bones. Too bony. Too lean. He looked nearly as starved as Jem often felt. No wonder the badger was worried about him, what with the lack of appetite and isolation. The loyal butler-coachman-serving maid must have sensed his master's despair but didn't know how to reach him or cheer him up.

Fortunately Jem did. He scooted closer to the warm body lying beside him and slid his hand down Alan's chest to his groin. The dark hairs were wirier there, tangling around his fingers as he reached for the man's erection. Ah yes, its owner might be asleep, but his cock was wide awake, thick and solid, and twitching at Jem's touch.

He crawled beneath the covers, his headache diminished as all the blood left his head to rush down to his penis. Single-minded—that was what his old granny used to call him, and she was right. When he got an idea in his head, he'd worry it like a terrier with a rat. Sometimes his focus might be an argument or prodding to get to the root of a question as he'd done with Alan last night, but at the moment his attention was on more basic needs—getting a mouthful of cock and making his bed partner groan and writhe.

As he wedged his body between strong, hairy thighs and well-muscled calves, Jem breathed in the musky, salty aroma of the man. A clean smell compared to many of his clients who bathed so rarely their ripe stench was eye-watering—and some were rich gents from whom one would expect better hygiene. But some seemed to think a splash of strong cologne was sufficient to replace a good wash.

Alan stirred and shifted and made a quiet mumbling sound, but didn't fully awaken. Jem took his cock in hand and placed the tip to his lips. He gently drew back the foreskin and licked over the smooth head before sucking the length into his mouth. *That* woke up his lordship. He groaned and tensed. Lovely.

As he sucked, Jem stroked his hand up and down, slow and leisurely, the way a morning frigging should be, as if they had an entire day to loll in bed together. Beneath the covers, sandwiched between Alan's hairy legs, Jem was toasty warm and secure. Too bad it couldn't last, but he'd play out the situation as long as possible. Perhaps he'd at least get another meal before he had to leave.

Alan thrust gently, rising and falling beneath his skilled mouth and hands. Jem swirled his tongue around the salty length of his shaft and sucked deeper. He cupped the other man's sac and fondled his balls for a while, then slid his fingers along the sensitive strip behind Alan's balls and traced delicate circles around the rim of his anus.

A soft gasp came from above. Jem grinned around his mouthful of cock and darted the tip of his finger in and out of the clenching ring of muscle. Oh yes, the master liked that. His hand stole beneath the covers and settled on Jem's head, fingers twining in his curls.

Jem let the other man's cock slip from his mouth to flop against his stomach, solid and hard. If he wanted to make this last, he had to slow down and build up more anticipation. He turned his face into the hand that cradled the side of his head and kissed Alan's palm. He stroked it with soft, tickling laps of his tongue like a grateful dog and was rewarded with another soft groan. It was a rich reward. Jem enjoyed giving pleasure nearly as much as receiving it when the man was one he was attracted to, someone he could envision being with as more than a customer. And Alan definitely fit that bill. Hell, Jem would happily fuck him for free. If he walked away from this experience with a couple of meals and the memory of a night in a soft bed, that would be ample payment.

Alan curved his hand around Jem's cheek, touching him, feeling the shape of his brow, his nose, and jaw. When his exploring fingers reached Jem's lips, Jem drew one into his mouth and sucked it, hard. All the while he continued to explore the other man's arsehole, gently probing, stretching it wider, feeling the muscle spasm around his fingers. Alan thrust back onto his hand, urging him deeper. Jem didn't want to go too far, not without some unguent to ease the way, so he continued to tease around the opening.

He burrowed his face between Alan's legs and kissed his inner thighs, then licked his scrotum, making him arch his back with the need to have Jem's mouth wrapped around his cock again.

At last Jem took pity and kissed his way around the thatch of dark hair to where the man's cock lay twitching against his belly. As he drew Alan's penis into his mouth once more, he tasted the musky fluid leaking from the tip. This wasn't going to last long at all.

Jem resumed pumping with his fist and sucking the head while drilling the master's bunghole with insistent fingers. The heat and tightness of that spot was making his own cock throb and weep with the desire to fill it.

Within minutes, Alan was rocking forward and back, trying to relieve his cock in Jem's mouth and impale his bottom on Jem's fingers. He groaned and shuddered. Jem felt warm jets of spending hit the back of his throat. He swallowed it down, squeezing his thighs tight to control his cock's need to explode.

Alan's wild thrashing, like an unbroken horse, calmed after a moment. He lay panting against the mattress with Jem's fingers still spearing his rear. Jem released the man's spent cock and withdrew his fingers from the clenching bunghole. He crawled up Alan's body to lie full-length on top of him. He poked his head out from under the covers and grinned down at his host.

"Morning. Ain't you glad you asked me to stop the night?"

The pale ghost of a smile haunted Alan's mouth, softening his hard features. "How's your head?"

"Got me a goose egg, but I'm fine. I've a hard head. Nearly as hard as yours was this morning." He winked and rocked his groin against Alan's softening penis, leaving no doubt as to his meaning.

The rocking felt damned good on Jem's erection, so he did it some more, thrusting lightly and enjoying the friction against Alan's warm belly. He'd be happy to stay pressed against the other man's hard body for as long as he'd let him, but supposed he should make some indication toward leaving.

"Thank you for your hospitality, sir. 'Twas a lovely night. Some moments excepted."

"Yes." The smile was gone and the frown lines back as Alan took hold of Jem's shoulders and gently moved him off his body. Acknowledgement of what they'd done, what Jem had just finished doing for him, in the light of day was too much for the older man to face, Jem guessed. He couldn't look Jem in the eyes, so close and intimate, so he pushed him away and rolled to a sitting position. Jem watched his long back, the perfect canvas marred by scars and several freckles and small moles. He gazed at the other man's bowed head and wondered what was rattling around inside it.

"Would you like some breakfast?" Alan asked abruptly. "No need for you to leave without a proper meal first. Likely it's another cold, foggy morning, and you should have something hot in you."

"Bit of brekkers sounds like just the thing." Jem sat up, legs crossed, arms resting on his bent knees. He continued to watch the curious creature who'd brought him home and surprisingly didn't seem to be in a hurry to see the back of him.

As Alan used the chamber pot and then went to his wardrobe to select clothes, he seemed to be trying to pretend Jem wasn't there—or at least that he wasn't sitting naked on the bed with his erect whang on display. Jem had half hoped the man would think turnabout was fair play and at least give him a release by hand, but no such luck. Alan was not acknowledging his erection.

"We'll go down for breakfast. You should dress," he advised without turning to look at Jem.

With a sigh and a halfhearted stroke of his cock, Jem slid out of bed and used the chamber pot himself before dressing in the clothes he'd been given. He cast a last, wistful glance at the rumpled bed with those lovely, soft sheets, then followed Alan out the room and downstairs.

The smell of sausage hit him halfway down the stairs, and he could've found his way to the massive dining room by following the scent alone. His stomach rumbled, and his aching head was nearly forgotten as he focused on the table laden with gleaming silver-covered dishes. It was like magic, as if a wizard had made the breakfast appear from thin air, because there was no sign of servants. And how had Badger known when his master would rise or that he'd be hungry enough to eat sufficient food to feed a regiment?

Jem took the seat Alan indicated, enjoying the feel of the carved wood beneath his hands as he pulled out the heavy chair.

Dark, glossy wood pieces like the table and chairs dominated the room. He stared around, memorizing the details, storing them up for later. Jem had an eye for beauty, his mum used to say, sometimes fondly—more often mockingly.

The big badger also dominated the room, but wasn't nearly as handsome as the furniture. He lifted the lid of each serving dish and directed a look at Alan, who silently nodded or shook his head. After placing the dangerously well-loaded plate in front of his nibs, the badger turned to Jem.

He looked straight into Jem's face for several long heartbeats. No need to guess at the threat in that harsh gaze. "Thank you ever so much," Jem said and grinned. "Just give me what he's got, if you please."

Badgeman served Jem silently, then poured two cups of thick steaming chocolate and placed one in front of each of them. He stepped back, bowed, and left without saying a word.

"Don't you have anyone else about the place?" Jem asked. He picked up the toast and spoke through the mouthful. "Servants, I mean."

Alan picked up his thin porcelain cup. "I gave them all last night off."

Of course. The obvious move for any gent planning to bring home a male whore would be to dismiss the servants so they wouldn't find out about his dangerous tastes. "Where are they now? On a normal morning wouldn't you have, I dunno, footmen and whatnot staring over you while you eat?"

Alan shook his head. "Badgeman seems to believe I can't serve myself, but I draw the line at more help. I don't require anyone to cut my meat for me."

He looked pointedly at Jem's hand and raised his eyebrows. Jem had grabbed a slice of ham from his plate with his fingers.

Laughing, he dropped the ham back onto the plate and picked up a fistful of cutlery, which he shook at Alan. "Surprised you'd allow me a knife. After all, I might be prone to violence. You don't know about me."

"I know you have very little in the way of manners, but that's not my concern."

Jem dropped the silver back onto the table with a clatter. He selected a fork and a knife, and sawed away at the slice of ham.

"Tell me, Jem, what would you steal in this room?"

His words stung. Jem felt a flash of anger. He put down the fork he clutched and drew in a long breath to steady himself. First Lord High-and-Mighty mocked his manners, and now he reminded him of his stupidity the night before. The gent was obviously tolerant, but Jem suspected he wouldn't stand being called a buggering bastard.

"I'd steal naught from you, sir, especially now, for should anything go missing, you'd know where to hunt. Easy enough to set your badger or the watch after me. No, thank you. I don't court hanging—leastwise not for thievery," he added as an afterthought.

He prodded the ham with the point of the knife to avoid looking at the handsome man who leaned on the arm of his chair and watched. Jem gave the ham a particularly sharp poke. "Last night I musta been dicked in the nob to take from the likes of you. I'm a half-a-loaf man."

"You are offended," Alan said. "I'm honestly curious, I assure you. I've never had a conversation with a thief."

Oh. Now he understood. Jem decided he might sing for his breakfast, but he wouldn't tell a tale on any of his mates. He looked around the room, then examined the handle of the knife. "The silver don't have letters on it, so that'd do if I'm feeling lucky."

He pointed the knife at a large silver thing with pedestals, bowls and strange silver animals perched all over it. A monkey hung from the side, and an elephant stood at the very top. "That thing is too bulky and too what-you-may-call-it. Distinct-like. Jimmy wouldn't care to take such a thing."

"That thing's an epergne. Jimmy's the merchant you'd sell to?"

Jem nodded. "Runs a stalling ken, or he's a fence, we'd call it."

Alan smiled suddenly. A real smile with white teeth.

Jem narrowed his eyes. "Don't tell me you know Jimmy, sir, because I changed his name."

"I'm amused because you're teaching me your words, and I'm teaching you mine. Epergne for stalling ken."

Jem chuckled. He liked this Alan when the man shrugged off that mantle of sorrow that hung about him like a fog. Hell, he liked him even when he was Lord Gloom.

"Anything else you'd take?"

Jem waved a hand airily. "The whole of it. 'Cept maybe that epergne thing. 'Tis too silly and wouldn't fit my dining room."

"Ah. But this is the breakfast room."

Jem hooted with laughter. "Naw, you're pulling my leg, sir. Truly? You have a special room for each meal? What if you grow peckish between the meals? Do you stand in the corridor between 'em?"

The corners of Alan's mouth twitched, and he leaned back in his chair. "After breakfast, would you care to see the other rooms?"

"So I might tell you what else I'd pinch?"

"Certainly."

"If you want God's honest truth, there's not much I would lift from this place."

Alan's eyes narrowed in obvious disbelief.

"Not because I'm an upright cull, but I'd wager your possessions are too costly." Jem shook a finger at Alan and slipped into cant. "You got to be awake on all counts if you're to be an angler or crack a crib. Don't be caught with more 'n a pound in your dabblers, or the beak will pass the cramp word, and it'll be the hemp for you, lad. Better to be a clouting lay."

"And what is that?"

"Those who dive for handkerchiefs on the sly. A humble trade, yet if you're nabbed, you still end up a lag and perhaps get some air and exercise."

Alan nearly smiled. "You get air and exercise in prison?"

"Nay man. No real airing in the trib. Means to be drubbed at the cart's arse. A good basting."

"Beaten behind a cart?"

Jem nodded.

Alan's smile actually reached his eyes, and he was almost completely transformed from the granite-faced Lord Doom. "Fool that I was, I thought I knew cant."

Pleased that he'd managed to again get Lord Grim to smile, Jem grinned back. "Epergne. Hmm. Can't recall any other words from you. Now it's quite a lot of fine language you owe me, sir." He crammed the rest of the ham into his mouth and stood. "You ready? I am."

Alan wasn't sure why he wanted to show the man the rest of the house. It was hours past the time they should have parted ways—setting aside the fact that they shouldn't have met at all. He searched his heart for the sick regret and contempt he'd felt the two other times he'd indulged in his perversion, and felt nothing but a curious lightened sensation.

Odd, because yesterday he'd hit upon a solution that had given him a sense of peace, and now he'd abandoned it. Sometime during the night he'd decided against the sin of suicide. If the heavy blanket of misery could lift for a few minutes now, perhaps in time he'd live without it for hours, and he might eventually even shed that weight for an entire day.

He supposed if he had decided to live, he'd best grow used to such frighteningly changeable moods. The ground under his feet had shifted, and as a result, he was no longer the same steady, calm man. No longer a soldier, son, or brother. What would he be instead?

He led Jem through the red drawing room and answered his many questions about the marble fireplace, the inlaid wood floors, the paintings, and the pianoforte his mother used to play. The man seemed honestly curious, not simply looking over Alan's home for the best items to steal.

When they entered the library, Jem gave a low whistle. "Take a look at that. Never seen so many books in one spot. Must have paid a goodly sum in paper taxes. Nearly makes me wish I could read better." He glanced at Alan and shrugged as if he'd asked a question. "I can scratch out my name and a bit." He jammed his hands in his pockets and walked up and down the room until he came back to Alan's side and caught sight of the mahogany desk.

Alan had avoided this elaborate, ugly thing, with its vast surface that still carried the hint of his father's snuff and cologne. He still thought of it as his father's and used the much smaller escritoire in the cramped study for his correspondence and work.

He'd avoided the library altogether, and now, as the memories poured in, swamping him with bleak and bitter loss, he remembered why.

He wondered how he might end this tour. Which brought up the question of what he would do once Jem left the house.

Why had he come home to London? He should go to his family's seat in Shropshire. He imagined riding through fields that weren't scarred with blood or cannon fire. His army charger had been shot from under him during the second-to-last campaign, and he hadn't replaced the big gelding, hadn't wanted to.

Jem stopped running his hands over the carved lotus flowers on the desk leg. He straightened and sauntered over to Alan. “Come now, sir. Didn't yer mum or old nanny tell you yer face will freeze like that?”

“Never.” Alan forced his scowl to relax, amused that he would give in to the bullying of a thief who sold his body on the street. “I'm certain this is dull for you,” he said and left the room. When Jem didn't immediately follow, he reluctantly reentered the library.

Jem stood in front of the family portrait. “Tell me about 'em,” he said without taking his gaze off the painting.

When Alan said nothing, Jem pointed to the boy standing behind the mother's chair, his hands on her shoulders. “That's you, no doubt. The eyes tell me. And that's your brother next to you. He looks less merry than you, I'd say—leastways, less merry than you was back then. Older 'n you?”

Alan turned away.

Jem put his hands behind his back and rocked on his feet as if he hadn't noticed Alan's disinterest. He kept chatting about the painting as if they held a conversation.

“Yes, I'd say so. Though not as tall, he's the older brother. Oh, and your mum is pretty and your dad a solemn old cove. Quite distinguished, but not such an old stick as some. Are you lot as happy as you look there?”

Alan didn't want to answer. “I'm the only one left,” he said flatly. “I'd prefer not to discuss the matter.” His voice was steady and cool, thank goodness.

“Oh.” Jem looked at him at last. Thank God he didn't offer any driveling words of sympathy.

“Come on,” Alan said, and they left the room in silence.

As they entered the dining room, Jem spoke again. “Is your loss a recent one, sir?”

“I said I do not wish to speak about the matter.”

“Yah, you did. But I wasn't sure if you meant it.”

“Christ, man,” he snapped. “I speak plain English.”

“What you speak of and what you long for are a fair distance apart, pardon my saying so.”

Alan's breath hissed out on a curse. He suspected Jem taunted him for his cowardice in not facing up to his sick tastes. “And if I don't pardon your impudence?” He'd moved closer to Jem, anger pulsing through him.

The corners of Jem's eyes crinkled, the hint of a smile. “You'll get your bloody big badger to scoop out me insides, or do it yourself. Not that I'd blame you a bit—a nosy beggar like me, prying into your business. Thing is, you interest me, Lord Alan.”

Alan steadied himself. He didn't want to speak of his family, and he didn't want to throw Jem out—although God knew why.

He could hear Jem's soft, fast breath, and Alan's anger began to turn into something worse. Arousal beat in his veins and stiffened his cock with every heartbeat. He stepped back from the temptation.

“I'm not Lord anyone.” He headed for the window to put some space between them. The bright spring morning beckoned. The doctor had pronounced his leg still too weak to ride. He wondered if Jem rode horses.

“No title, then?” Jem asked.

“I'm a baronet, which makes me Sir Alan.” Turning from the window, he met Jem's eyes. Why the hell not tell his name? He didn't fear blackmail from this source, not really.

"Sir Alan Watleigh," he finished.

Jem's eyes widened, and his arched brows rose higher. He touched his forelock in a proper salute. "An honor, Sir Alan Watleigh." There wasn't a trace of playfulness in his manner. "Jem Brown, at your service." He bowed.

Alan felt a surge of warmth which wasn't lust this time. He was oddly touched by the small sign of respect from a man who appeared to regard everything in life with glib irony and a dismissive casualness.

"I suppose I might show you the garden," he said, changing the subject.

As he led his guest outside, Alan realized he was doing everything in his power to prolong Jem's stay. What would he show him next, the attic? The kitchen and the servants' quarters?

The thought was born in sarcasm but blossomed into an idea—a way he could keep Jem around longer than one night. The concept was preposterous, yet even as he examined it from every ludicrous angle, Alan knew he was going to make the offer.

"Mm, smells good." Jem turned in a circle on the stone path that led through the shrubbery and inhaled the bit of nature. "Ain't seen this much green in a long time. Not a lot of gardens in the circles I frequent."

When Alan didn't respond, the young man looked sharply at him. "What's troubling your nob now? You're the hardest-thinking man I ever clapped eyes on. Should give your brain a rest before you break it."

Alan cleared his throat. His heart pounded and his cheeks were burning. How ridiculous to be blushing, to be making this suggestion, to be afraid Jem would laugh when he heard it and refuse. Alan's misgivings clamored to be heard, but he spoke over them.

"I was wondering if you might consider a position on my household staff."

Jem stared at him and waited.

"Perhaps permanent employment if it works out. But perhaps you wouldn't be interested." He felt as nervous as a youth asking for a dance. Ridiculous! He who had commanded men in battle, who'd ridden into cannon fire, what did he have to fear from this street rat?

"Employment? Here?" Jem's surprised stare melted into a devilish grin. "Doing what, exactly?"

"I need... That is, it's customary for a man to have a valet. Other than Badgeman, I don't have any servant to fill that capacity. He has enough duties to perform without caring for my clothes and effects. The man deserves a rest and more time to himself. I've been considering hiring someone."

"Oh, so it's for poor, tired old badger, I see." The grin grew wider and possibly more devilish. "That is so kind and generous of you, Sir Alan."

Alan felt his flush grow hotter and his temper rise along with it. How dare the impudent whelp make light of him? Who was this common whore to disrespect his betters and to jeer at an offer of honest work?

"You needn't take the position if you don't wish to. It was a mere passing thought. Of course, you wouldn't be suitable at all." The sharpness of Alan's voice sliced the smile from Jem's mouth.

Suddenly sober, the young man moved closer and gazed into his eyes. "Sir, I apologize for my yawning gob. I'd be pleased and grateful to take any position you like." He suggestively stressed the final words, but Alan chose to ignore it. The lad couldn't seem to help putting a saucy spin on most everything he said. "If you forgive me asking, what would my duties and wages be?"

Alan paused, pretending to consider but actually collecting his wildly ricocheting emotions. Disbelief, delight, excitement, and horror at what he'd done warred within him.

"Badgeman can tell you the specifics. Since you'll be in training, as it were, your wages will be commensurate with your inexperience. I'm not certain of the going rate. Badgeman will know the proper wage, but I should imagine four pounds monthly would be sufficient to start."

Jem's expressive eyes opened wide. Standing this close, Alan could see the dark rim and striations of navy against the lighter blue. The way they caught and reflected the sunlight made them shine like two bits of sky. His chest tightened painfully with some inexplicable feeling, and he cursed his increasingly emotional nature. What had happened to the officer whose men used to call Captain Iron Drawers behind his back?

"That would indeed be sufficient," Jem agreed with a broad and not-so-devilish grin. "Thank you."

Alan inclined his head. "Badgeman will outfit you in proper attire and show you your duties. The servants will be returning to work soon, and he'll introduce you to them as well." He paused again, and a stab of fear went through him as he realized the danger he was putting himself in on a whim. "I trust you will comport yourself as a valet in training and not…"

"A foul-mouthed whore? Yes sir, I believe I can manage the role. I wouldn't give anyone reason to question the terms of my service here, I promise." Jem folded his hands together and lifted his eyes to the heavens. "Pure as a choirboy and sober as a judge, I'll be. Jem Brown, late of Southwark, who was given the opportunity to rise above his pitiable life and enter service. I'll keep the story simple. Embellishments only get a cove into trouble."

Alan grunted an acknowledgement, still mentally kicking himself for inviting this thieving stranger into his life. But then, it hadn't been much of a life before yesterday, and now it felt rich with color, like a black-and-white ink sketch turned into an oil painting.

"Come along then, I'll pass you over to Badgeman." He led the way back toward the house.

"One last question, sir. Where might I be sleeping? Isn't it customary for a valet to have a small room adjacent to his master's in case anything is required of him in the night?" Jem's cheeky tone and grin were enough to make a saint lose patience, and Alan was no saint.

He stopped, turned, and favored the delinquent with his most quelling look, the one that had always made soldiers' gazes drop to their boots. His tone was ice. "As you can imagine, I have some serious misgivings about making you this offer. Please don't make me regret my decision. You can be returned from whence you came in a heartbeat."

Jem sobered again, although he did manage to meet and hold Alan's stare unlike many a man before him. "Yes, sir."

Alan turned on his heel and stalked away. Of course, the lad had a legitimate question. What was he to expect his duties to include in service to a man who'd recently buggered him? Alan couldn't deny he'd thought about sex when making his decision, but that wasn't at all his primary purpose in asking Jem to stay. It was the companionship he craved and the buoyant spirit the irrepressible thief raised in him.

Keeping him close for a while was a matter of Alan's survival.

Chapter Six

It was a posh new life, but with so many rules, constraints, and manners. Jem felt stifled by the very air of belowstairs where the household staff was headquartered. The hierarchy of the servants wasn't as rigid as one would find in most wealthy houses. Sir Alan kept his staff to a minimum, with Badgeman serving as steward, butler, and even as coachman when needed—unheard of for the butler to do outdoor work. But it was the awful housekeeper, Mrs. Crimpett, who Jem hated like a cat hates rain and who brought out the worst in him. She was a tyrant queen ruling with an iron fist over the parlor maids, the scullery maid, and the lone, feeble-minded old footman, Dicky, who by rights should've been Badgeman's responsibility. Even Cook, who controlled the kitchen, kowtowed to Mrs. Crimpett.

Jem hated a bully, had had his nose bloodied on more than one occasion, standing against those who would persecute the weak, and Crimpett was every bit as bad as some of the nappers who'd terrorized Southwark. He pitied poor Bridie, Jenny, little Susan, and that girl with the squint who slaved in the kitchen—he'd forgotten her name. Poor slobber-mouthed Dicky, who must be at least fifty, nearly wet his drawers every time Mrs. Crimpett addressed him. Shame on Badgeman for not taking his part.

As the master's new valet, Jem's duties didn't fall under Mrs. Crimpett's jurisdiction, so he could spend most of his time upstairs mucking about with Alan's clothes or pretending to polish his boots. But the old hag wanted to knock him down a peg; he sensed it in her every baleful glance and sharp word. She was biding her time until she could find a way to get him tossed out on his arse. Meanwhile, he only had to suffer her at meals when he sat with the rest of the staff at table. Of course, he couldn't manage to keep a civil tongue in his head, but had to tease and bait her with snide comments guaranteed to turn her already-florid face an apoplectic scarlet.

On the brighter side, it turned out old Badgeman wasn't the horror Jem had expected him to be. Oh yes, they'd had several set-tos on Jem's first few days in the house. The mountainous man didn't bother to hide his distrust as he grudgingly demonstrated Jem's new duties. But things got better after the third day, when Jem wheedled the story of his master's injuries from the badger.

"No. You brush *with* the nap," Badgeman barked, taking the brush from Jem and demonstrating the proper way to remove lint from the velvet collar of one of Alan's jackets. "Be sure to check his boots at least once a day. A gentleman can't be seen in public with scuffed shoes."

Jem watched him briskly brush the velvet until it lay smooth and lint-free. He could've done it right himself, but he enjoyed irritating Badgeman too much to resist playing dumb. "Check his boots every day. Got it. But the gentleman never goes out, does he? Hardly seems worth keeping a chap like me around."

The badger grunted in hearty agreement.

"He's a bleak sort, but you admire him greatly, don't you?" Jem continued, determined to prod until he'd learned more about Alan.

"He saved me life." Badgeman turned from hanging the jacket back in the wardrobe and stared at Jem with steely eyes from under his jutting brow. "And I'd cheerfully kill anyone as would harm him."

"Aye, loyalty. I respect that. What were the circumstances of his saving you?"

"No business of yours."

"'Spose not. But I'm asking all the same. If I'm going to work for the man, if I'm going to 'spend time' near him, it might help me to know what brings on his nightmares." Jem opted for frankness. No point in acting the part of valet with Badgeman, who knew better. Draw a picture for him of sleepless nights and Jem offering a sort of comfort Badge never could. Assert his new place in the master's life. Although, truth be told, Alan hadn't summoned Jem to his bed once since that first night they'd spent together, and he was only guessing about the nightmares.

He met Badgeman's hard stare with one of his own, frank and guileless. "I may be a thief, a whore, and a liar, but I'm not here to hurt anyone, and if I can, I'll help. So why don't you and I come to an agreement? You tell me a little more about Sir Alan's past, and I'll stop acting like I don't know bootblacking from bacon."

Was that almost a smile that curled the man's hard lips?

"Tell me about Badajoz," Jem finished. "Please." Oh, he could be a right winning lad when he tried. Even foul-tempered badgers softened at his innocent eyes.

"It were a cold day like this one here. We'd been digging trenches for weeks in muck so thick it could drown a man, and all the while the howitzers blasting over our heads, pounding holes in the stone wall around the town. Now it was time to attack. You ever tried to pour summat through a funnel only to get a bit o' shite stuck in the tube and back up the whole works?"

Jem nodded, but Badgeman's expression was far away as he painted the picture. "Two thousand men dead or injured in less than two hours' time, all clogging up those breaches in the wall. The French had mined 'em and was pouring musket fire and grenades down on us like fucking manna from heaven." His voice was harsh with irony as he compared bombs to blessings.

"Did we retreat? Hell, no. Brave, bloody soldiers one and all, we clambered over our dead and dying, infiltrated the town, drove back the Frogs, and won the day. Heroic it were, what followed, but I missed out on that particular party, as my nob got cracked wide open, and I was unconscious. Still don't know how he managed to haul this slab o' flesh, but 'twas Captain Watleigh who dragged me, his batman, someplace safe before plunging back into the wild rumpus."

Jem didn't have to ask what rumpus he was referring to. Everyone knew about the disastrous losses at Badajoz followed by the horrifying rape, murder, and pillage the victors had inflicted on civilians for nearly two days, long after the French and Spanish troops had withdrawn from the city.

"They say Wellington wept when he saw the dead." Badgeman's laughter sounded more like a snarl. "He should weep in hell for orchestrating that buggering disaster."

"Sounds like a right mess," Jem said. "I shouldn't wonder if all the soldiers who survived would be walking ghosts after such an ordeal, you included, sir." It was the first time he'd addressed Badgeman with the title of respect.

The man seemed to come back from his memories. His eyes flickered, and he cast a sharp look at Jem to see if he was once again mocking. When he registered his sober expression, Badgeman nodded. “Aye, that's a proper term, lad. Walking ghosts we are. None more so than the master, I'm afraid. What happened to him while I was out of me senses, he won't say. But it must have been frightful bad, and I don't mean the injury to his leg.”

“Well, time he came back to the living, I say, and I mean to see him do it.” Jem ventured a smile, and Badgeman didn't scowl, which was as near as he'd come thus far to politeness where Jem was concerned.

Since that incident, the two men had coexisted in wary civility, and Badgeman was, if not an ally, at least a more kindly face than Mrs. Crimpett's. Now it was nearly a week since Jem had taken up residence at the house near Mayfair, and he was bored out of his skull with being indoors, warm, safe, secure, and with having far too much time on his hands. Being a valet for a man who had no social obligations was not a strenuous task, so he'd done his share of exploring the house when he wasn't in Alan's company, including looking through the many library books he could scarcely read. He'd seen plenty of items ripe for nicking, but hadn't touched one of them.

Today he was ready for a bit of fun, perhaps a ride through the park in Watleigh's phaeton—the man had two carriages, one enclosed, one open—or a shopping trip. What was the good of having all that money if a man didn't use it to enjoy life? At the very least, if he couldn't cajole Alan to go out, he planned to land him in bed today. It was past time for a tumble—nearly seven days—and Jem didn't know what Sir Doom-and-Gloom was waiting for, why they were spending every night only a room apart.

He made his way to Alan's study, where the man was bent over his escritoire writing something. In Jem's opinion, he spent far too much time at the damned desk, poring over ledgers, letters, and God knew what all. What he needed was a good airing and a bit of fun.

Jem leaned against the edge of the small desk, picked up a small brass elephant perched on the top shelf, and hefted it in his hand. "Lovely day out. Seems winter's broke at last."

Watleigh glanced up, distracted, from the correspondence he was reading. "Yes."

This wouldn't do at all. He was looking *through* Jem rather than at him. Was he a stick of furniture to be ignored so, especially when wearing his spruce new jacket, fancy cravat, and with his hair freshly cut and styled like Brummell himself?

Jem set the elephant down. "Thought we might take a tour of the park today, or p'raps stop by your tailor. The state of your wardrobe is deplorable, sir. You need a new jacket or a waistcoat or two at least."

His employer stared at him. "I don't require any new garments at this time. Thank you for your concern."

"Just doing my job, sir. Valet," Jem reminded in case he'd forgotten. "Care of your clothing is my life's work." He grinned.

Alan's lips twitched. "Are you bored already, Jem?"

"Not bored, precisely. Our chess matches are a lark now that I'm getting the hang of the game, but I wouldn't mind going out and seeing a bit o' the town now and again."

What am I doing here? he longed to ask the man who refused to fuck him. Alan had kept him at a distance over the past week, speaking politely but not sharing intimacy as they'd done that first night. They spent time together discussing events of the day, which Alan read from the newspaper. Jem learned to play chess and card games and taught the other man to throw dice. But he must refer to him always as "sir" now—no more plain "Alan"—and this Watleigh treated him as naught but a servant, although quite a familiar one. Theirs was a strange and stilted camaraderie, not what Jem had expected or hoped for. Every night he gave the man plenty of opportunity to ask him to sleep in his chamber, but every night he was sent away.

Now Alan glanced at the papers on his desk, wiped the quill, covered the inkpot, and rose. "I suppose it would be good to get out of the house for a while. This winter has been confining, and my physician suggests it's time I exercise my leg more."

"Good. A stroll in the park it is, then." He paused. "But is it acceptable for me to walk with you?"

A flicker of some emotion crossed the other man's face. "I believe if you stay a pace or two behind, bearing my umbrella and topcoat, it will suffice."

Jem mentally shook his head at the silly devices a gent had to take to protect his reputation and place in society. A cove had more freedom in his world, where no one was too high-and-mighty to pass the time of day with anyone he chose.

Within the hour they were seated in the closed carriage that had brought Jem to his new life. What a strange week this had been, full of unexpected twists and turns, and now here he was, clean, well fed, dressed nearly as nice as a swell himself, and still finding reason to complain. Men were fools, never content even when good fortune fell right into their laps. So what if Sir Bumbuggerer never buggered his bum again. It was up to the gentleman to decide what course their relationship would take. Jem needed to stop fretting, have a good tug at himself if he was getting too tight in the seam, and let nature unfold as it would.

They took the larger traveling coach, with Badgeman on the box, instead of the sportier phaeton. Jem would have liked to be out in the open, perched on the high seat. Fresh air blew into the carriage through the small window. It smelled good and clean, of rain and coal smoke, horse dung and alley refuse. It smelled like London.

Jem relaxed in his seat, enjoying the ride since he was used to walking, listening to the wheels rattle over the cobblestones then grind over pebbles on an unpaved road. The racket of traffic on the street outside was loud—horses whinnying, draymen yelling, vehicles clattering along.

He glanced across at his traveling companion.

Alan was gazing out the window, the light illuminating the harsh planes of his face in an artistic way. He was a very handsome man, brooding and dark in a way that attracted Jem like a cat to a bowl of cream. Jem "accidentally" bumped his knees against the other man's, trying to get his attention. When that didn't work, he tapped his foot lightly against Alan's shoe.

Hooded eyes turned toward him, and Sir Alan stared down his patrician nose at him. "Have you lived in London all your life, Jem?"

"Southwark born and bred. Yes, sir."

"Do you care for riding at all?"

"Never have had the opportunity. Horses and me, I don't know as we'd get on."

"I was thinking it might be time to take a trip to check on my country estate soon. Have you ever been to the countryside?"

"Can't say as I have."

"The land is beautiful in Shropshire. A man can walk or ride for miles and enjoy absolute solitude. I think you would like it there."

Jem felt Alan was trying to tell him more than what his words were saying. "Sounds lovely, sir."

"A man can feel more...alive there than he does in the city. More free."

Ah, Jem understood. Poor Sir Alan Watleigh was bound by convention and moral and religious strictures that would choke the very life from him. He feared his sexual needs, tried to deny them until he couldn't stand it any longer, indulged his vice, then hated himself all the more afterward. Jem had figured all that the first night; guilt was a common malady and luckily one he wasn't prone to himself. But it seemed Alan felt freer to pursue what he wanted while in the country. Very well, then. They should go there, and soon.

"I'd be delighted to accompany you," Jem said. "Always wanted to see a cow or sheep at home."

The carriage lurched to a stop, and a moment later, Badgeman opened the door for them to get out at the park.

"You may take yourself off to a tavern, if you like," Alan told him. "Have a drink or two, then return for us."

"Yes, sir." Badger had never looked brighter. Jem guessed he was just as tired as Jem was of lurking about the house. Give the man a tankard of ale and a wench, and he was in his element, no doubt. A Yorkshireman through and through, if Jem didn't mistake his accent.

The sun was warm but the breeze chilly as it lifted Jem's hair and tried to burrow beneath his jacket. He had the master's topcoat tossed over one arm and his umbrella in hand. They walked together yet apart down the gravel path, past a wide pond full of water lilies and geese, and under the arching boughs of a gnarled old tree.

Jem glanced down with a swell of pride at the buckles on his shoes, glinting in the sunlight with every step. He'd never owned footwear so fine. The sight of them pleased him immensely. He sidestepped a dollop of goose shit with a grimace.

"Ever heard the story of Narcissus?" Amusement tinged Alan's voice.

"No, I believe I missed that one."

"It's about a man so enamored by his own reflection that his vanity angered the gods. Ultimately he was turned into one of those." He pointed to a cluster of yellow flowers which drooped near the water's edge. "Ever straining to catch a glimpse of his own handsome face in the water."

Jem scowled at the tease. "You've a right clever tongue in your head when you care to use it. I ain't putting on airs. It's these new shoes. I just like the way they look. They're not of my own making, so it can't be considered prideful, eh? Nothing wrong with admiring them, is there?"

"Nothing wrong at all." Alan's voice was warm, and the smile continued to curve his lips. It looked good on him.

They skirted the pond, passing several strolling couples along the way, before walking farther back into a wooded area. Here the path was shaded by thick branches, and the way was empty of other people. It felt as solitary and private as if it were a darkened cathedral made just for them. Overhead, birds chirped and rustled in the leaves. Beneath, only the sound of their footsteps on gravel disturbed the quiet.

In the hushed stillness, Jem became intimately aware of his master walking beside him—the stride of his boots, the swish of his jacket sleeve, the scent that wafted from his heated body. Arousal stirred and grew within him, his cock hardening as he cast a glance at Alan's handsome profile.

At the same moment, the man looked toward him. Their gazes met and held, and Jem's erection swelled larger. Sweet Jesus, something had to break soon. He couldn't wait for a trip to the country or for Alan to come around on his own. He simply wasn't that patient.

Their steps slowed then stopped, and they stood side by side on the path, simply staring at each other.

"What's it going to be then, Your Grace?" Jem asked.

By God, the boy was relentless! Alan drew an unsteady breath. The desire he'd been fighting for days pulled against his reins of control like a mettlesome horse. Jem had suggested, prodded, and teased—not always intentionally, but by his mere presence in Alan's house. For days he'd enticed and drawn him toward what he craved. And now this. Did he truly not understand the danger of what he was suggesting, here on a path in a public park?

Alan strode toward him, crossing the ground between them in two steps. He took Jem by the upper arms and shook him. "What the hell are you playing at?" he growled. "Are you insane or just insanely reckless?"

Jem's eyes were as wide and innocent as always. He looked like a schoolboy caught putting jam in the inkwells in the classroom. "There's no one here. No one but you and me."

Jem's tongue darted out to wet his lips, and Alan was fascinated by the flash of pink. His heart pounded, and his cock felt like it would explode in his trousers in a moment. He wanted to kiss those moist lips so badly, he thought he'd sell his soul for the chance. The reins of his control broke, and lust thundered through him.

Alan shook the youth once more before bending his head and seizing Jem's lips with his own. Their mouths clashed together with the power of a flood against a tide wall as passion flowed through him. His teeth cut the inside of his lip with the force of the kiss, and the warmth and softness of the other man's lips were everything he'd yearned for. When Jem's tongue slipped into his mouth, Alan gasped with surprise at the wet, sinuous intrusion.

He let go of Jem's arms to cup his face in both hands, feeling the hardness of his jaw, the faint scrape of stubble, and the softness of his skin beneath his palms. The umbrella hit the ground with a thud as Jem wrapped his arms around Alan's back and held him.

Christ, they were hugging and kissing, right there on the path in the middle of God's green earth where anyone could see them. The thought horrified, aroused, and thrilled him all at the same time. His senses left him as blood rushed down to his cock. His pulse pounded in his ears so he could hardly hear, and his body felt like it would shudder apart from the powerful emotions surging through it.

Jem shuffled closer, groin pressing against Alan's, the bulge of his erection apparent. Alan's cock responded, straining as if it would drill its way through his trousers to get to where it wanted to be. He ground his hips, rubbing in an effort to relieve his desperate need. All the while he never stopped kissing Jem. What a marvel it was to share a kiss with someone. The intimate exploration of mouth to mouth was even more personal than two bodies coupling.

"Mm," Jem groaned and pulled away to draw a breath.

Alan released the man's face from between his hands. Opening his eyes, he looked at Jem's closed ones, long lashes brushing against his cheeks. His chest ached with sudden emotion, and the strength of the unnamed feeling frightened him.

Alan stepped back.

"This can't happen," he said gruffly. "Not here. We must keep walking."

Easier said than done when his dick was throbbing so badly, it was painful to stalk away. He strode fast enough that Jem had to practically run to catch up after retrieving Alan's umbrella and coat from the ground.

"It's perfectly safe. There's no one around," he repeated, sounding breathless. "P'raps just behind that tree over there. Won't take long. I can do you proper."

"I said no!" Alan bit out the words through clenched teeth because the rest of his body was clamoring for him to say yes. And despite his show of anger, he was already imagining the things they could do later in his bedroom, or maybe even in the carriage.

Jem fell silent then, and they continued to walk at a brisk pace through the thick of the wood and around a loop back to more civilized paths.

Alan pondered his perverted desires, the things he wanted that a man should be ashamed to think of. He wondered, as he had all his life, why he felt that way. Over the years, he'd tried to deny his nature. He'd slept with a few women, but the experience had been weak and tepid compared to the desire a man could arouse in him. Remaining abstinent only worked for so long before he had to find relief for his tension. Now with Jem, for the first time he'd experienced more than a simple physical release. He liked the lad, felt an odd connection with him, which was even more frightening than his twisted sexual desires.

"Sir." Jem panted as he trotted alongside him. "Remember Old Sally I told you about? Well, she weren't the only one in her family to come across magic folk. Her brother Donald has his own tale of meeting the fae. Would you like to hear about it?"

Alan glanced at him and slowed down a little.

"Donnie was a drinker, as was his friend Pat. The pair also loved to fish. Went out every day on their favorite pond, although neither brought any catch home to his wife at night. Spent the entire day drinking, they did.

"So one day Donnie felt something big pulling on his hook. He drew it up and found a wee man struggling on the line. He recognized a leprechaun when he saw one, but did he demand the little fellow's gold? No. Did he ask for a fine mess of fish to take home to his wife and hungry brood? Oh no, Donnie had a better idea for his one wish. It was only midday, and the drink was getting low, so he asked the wee man to turn the entire lake into the very best ale.

"'Fool,' his friend Pat raged as he gazed at the pond brimming with delicious brown ale. 'Now we have to piss in the boat!'"

Jem cocked a glance at him, waiting for a response, and Alan couldn't help but smile. The joke wasn't all that funny, but Jem's natural way of telling a story was a pleasure to listen to.

"The world's full of fools, I say," Jem continued. "People always longing after something different 'stead of enjoying what they have right in front of 'em."

"You know a lot of interesting people," Alan remarked, ignoring the little homily.

"Yah, my nob's chock-full o' tales like that. Could keep you entertained for years." He winked, eyes sparkling, and Alan noticed the blue of his waistcoat almost exactly matched them. Jem looked very fine in his new attire and knew it.

"I don't know about years, but you amuse me for now." Alan paused. There no longer seemed any point in denying the physical element floating in the air between them, which had erupted just now. "As for the other… If something is to happen, we must be extremely circumspect."

He looked sharply at the younger man. "No public incidents like this again. Ever."

Jem bobbed his head. "Yes, sir. Understood. Too dangerous." He walked several more paces, his high-heeled shoes crunching the gravel. "But p'raps in the carriage on the way home…?"

Hopeless! The youth's hunger seemed to be irrepressible, and since he ignited a fire that burned away Alan's common sense, it was quite likely they'd follow his suggestion. Alan began to walk faster again, anticipating the ride.

Chapter Seven

By the time they'd finished their stroll in the park, including stopping while Jem cleaned his shoe after he'd stepped in goose shit after all, the carriage awaited them. Badgeman stood beside it rather than sitting on the box, and Alan knew the instant he saw him that something was the matter. After all their years together, he could read the man's anxious posture like a book. He was shifting his weight impatiently from foot to foot, hands jammed in his pockets and shoulders hunched.

Alan strode quickly toward him. "What is it?"

"T'aint nowt, sor."

He was lying, of course, and the shift in his accent confirmed he was truly upset.

Alan turned to Jem. "I think I must have dropped my snuffbox. Please retrace our steps and see if you can find it."

For once Jem said nothing. His eyes shifted to Badgeman and back to Alan. He gave a brief nod and strode toward the trees without even pretending to hunt the ground for a snuffbox.

"Now then, Sergeant, cut line and tell me what has happened." Alan hadn't called Badgeman "sergeant" since their return to England and hoped that pulling rank would serve to loosen the man's tongue.

Badgeman adopted the proper stance—at attention, shoulders back, hands at side. But he didn't obey the order. "Begging pardon. 'Tis nowt to do wi' ye, sir."

So much for the absolute authority he'd once wielded over the man, Alan thought wryly.

Still at attention, Badgeman said, "I pray I might take a bit o' time off, though. To attend to personal business."

"Of course you shall have time off." Alan hesitated. "I shan't interfere, Badgeman. And you know we keep one another's secrets."

Badgeman blinked and looked away. "Aye. Only...'tis...I'm ashamed. Simple as that."

Alan waited.

Still pretending to examine a nearby tree, Badgeman blurted, "I made a promise to Charlie Cutler, and I ain't even tried to keep it. Been more 'n a year, and I never even..." He pulled in a deep breath. "I just went on my merry way."

"Don't be a fool. Any promises you made to Charlie had to have been before Badajoz. I recall he died of fever weeks before, poor devil. He'd understand your situation. Getting blown to bits isn't exactly going on your merry way. You had your own worries."

"But Mrs. Charlie and the Major. I promised to look out for them, sir."

"Ah." Dismay flooded Alan. During his absence, Badgeman must have learned some bad news about Mrs. Cutler and her daughter.

Alan hadn't known Private Cutler's wife well, for all that she followed the drum. Mrs. Charlie had a strict sense of protocol and kept out of the officers' way.

The Major was a different story. Cutler's daughter had been fearless and quietly inquisitive. Conditions in the camp were primitive. The Major—Alan couldn't recall her real name—didn't complain, for she had never known any other life. She'd had the propriety of the military drummed into her but still managed to slip through the rules when her mother wasn't watching. More than once he'd been sitting in his tent and looked up to see her solemn gray eyes watching him from the open flap.

Badgeman choked out the words. "I promised Charlie I'd watch over his wife and the Major, but then with one thing and another... Right after Charlie perished, Mrs. Charlie told me she wanted for nothing. That she'd help with the wounded like she always had."

"A strong woman," Alan said, recalling the dark-haired lady who never smiled and who tried to hide her permanently reddened hands whenever she encountered an officer. "And she had some pride."

"Made of iron," Badgeman agreed. "Said working with the surgeons and the wounded made her forget her own troubles." He rubbed his scarred cheek absently with a hand. "But you see, sir, she was not the best judge o' character. She greatly admired that Mr. Schivvers."

"You're worried that she might have taken up with him? Whatever news you've heard, I doubt it could be that. Not that bastard. He thought too highly of himself to take a woman like her even for a moment's fun."

Mr. Schivvers, the head army surgeon, was a fine figure of a man—tall, lean, with a ready smile and thick, pale hair. Yet the man had repulsed Alan from their first meeting. For months he couldn't understand why. After all, Schivvers was cultured, trained by the best, and skilled at his work. More than a mere stitcher and bone-cutter, the man had aspirations to be a physician.

Then Alan had discovered he'd kept his skill finely honed and learned new ones by chopping up the corpses of those who'd died on his table. Not that he'd killed them. No, he did his cool best to save the men under his knife. But if they expired on the table, Schivvers would continue carving them up, casually poking through their insides, all the while whistling under his breath.

Lying injured on the ground, Alan had also watched the man go through the pockets of the dead and slip money and goods into his own pockets like any battlefield vulture.

"*Not me, you bastard*," he'd whispered.

Schivvers had smiled, showing his strong white teeth. "*We'll see.*"

"That man is the devil, sir. I think he's got no soul," Badgeman said now and began to pace again. "Soft-spoken. Acts the gentleman, but I swear, sir, nothing's there."

"True enough. But if Mrs. Charlie has taken up with him, there's nothing you can do."

"Naw, naw indeed, sir. That would be bad enough. But 'tis worse. I met up with a man from my village just now at the King's Arms. He'd been in the Ninety-fifth Fusiliers and got injured. Missing most of his hand now."

Alan wanted to interrupt and tell him to get to the point, but country-bred Badgeman would tell stories at his own slow pace. "My old pal Ned was in Portugal. Not Spain like we was. He saw Schivvers there, so the surgeon's shifted quarters. Ned only noticed him because of the man's shadow—went with him everywhere. Ned told me she was a pretty little thing. Young. An orphan."

Alan closed his eyes, dreading what would come next.

Badgeman continued. "Mrs. Charlie had met her maker, poor thing. Ned thinks she died of fever or some accident in Spain. That's the thing, sir. Schivvers has the Major. Ned says she's the one 'at's his shadow. Do ye see, sir? The Major was left in the surgeon's tender care by Mrs. Charlie."

"Shit."

Badgeman gave his crooked half smile. "Sums it up, sir. So now you understand. I gotta go."

Alan nodded. "I'll have Jem pack my things as soon as we—"

"No, sir. Not you. I were the one that promised Charlie. 'Tis not your affair. 'Tis my failure, and I must make the remedy."

"Sergeant!" Alan barked the word from their past life. "Cutler was under my command. The fate of his family is my concern. You will allow me to help you."

Apparently his discipline had broken down entirely since army days, for instead of instantly obeying, Badgeman only shook his head. "No, sir."

"And why not?"

Badgeman glared back, but eventually his gaze dropped. "He has her legally, sir."

"And you plan on taking illegal action?" Alan swore again.

"I'll do what must be done. With all due respect sir, I do not want you there." The servant's quiet voice was apologetic but firm. His accent had vanished again, so he was in control.

Alan gave up. No doubt Badgeman was right to put him off. Alan no longer wallowed in miserable self-pity most of his days and nights, yet he was still weak and hadn't ridden more than a mile on horseback for over a year—he'd be a greater nuisance than help. "I'll fund your journey."

"It's not necessary, sir. I have the funds saved."

"Damn you, Badgeman, you must learn to compromise. I shan't insist on going with you, and that's my concession. You will take my funds and stop your whimpering about it—that is yours. And as soon we return home, I'll consult a lawyer. There must be something to be done short of killing the bastard."

Badgeman looked relieved. "Thank you. That'd be useful, sir. With your permission, sir, I'll start as soon as may be for Lisbon. That's where Ned saw that bastard surgeon." He stopped pacing and thumped a hand against the carriage wheel. "Captain Watleigh, sir. Oh, no. Your household. Who'll run it when I'm gone?"

"Why me, o' course." Jem appeared next to them. "No snuffbox, sir," he told Alan with a wink. Alan had actually forgotten his existence for five whole minutes—for the first time since the man had entered his life.

"No need to glare like you'd love to tear me limb from limb, Mr. Badgeman." Jem opened the carriage door and waited for Alan to enter. As he stood with a hand on the handle, he bowed to Badgeman. "'Twas a joke, I promise."

"A poor one," Badgeman muttered.

"I heard nothing much, Mr. B., if that's your worry. Only that you'll be traveling to a surgeon."

Alan ignored Jem. He squeezed his ex-batman's upper arm as he passed him. "We'll miss you, Badgeman, but there's no need for you to worry. I promise the house shan't tumble down during your absence. And I will do what I can to help."

Badgeman muttered his thanks, and Alan climbed in.

"I overheard more 'n I told the badger," Jem said as he settled onto the seat next to Alan and the door closed behind them.

Propriety dictated that he should have taken the seat across, with his back to the horses, but again Alan didn't say anything.

Jem cocked his head. "He's truly tearing off to foreign parts to kill some bastard?"

Alan considered telling him to mind his own business, then he noticed the glowing blue eyes showed more than curiosity. "Do you like Mr. Badgeman, Jem?"

"Him? That fearful, ugly devil? P'raps." Jem leaned back in the seat and looked out the window as if wishing he hadn't displayed concern.

"It won't come to murder." Alan spoke with more confidence than he felt.

Jem's attention seemed fixed on the scenery outside the coach, and Alan used the moment of his rare distraction to admire Jem's lean, muscular body. His hands, with their long, sensitive fingers, lay relaxed, splayed on his thighs. The light from the window gilded Jem's throat. The glow picked out his Adam's apple and then the lines in his cheek as a smile flashed across his face.

"Like what you see, sir?" he asked in low voice without turning from the window. Damn the man, he must have eyes in the back of his head.

Alan folded his arms over his chest. "I'm only noticing you've gained some weight in the time you've been in my employment."

"I have at that. You have as well. But truly, is that all you notice?" Jem looked away from the window, and Alan saw he wore the smile of a ravenous predator.

Alan's breath quickened, and his cock stirred. "Yes, that is all. We will not behave like animals in the coach." He commanded his unruly body to relax. Very well, if his desire refused to abate, he would have to fall back on sheer resolve. Not in the park and not here, Alan told himself, and then realized the implications. He hadn't added *not in my house.*

It would happen, of course. The ever-present, nagging hunger weakened his resolution. He held his breath, waiting. If Jem so much as touched him now, the last of his qualms would vanish as they had in the park. As they rode through the busy streets, he'd seize Jem and taste his mouth and his skin again.

Alan sat in the quiet coach, dreading and hoping that Jem might lean against him or brush fingers over his thigh. But the man kept his hands to himself, and they didn't speak again until Badgeman flung open the door in front of the town house.

"Thank you, Badgeman," Alan said. He rubbed his leg hard, pretending it hurt, as he waited for his erection to subside. "I'll compose a note to my solicitor immediately."

He soon climbed out of the carriage, and without looking back to see if Jem followed, mounted the steps to the house.

On his way to the study, he was startled by a crash from a room down the hall, accompanied by a distressed oath. "God's blood." Dicky's favorite.

Alan paused, wondering if he should go to the room and confront Dicky. What would he say other than "clean up that mess," which the footman was bound to do anyway.

The efficient Mrs. Crimpett had recently come to Alan, complaining about Dicky. "*You must see he's not good anymore. You might hire two handsome lads, the same height, sir*," she pleaded.

Alan had refused—and not just because he had no interest in filling his house with attractive young men. Bad enough some men lusted after their female servants. Although, God, he'd done just that with Jem, hadn't he?

He'd told Mrs. Crimpett that as long as Badgeman had no complaints, neither did he. Since the housekeeper was terrified of Badgeman—who had a soft spot for the almost-addled footman and did most of his duties for him—Dicky was there to stay.

"*One more lie from him, sir,*" Mrs. Crimpett had warned Alan, "*and you must show him the door.*"

Alan hadn't bothered to answer. The old dragon had been with his family forever, and letting her have the last word was the best way to keep her from breathing fire.

And now Dicky had apparently broken something in the sitting room. No doubt he'd be able to hide the evidence, and no one would notice for days, if he was lucky.

Alan continued on to the study, reflecting he was a poor steward of his family's possessions. He couldn't care less about many of the things he'd inherited, especially the decorative nonsense. As far as he was concerned, most objects turned into meaningless junk after the people who'd bought and cared about them died. Others, like his father's desk, held too much meaning.

The crash from the sitting room didn't dismay him in the least. Perhaps that was why he hadn't lost any sleep over hiring a thief. He'd lost a great deal more sleep thinking about the thief's welcoming body lying so close to his own bedchamber.

Enough useless, painful lust. He sat to write his note summoning Mr. Gardner for Badgeman and promptly forgot about whatever Dicky had broken.

An hour later, as he awaited the response from the solicitor, he heard another cry of distress coming from the sitting room. Soon after, a babble of excited voices started up. He sighed, put down his book, and went to investigate.

The housekeeper stood in the middle of the sitting room, fists on hips, glaring at the half circle of servants—the ones who had permission to enter the family quarters. Dicky, the maids, and, of course, Jem. None of them noticed Alan in the doorway. The servants' attention was focused on Mrs. C., Jem's name for the fierce protector of the Watleigh house. She pointed at shards that had been carefully wrapped in a handkerchief. Now it lay on the cloth atop an occasional table—a smashed figurine. Judging from the pieces, it was the shepherdess, one of the more repulsive ceramic pieces collected by a forgotten ancestor.

"I know Jane is not responsible," Mrs. C. declared. "As I sent you in here, Dicky, you and only you could be the culprit. This is *the end*, I tell you."

Alan hadn't ever seen her on her high horse with the other servants, and this was impressive. She was as loud and full of hellfire as a preacher from the pulpit. Poor Dicky looked on the edge of tears. Mrs. C. went on. "The master agreed with me. One more incident, and you'll be turned out. I promise you, Dicky, this is—"

Before Alan could reveal his presence and point out he'd agreed to no such thing, another voice interrupted her tirade. "Here now, Mrs. C. You got the wrong end of the stick. Weren't Dicky. Not at all. I took a fancy to the thing, see. Just wanted to take a closer look, and *wham, smash*, it slid right out o' my butter fingers. Terrible mistake. I shoulda confessed my sin right away, of course."

Dicky visibly started. “But,” he began. He opened his mouth once or twice, then jerked again when Jem's elbow jammed into his side.

“My excuse is like this.” Jem might have been chatting with the housekeeper over a cozy cup of tea. “I got busy polishing Sir Alan's boots and fobs and whatnot. Clean forgot my crime when Mr. B. told me about a recipe for boot polish. I'm supposed to use champagne, if you can believe it. On boots. Such a terrible waste drove all other thoughts outta me nob.”

Alan tried to hold back a laugh that emerged as a cough. Mrs. Crimpett started, just as Dicky had, except with considerably more grace. She whirled to face him. “Sir. I beg your pardon. You're just in time.”

“So I understand.”

“I would consult Mr. Badgeman, however, he is preoccupied, packing to visit his sick aunt,” Mrs. Crimpett said.

“That's the story, is it?” muttered Jem.

She ignored him and went on. “And I'm not sure I believe Jem's version of events.”

“Why not?” asked Alan, determined not to meet Jem's eyes. “Have you had any indication that he is a liar?”

“He's attempting to protect Dicky from dismissal, sir. And as we decided when last we spoke on the matter—”

Alan had had enough. He raised his voice. “I made no sort of agreement. And while I'm sure we're all sad to see that objet d'art go, I'm sure we won't dismiss any servants over its destruction.”

“But sir, we can't allow clumsiness to go unchecked in a household so filled with treasures. It's as bad as hiring a thief.”

Alan definitely didn't want to meet Jem's eyes now. "I hardly think one ugly smashed statue is worth such a hue and cry," he said.

"But sir…" She tried again.

Alan wished he could shake this off and allow her to have the last word. Mrs. Crimpett was afraid of Badgeman, but he would be absent for God knew how long.

She had always called him Master Alan, and he'd been the younger son. Then he'd limped home from battle, in constant pain and uninterested in the household. It was past time to establish himself as the highest authority on the premises.

"Mrs. Crimpett." He drew himself up to his full height and glared down at her like the captain he'd been. Twice in one day he'd drawn on his abandoned role. "No more. We will not discuss this matter any longer, do you understand? You will all return to your duties. At once."

Without a murmur, the servants filed from the room. Even Mrs. Crimpett didn't look back.

"Jem," Alan called out.

He sauntered back into the room, grinning. "Sorry I broke that dreadful bit of ugliness, sir."

"You didn't." Alan tried to keep from smiling. He waited until the last of the footsteps died away. "You don't have to lie to keep Dicky safe. I shan't dismiss him." A sharp pain shot through his leg, so he slumped onto the sofa.

Jem came over and, without permission, sat next to him, too close. Alan could feel the heat of his leg almost touching him. He was far too aware of the man. Surely it was his imagination that the air shifted slightly as Jem breathed.

Jem moved, and the pressure of his thigh against Alan's vanished—not in time to slow his sudden quick heartbeat or stop the rush of blood to his cock.

"Good for you, sir," Jem spoke easily, as if he hadn't been affected by their bodies' contact. "Near an addle-pated cully, our Dicky. He'd never set the Thames on fire, but he's no thatch-gallows."

"Meaning he's not a bad person?"

"Just that, indeed."

"Why did you protect him?"

Jem shrugged. "He'd have a hard time out and about in the cruel world."

Another thought surfaced in Alan's lust-blurred brain. "And you counted on me to keep you safe from dismissal."

Jem's eyes lit with amusement. "Perhaps," he drawled

"You're a rogue, Jem," Alan said softly.

"Perhaps."

"Most definitely."

He'd learned something important about Jem that afternoon. Despite his sharp tongue and constant barrage of quips, the youth was tenderhearted and had an unexpected decency. His inborn protectiveness toward one he perceived as weak showed an honorable nature at odds with his thieving and whoring. What manner of man might Jem have become if the circumstances of his life had been different? Perhaps a fine and decent one. Perhaps a leader.

Alan had never spared much thought for the lower classes. He'd been raised, as all his peers were, to think of them as practically a separate species, without the sensitive spirit, higher thought, or nobility of their superiors. In the service, although his men had respected him, there had naturally been the distance of rank as well as class between them. With Jem, for the first time, Alan considered that perhaps all men were the same, and only the hand life dealt them created differences.

By late afternoon, when Mr. Gardner responded to Alan's note with one of his own saying he would meet with him on the morrow, Badgeman could restrain himself no longer. The normally unflappable man seemed bent on heading off immediately to rectify the situation with Cutler's family.

"I'm sorry, sir. When I think of what the likes o' that evil man might be doing to the wee lass, I can't abide it. I must leave today. As it is, 'twill take many days to reach Lisbon, where Ned spotted Schivvers and his ward. Poor little Major, always so brave and soldierly—a heroic young lass growing into a fine woman like her mum. Whether your solicitor can find a way to take the girl from the doctor legally or no, I've got to rescue her."

He strode toward the mews. Alan watched him go and then remembered he had forgotten the funds.

Rather than race after the man, Alan shouted, "Hup!" and made the signal for him to join him. The sergeant marched back double time. Alan pulled out the purse of money. "Take it."

"Thank 'ee sir," Badgeman said. He turned and walked away quickly, almost at a trot.

"What was that you did to your head?" Jem stood behind him.

Alan looked at him, still lost in thought. "Hmm?" Badgeman was usually so imperturbable. Schivvers must have done something to have shaken the man back in Spain. He wondered if Badgeman knew something he hadn't told Alan.

"You shouted after him and did something with your hand on your head," Jem persisted. "What is it?"

"I told him to come to me."

"It's some kinda military signal?"

Alan rubbed the top of his aching leg and nodded.

"Are there more you can show me later, maybe?" Jem suggested. "If we get caught behind enemy lines, we can chatter, eh?" He was probably trying to distract Alan, who stared in the direction in which Badgeman had torn off, riding hell-for-leather.

Some planning on exactly how Badgeman might remove the girl and take her into his own custody would have been advisable. But there was nothing to be done once Badgeman made up his mind about something. He was like a rock that seemed immovable until it started rolling downhill; then nothing could stop it.

Alan put the matter out of his mind as best he could. It wasn't impossible with Jem there to divert him. After dinner they retired to Alan's study, where Jem laughed and imitated the various military signals he begged Alan to show him.

"It's like a dance," Jem said as he circled his hand at hip height, the motion for *go back*. "The only one that makes sense is the *stop and listen*." Jem made a comical display of stopping in midstride and cupping his hand to his ear. "Did all your men know these?"

"Their lives might depend on silent communication, so of course they did." And his words brought back the dreary truth—knowing a few signals hadn't saved most of those lives. "Enough of this. We'll play cards instead."

They played a few hands of piquet, which held neither man's attention.

After awhile, Jem gave up all pretense of concentrating and tossed his hand down on the table.

"Your leg's been troubling you this evening," he stated baldly. "You limped on the way up the stairs, and you've been grimacing as you sit there. Let me ease it for you."

Before Alan could ask what he meant by that, Jem was on the floor by his chair, moving the small card table aside and reaching for Alan's boot. He grabbed the heel and wrestled it off his foot. Alan had worn the boot thinking it would support his leg during their walk, but hadn't thought about the fact his foot might swell, making it hard to take off the footwear.

Jem clicked his tongue as he removed the stocking from Alan's swollen, scarred leg. "Look a' this. You've messed yourself up good."

Carefully placing his foot on the floor, Jem removed the other boot before returning his attention to the injured leg. As tenderly as a mother cat grooming her kits, he lifted Alan's foot and placed it on his lap, then gently massaged his sore calf. His hands were warm and careful as they rubbed from knee to ankle and back up again.

Alan studied the young man sitting at his feet, ministering to him in a sweetly subservient manner. He was both touched and strongly aroused by the service. He groaned softly as Jem took his bare foot between his hands and kneaded the instep, heel, and each toe. The tousle-haired youth looked up at him and smiled, a knowing smile that made Alan's breath catch. His heart pounded, aware this was headed to his bedroom, which would change everything.

This was not like that first night, when he'd hired Jem for a last chance at pleasure before ending himself. Once he'd invited the man into his bed this time, he would not be able to resist having him there again and again. They would have something akin to a relationship, an unpardonable crime in the eyes of both God and man.

Blithely unaware of Alan's inner turmoil, Jem moved his attention to the uninjured leg and foot, spreading more joy with his hands. Alan pushed his doubts and fears aside, relaxed back into his chair, and watched the assurance with which Jem manipulated his limbs.

"You've had some experience at this?"

"Aye, me old granny—well, she wasn't really my granny, but I called her that—had sore joints and used to pay me a penny to ease her pain." He winked. "Not nearly as attractive a proposition as rubbing your joints, sir."

He returned his attention to Alan's war wound, tracing a finger up the length of the scar. "Looks like you nearly lost your leg with this one."

"Mm. It was the injury that sent me home."

"Happened at Badajoz?" Jem pressed. "Old Badger told me a bit about that mess. He said you was a trusty trout to him, pulling him to safety. What happened after that?"

Screams, blood, horror, his men out of control and committing atrocities the likes of which he'd never seen in all his years of active service. It was as if they were possessed, and he could do nothing to rein them in. Then, a sharp pain in his leg, and he went down. A glancing blow to his head, and he was out of it until he woke with Mr. Schivvers bending over him.

"I got shot," he answered simply.

"Is that when you got this one too?" Jem knelt between his knees and reached to touch Alan's side. Beneath his shirt was the cratered scar where another musket ball had once caught him.

"No. That was from years before."

"You've been hard used, sir." Jem began unfastening the shirt, and Alan didn't stop him. "You've earned a rest from battle and a little pleasure after all your heroics."

"I'm no hero. I simply did my job," he muttered, thinking of all those he hadn't been able to save in the ruined city. "And not always well."

"I'm sure you did the very best you could, sir." Warm hands slipped beneath his shirt and undershirt to glide across his stomach. "And old Badgeman, at least, is eternally grateful to you."

The pressure of Jem's body between his spread knees, his hands roaming across his skin, had Alan's cock throbbing with every heartbeat. God, how he wanted those clever hands to finish disrobing him and wrap around his shaft. How he wanted that pursed mouth to encircle his cock and draw him into warmth and wetness. He'd not forgotten the feeling of Jem sucking him when he woke that other morning. In fact, he'd relived the experience every morning, and evening, and at odd hours of the day, ever since then. The only memory to supersede it had been the even more intense one of having his cock buried in the other man's rear, Jem's sweaty, heaving body trapped beneath him.

"Not here." Alan shoved Jem's hands away from his rib cage. "In my room."

"Yes, sir." Jem grinned and rose to stand above him for a moment, looking down. He offered his hand to pull Alan to his feet. Their hands remain clasped as they stood facing each other. "You won't regret it. Not if you don't insist on feeling regret. Let go of your guilt, I say, and allow yourself to have what you want."

Looking into the young thief's earnest eyes, Alan found he believed him. He *could* let go of his guilt. He *wanted* to simply relax and give in to temptation, to have what he wanted...but not right here where the servants might interrupt them.

He grabbed Jem into a hard embrace and pressed a swift kiss on his mouth before pulling away.

"Upstairs," he reiterated, and led the way from the room.

With the bedroom door safely closed and locked behind them, clothing was torn off and fluttered to the floor like discarded rags. Soon both men were naked and locked in an embrace.

To clasp Jem's lean, hard body in his arms and feel skin sliding over skin, muscular arms welded around his back, hairy thighs and groin pressed against his own, a hot mouth latched on to his, was the fulfillment of all Alan had longed for.

Or nearly all. There were other things, and he proceeded to make those fantasies come true. He slid his hands down Jem's back and grasped his rear, the taut globes filling his hands with satisfactory heft. He drew his mouth away from Jem's with a deep inhalation and began to kiss his jaw, his neck, and his chest. The salty taste of the other man's skin was a delectable treat and made Alan want more. His cock ached nearly as much as his bad leg, which was beginning to tremble with the need for him to remove his weight from it.

Alan pulled Jem onto the tall bed with him. They collapsed together in a tangle of limbs, two bodies wrestling but not in conflict. He loved the feeling of Jem's weight on top of him, the heat of his body pressed close, the slickness of his plunging tongue as they kissed again. He'd be quite happy simply to kiss and hold him for the rest of the night, but his cock was already demanding more.

Jem rocked against him, the friction of his body inciting Alan's lust even further. The youth pushed up to a kneeling position and straddled his body, knees digging into the mattress on either side of Alan's hips. He reached out to smooth Alan's hair back, and his hand lingered, caressing his face.

Alan closed his eyes and pressed his cheek into the cupping palm. Jem's soft touch made his heart clench and his chest tighten. This was what he'd denied himself for too long—a simple connection with another human being. As he opened his eyes again to look up into the other man's blue gaze, a solemn, hushed moment filled the air between them.

Jem wasn't smiling for once. In fact, a slight frown furrowed his brow. Did he feel the same strange sense of gravity that Alan felt, or was this perception of something important passing between them all in his mind?

Jem broke the mood with a little laugh. He bent to kiss Alan's chest, licking from nipple to nipple and taking each one into his mouth to suck. A little shocked, Alan gasped and thrust his chest toward Jem's mouth. The furtive and brief couplings he'd shared with men in the past hadn't included such foreplay. The moment was always rushed, with limited contact, and over too soon.

But Jem was ready to take his time and play. He nipped Alan's nipple sharply, making him groan, then kissed his way down his stomach. He took his cock in hand and kissed the tip before sucking it into his mouth. Alan sighed and closed his eyes once more, surrendering to the pleasure.

After pulling and sucking until he had Alan's cock as hard as stone, Jem let go and sat up. “Do you have something, sir, to make the going a bit easier?”

Alan nodded and gestured to the drawer by his bedside. Jem knew the oil was there, had seen him take it from there the other night, but he hadn't been about to rummage in the bedside table uninvited. Now he rolled off Alan and retrieved the small vial of oil, then poured a bit on his palm and smoothed it the length of Alan's shaft.

When Alan groaned at his touch, he whispered, “Feels good, don't it? You're a big one, you are. Would go hard on me without a little oiling first. You'd likely tear me asunder.”

It was flattery. What man doesn't like to be told how enormous his cock is? But the words and Jem's soft, seductive tone inflamed Alan as they were intended to do. His hips lifted as he pushed into the man's stroking hand.

Jem shifted, kneeling high and reaching back between his legs to thrust his oiled fingers into his hole. Eyes closed, he bit his bottom lip and fucked himself with thrusts of his fingers. When he'd stretched the opening to his satisfaction, he reached behind himself and carefully positioned Alan's penis at his back entrance.

The tip penetrated, the ring of muscle clenching around him, and Alan groaned. It was so lovely. Jem sank down on him, slowly, surely, taking him in deep. The oil made the passage smooth, a tight glide like pushing one's fingers into the finest kid glove that was just a shade too small.

Alan watched Jem's face as he penetrated him. His eyes were half-closed and his mouth slack. A soft groan rumbled from his throat. His body was tilted back slightly in order to fit to the angle of Alan's cock, and his own cock thrust like the prow of a ship before him. Alan wrapped his hand around it and gave a good tug. Hard to concentrate on giving Jem pleasure when he was buried so deep up his ass, he could scarcely fathom anything else, but he made the effort. He pumped his hand up and down.

Blue eyes flickered open and regarded him as Jem rose and fell in a leisurely cadence. Alan's cock felt as if it were on fire, so hot and tight was the channel that engulfed it.

"You like that, eh?" Jem muttered. "Say it, then. Say you like fucking me up the arse. It's what you crave. You dream about it all the time. Admit it aloud, Alan."

It was the first time he'd called him his given name since he'd taken formal employment with him. Alan loved the sound of his name on Jem's tongue, the rough tone of his speech, and the filthy things he said.

"'I love to bugger you, Jem.' Say it!" the lad demanded, clenching his muscles hard around Alan's cock. He froze with the shaft buried deep inside him and stared at Alan like a schoolmaster waiting for the right answer.

Alan could barely summon enough moisture to speak. His voice was gruff when it issued from his lips. "I… Aw, Jesus. Fuck!" he groaned.

"Say it!"

"I love to f-fuck you."

"'Up the arse.' Don't fear to admit it any longer." He lifted and rammed down onto Alan's cock—hard, impaling himself.

Alan groaned harshly. "I love to fuck you. I love to… I love this."

"Good. That's good." Jem's voice was as soothing as water pouring over him. "That's what I wanted to hear. Now do it."

Easier said than done, as Jem sat astride him and had all control, but Alan obliged, thrusting his hips and driving himself up into the other man like a battering ram. Again and again he filled him. He gave up on pulling Jem's cock and gripped his hips instead, guiding him up and down.

Pleasure built and rolled through him, filling his body and mind until there was no room for any other thought or feeling but this. The joining of their two bodies was the center of the world, the fulcrum on which everything balanced. Joy coursed through his veins and burst in his chest. He was uplifted even as he lifted up to thrust into Jem one last time. His cock pulsed as he released in warm gushes.

"Christ Almighty," Jem cursed. His body was sweat-slicked, perspiration trickling down his chest and pooling on his concave belly. He was beautiful. Merely looking at him drove Alan mad with desire even as the last waves of pleasure receded.

Coming out of his haze of lust, Alan again reached for Jem's cock and continued what he'd begun. He pumped his shaft until Jem groaned. It didn't take long to bring him to climax. Jem rocked his hips, and Alan's depleted erection slipped from his backside. A few quiet grunts later, Jem was spilling onto Alan's fist.

"Lovely," he murmured, blowing out a long breath. "Thanks." He cupped his hand around Alan's, which was still encircling his cock.

With the sex finished, Alan half expected remorse and shame to flood back in as they had the other night, but this time his elation didn't fade. It took him a moment to recognize the almost unfamiliar emotion. He was happy. Content.

Jem flopped on top of him and rested his head against Alan's shoulder. Alan's arms automatically went around his body and held him close. He nuzzled the top of Jem's head, soft hair tickling his lips. Oh, he could get used to this very quickly. Whore, thief, or whatever else Jem was be damned, Alan wanted him around.

After several moments, Jem sighed and slid off him to lie by his side, head propped on hand. "So what's our Badger up to, exactly? I heard more than I should've in the park today, but less than I wanted to. Can you tell me the whole story?"

"He made a promise to a friend to look after his wife and child. Now both parents are dead, and the young lady's the ward of a dangerous man. Badgeman wants to get her away from him, but I'm afraid he'll use force and only land himself in trouble. I shouldn't have let him go after her alone."

"How old is the girl?" A frown knit his finely arched brows.

"Should be eleven or twelve by now, I'd guess." He recalled the little girl's heart-shaped face and straight, dark brows that always gave her a sober air beyond her years. "Her mother was a camp washerwoman who also tended the injured, and Major used to help her with the laundry. Neither Badgeman nor I can remember Major's real name. She was a quiet little thing, though with a self-assurance one doesn't meet in most children."

Jem shifted to rest his chin on his folded arm. "Likely old Badge'll be too late to save her if the gent likes 'em young. Maybe the girl's not so bad off as you think, though. If she's got a protector looking after her, she may get on all right in life. Better than being on her own."

Alan studied his face, the puckered brow, the drawn-down corners of his mouth, and understood Jem was speaking from experience. "How young were you when you first...when you were...despoiled."

Jem's gaze flicked up to meet his, but then he looked away. "Too young," he said flatly, shrugging his shoulders. "It's not something worth dwelling on. I do have a more interesting story for you, though, if you'd care to hear it. It concerns Pat, the fishing friend of Donnie, who I told you about earlier."

"Go on." Alan smiled, anticipating the tale but aware of the fact that Jem was avoiding a darker story he found too painful to tell. He understood that. They both had memories they couldn't speak of.

"As I mentioned, Pat was a great drinker like his friend Donnie, but he was also a great lover. He confided in me a tale from his younger days, when he was a tinker traveling far and wide. On the road, he once stopped by a tavern in a far northern village where there were no women. Halfway through an evening of drinking, Pat was feeling the need strongly and asked the tavern keeper what the local men did to keep loneliness at bay.

"'Well, sir, out the back is a great barrel with a knothole in the side. When we miss the companionship of the fair sex, we make great use of it.'

"Pat downed his drink and went out the back, where he pulled out his cock and took his pleasure from the knothole. When he was finished, he went back in and thanked the man for the tip. 'Sir, that was the grandest time I've ever had. What do I owe you?'

"Says the barkeep, 'Nothing. But 'tis your turn to get in the barrel.'"

Jem grinned—his wicked grin—and Alan burst out laughing.

“You are indeed a rogue, Jem.”

Jem lifted his eyebrows. “I only tell the tales as others have told them to me. Every word's truth, or so they swear.”

Alan reached out and ruffled a hand through his already-tousled hair. “What am I to do with such a liar?”

“Why, whatever you like, sir,” Jem replied with a smirk. “I'm here to please you.”

Which was precisely what worried Alan. He didn't want to be the lad's “protector,” as Mr. Schivvers was to the Cutler girl. He didn't want Jem to think he must serve him in every way, yet that was the situation he'd set up by hiring him as his valet. Where would all this end? Could he really trust a man who prostituted himself for profit and security?

Chapter Eight

Jem was already bored with playing the part of a footman, and it was barely after noon. Since Badgeman wasn't there to act as butler and open the door when callers came—not that there *were* any callers—and since Dicky was not the first impression one wanted to make on visitors, Mrs. Crimpett had decided Jem would be the official keeper of the door. This meant he couldn't stray too far from the ground floor. She'd also assigned him the task of polishing the brass urns in the hallway before she left to run errands.

The moment she left, he promptly tossed down the polishing rag and headed out to the garden.

Alan had gone to meet with his solicitor concerning the Cutler affair and wouldn't be back until later in the day. It was beautiful weather again, and Jem longed for another outing in the park. For now, strolling in the garden while drinking a glass of Alan's brandy would have to do. He swirled the liquid around in the large glass and pretended he was lord of the manor in his fine frock coat, silk stockings, and tight breeches.

"Excuse me, Jem. There's some gentlemen here to see you."

Dicky's voice startled him, and Jem turned toward the footman who'd emerged from the house.

"To see me?"

"I had 'em wait in the front hall." His forehead was furrowed like a basset hound's. "But I think maybe I should've told them to go to the servants' entrance. I think I made a mistake. Please don't tell Mrs. Crimpett."

"Rest easy, Dicky. I'll take care o' this." Who the hell would be here for *him*? It couldn't be anything but trouble.

When he reached the front hall, his stomach dropped to the heels of his new shoes. Oh yes, it was trouble, all right, in the form of Jerry Pickles and Noah Stackhouse, two of his best mates. Redheaded Jerry was short and dumpy, with a wide, round, freckled face. Noah stood tall and as lean as a scarecrow, with flyaway white blond hair that stuck out in all directions.

"Hoy, Jerry, Noah," he greeted them, stopping in the center of the hallway with his arms folded. Too welcoming, and they'd barge in. Reject them, and they'd make a set-to that would bring down the rafters. "How're yourselves?"

Noah turned from examining the painting of a deceased Watleigh ancestor and shoved his hair back to wedge his cap onto his head, briefly revealing the scar on his forehead which Jem had given him. "Look at you, my fine fellow. Ain't you togged in twig, though? What a handsome lad."

Jerry made a show of scraping his dirty shoes on the doormat before approaching Jem. "Lord, you've fallen into clover, haven't you? We heard it was so and had to come see for ourselves."

"How'd you find me?" Jem tried not to sound accusing but couldn't imagine they'd come simply for a visit. He wished he'd never sent that sweep who worked Sir Alan's street to the Hangman's Pub. He'd wanted to let his mates know he still lived, but should've paid the boy more to keep his gab shut about exactly *where* Jem lived.

"Flash place you've got here." Noah stared at the gilt wall sconces, then at a portrait of a long-dead Watleigh. "Saw you get in the carriage that night and go off with the gentleman. Jerry and me bought that boy you sent a drink or two, and we was able to track you down."

Stupid, stupid, stupid, Jem! What the hell had he been thinking? His old life was over. He should've put it behind him. What did it matter if his mates thought he'd been kidnapped or murdered? Now how could he get rid of them, and what kind of danger did they pose?

He took a step toward the door. "Good to see you lads. I'd ask you in, but this is my place of employment. I can't entertain."

"'Cept we're already in, ain't we?" Jerry grinned. "Aw, come on, Jemmy. Don't be niffy-naffy. You ain't too high-and-mighty for your best mates, are you? At least offer us a tipple. Your gent wouldn't begrudge you that, would he? Is he a kind one?"

Jem glanced at the crystal goblet he still carried and wished he'd set it aside before coming to the door. The drink made it look like he was a man of leisure rather than a well-dressed servant. "Yes. He's a very decent employer."

He knew he wasn't fooling them with his story of becoming a valet. They'd worked the streets along with him. They knew what service he was supplying.

"That's good, lad. You deserve a cushy life."

Jem was torn between shoving his mates right back out the door and giving them a quick tour. Surely it couldn't hurt to offer them one drink. Mrs. Crimpett would be gone for hours and so would Alan. The maids all loved him. They'd keep their traps shut.

As if sensing him teetering, Noah prodded. "Come on. One drink, man, and we'll be on our way. Don't be such a marplot." He touched his finger to his nose. "No one the wiser, eh?"

Jem's inner voice, the one that had saved him from trouble so many times, was clamoring to be heard, but he quashed it. He was bored and bottle-headed, slightly drunk from the brandy, and he wanted to show off his good fortune.

"All right. Come on, then." He led the way to the parlor and seated his guests on the green-and-gold-striped divan. Going to the sideboard, he poured two glasses of amber liquid and handed them to Jerry and Noah, then sat across from them in the master's chair. He crossed one leg over the other and swung his foot a little so they couldn't miss the glint of his shoe buckle.

"What's the latest in the stews?" he asked as he took a sip of the brandy.

The pair launched into one tale after another of friends and acquaintances who'd been up to all sorts of mischief and mayhem in the time he'd been gone.

"…then Peg throws a bottle at his head, it shatters on the wall behind him, glass raining down and cutting people at the table below. Seconds later, everyone was at each other's throats. Hangman's was wrecked and both Peg and Bill Wheaton banned from it for life. But just try to keep them two out of a pub, eh?" Jerry's face was red, and tears streamed down his plump cheeks.

Jem laughed. He was feeling fine, warm in his belly and fizzy in his mind. It was good to see his old mates and to sit there in his fancy clothes, holding court.

Noah got up and started circling the room, examining the statues and paintings. "Christ, Jem, 'tisn't a bouncer. You've done well for yourself."

The fizzy bubbles popped, unclouding his mind, and Jem watched his friend with sharp eyes. Noah was notoriously light-fingered, better at thieving than he and Jerry put together. The tall blond could make things disappear as if by magic.

Jem rose to his feet and wandered over to stand beside Noah and stare into the ornate-framed looking glass hanging on the wall. He studied his reflection and Noah's. Jem looked like he belonged here. With his neatly cut hair and fine clothes, he could pass for the young master of the house. Noah, on the other hand, looked like the street riffraff he was. Purple shadows were smudged beneath his eyes, and his skin was sallow.

Noah met Jem's gaze in the mirror. "Can you give us a little something to see us on our way, Jem? Old times' sake, eh? You owe us."

He thought of all they'd been through together over the past years—the freezing nights huddled together in a dank basement; the hours in the pub or on the street, hustling customers or picking pockets; the times they'd nearly been caught; and the way they'd always had each other's backs.

"Sorry, Noah. I can give you a few coins, blunt from me pocket, but the rest o' this ain't mine, and I'll be fucked before I let you take so much as a piece of lint."

Noah's eyes narrowed as he hefted the silver figurine of a running horse in his hand. "So that's how it is? You scrape us off and move on?"

Jerry, ever the peacemaker, hurried up behind them. "Now lads, keep it civil. No need to come to blows."

"What is this?" A voice thundered from across the room.

Jem's stomach felt like it'd been punched. Brandy burned in his throat and in his veins as he turned to face Alan's towering rage.

The man stood in the parlor doorway, his broad shoulders filling it. Wearing dark clothes and with his raven black hair, he looked like death itself come to fetch Jem away. His scowl was fierce, and his voice rumbled like God on high.

"Who are these men? What are they doing here?"

"Friends of mine come to call," Jem answered weakly.

"Out!" Alan strode across the room in three strides and snatched the running horse from Noah's hand. "Get out of my house."

Jerry's freckles blotched across his suddenly bone white face. He hurried toward the door. But Noah stared coolly at Alan. "Sorry, guv'nor. Didn't mean to make trouble for our Jem. We just wanted to see his new home and the handsome man he's taken up with. Wouldn't want to cause trouble for him…nor for you." His emphasis on the last words was clearly a threat.

Alan growled. An actual growling rumble issued from his throat as he seized Noah by his collar and propelled him bodily toward the door. "Out!"

Jem meant to follow, to see them out of the house, but his trembling legs would barely support him. He backed up against the wall and waited for Alan's return, his stomach a boiling mess that threatened to spill out onto the floor. He heard the front door slam and the hard tap of Alan's boot heels as he returned to the parlor.

"I'm sorry..." were all the words he had time to utter before Alan grabbed the front of his shirt and slammed him against the wall. The back of his head cracked against the looking glass.

"What were you thinking, inviting your friends here? They could blackmail me. They could cost me a fortune and my reputation. You little fool!"

The back of Jem's head ached, and his teeth chattered as Alan shook him.

"Or did you intend something else? Some thievery perhaps?"

"No, sir. I swear. Nothing like that. I'd hardly invite them here in broad daylight if we intended to rob you." He'd said too much. Made it sound like the thought had crossed his mind, which in truth it had at one point early on. But not recently—not anymore.

Alan shook him again and bile rose in Jem's throat. He feared vomiting on his master's pristine white shirt.

"Why did you tell them where you lived, and why did you let them in? What possessed you?"

"I didn't think—"

"No, you didn't think. That's clear," Alan interrupted. "And now you're going to have to leave. I can't trust you. I can't keep you around."

Jem literally felt the blood rushing from his head. He thought he might pass out if he didn't throw up first. This was much worse than he'd expected. Not that he'd expected any of this. How had everything spiraled so quickly out of his control? By one foolish action, he'd destroyed everything—his entire future and all the good things he'd had.

Alan dropped him onto his feet, and Jem stood, swaying slightly.

"Go. Get your things and get out, and if you dare try to cause any kind of trouble, you can be sure my vengeance will be much harsher than you could ever imagine."

He didn't even sound like Alan, but every inch the military leader whose commands made soldiers quake.

"Yes, sir." Jem started to move, then stopped.

"What is it?" The voice was like a whip lashing across his soul.

Jem blinked away the sudden tears that prickled his eyes. "Badgeman burned my clothes. I can't get my things. I don't have…anything."

A wave of loss swept over him, and he bit his lower lip to keep it from trembling.

"You may have the clothes I purchased for you. I've no need of them."

"Thank you," he barely whispered and started the long walk to the door.

It wasn't like him not to explain, wheedle, or beg, but he couldn't do it. Not this time. Alan's accusations and mistrust had cut him too deeply. He thought the man knew him better, but he'd taken one look at Jem's friends and assumed the worst. Why wouldn't he? What had Jem done to convince him otherwise?

Alan followed him to the hallway. Before Jem could head toward the back of the house and the servants' entrance, Dicky erupted into the parlor, hands waving and eyes wide.

"Wait, sir! 'Twas all my fault. I let those men in. Jem didn't do it. Please, sir. Don't dismiss him. Sorry for eavesdroppin', but I overheard you a-yelling, and it ain't right for Jem to pay for what I done. Not again." His chest rose and fell rapidly, and breath wheezed between his lips. His gray-streaked hair was awry, as were his clothes, but that was hardly unusual for Dicky.

Jem laid a hand on his shoulder. "It's all right, Dicky. You done nothing wrong. I shoulda sent 'em away, but I didn't. My mistake, not yours, so calm yerself." He clapped him once on the shoulder, then continued on his way. "I woulda let 'em in too, I reckon."

"Wait." Alan's command stopped him in his tracks.

He waited, breath held, heart pounding.

Alan came up beside him. Jem wouldn't turn to look at him, but felt his presence and those dark, solemn eyes studying him. "Why didn't you send them away when you knew you should have?"

Jem risked a sideways glance at him. "Pride, sir. Vanity. They were old mates of mine from way back. I guess I wanted 'em to see how I done good for myself, to show off everything I got now." He paused, then added, "Only now I ain't got nothing, do I? I buggered myself proper."

"Ah, Jem." The words were a barely audible sigh, and Jem knew in that moment that Alan's bloody rage had evaporated like a sudden squall at sea that blows up and disappears in seconds. "You are a fool."

He gave a short laugh. "Hardly news, sir." Since he had nothing to lose, he said, "But see, they was my mates once upon a time." The truth hit him that he'd be back among them. His stomach twisted with sour, unfamiliar fear. He didn't want to go. "Maybe I can run after 'em and catch up."

"No. Wait."

Jem clenched his jaw tight, an unexpected flare of anger abruptly replacing his despair over the unraveling of his dreams. Why did his existence here depend on Alan's whim? Did he deserve to be treated like a villain or an object?

"I forgot my place, sir," he replied stiffly. "Showing off like a swell. As if this were my home. I'm only a servant, after all. I should get sacked."

He turned then, ready to face Alan, whose dark brows were drawn into that fearful scowl. Their gazes held for almost a full minute, and Jem frowned right back at him. Let the man think what he wished… But no. God above, the truth was that Jem cared too much about that lean, hard face.

Jem swallowed, but the lump in his throat didn't dissolve. "I apologize, sir. And that's all I can do."

He wanted to keep his dignity, what little he had, but he found his eyes smarted with the threat of tears, and he looked away again, angry with them both now.

Alan took a step forward. His voice dropped even quieter so Dicky wouldn't hear. "You haven't the least notion of how a servant ought to behave."

Jem clutched his fists at his sides to stop himself from shoving the great fool. Instead he whispered fiercely, "Didn't I say as much already? Didn't your badger? Didn't Mrs. C.? I was neither born nor bred to be in service, and it's no surprise to any of us. Don't know why you should be shocked."

Alan remained silent, and Jem had more than enough of this torture. "You're right," Alan said quietly.

Jem nodded, glad that at least the cold anger was gone from Alan. "*You're right*" spoken in a mild tone would be fine to have as his last memory of the man.

"No, Jem. Wait," Alan repeated.

"Sir, I don't think we owe each other another word—"

"I do. Please. I want you to stay."

Jem cut another glance toward Alan from the corner of his eye.

"I'm sorry." Were they actually words, or a mere thought that floated from Alan's mind to his? He'd spoken so softly, Jem wasn't sure.

His chest ached from the wrestling emotions tumbling around in it. Fear, guilt, anger, joy, and other feelings he had no name for played tug-of-war with his guts. But he'd leave 'em to sort themselves out and go with the simplest emotion, something he could wrap his mind around—relief.

He folded his arms across his chest and grinned at Alan. "Well, that's all right, then. Since I've no place better to go, guess I'll stay."

Alan smiled back, the slow curve of his wide mouth turning his saturnine face stunningly handsome. With predictable reliability, Jem's cock hardened.

"I'm sorry for letting my friends know where I am," he offered. "I sent word round to the pub where I used to spend my time to let folks know I was alive. All's I said was I'd taken a position as a valet." He lowered his voice, although Dicky, standing nearby, would likely not understand his meaning. "Nothing anyone could take any other way, but my friends know me well."

Alan nodded, then addressed the footman. "You may go now, Dicky. Jem will not lose his place. But I wish you would keep this incident to yourself. No need to mention anything to Mrs. Crimpett or any of the maids, right?"

"Yes, sir." Dicky retreated backward a few paces before turning and scurrying off belowstairs, clearly relieved to have the crisis behind him.

Jem figured the maids had their ears pinned to the doors and had heard much of the row, including the fact he'd had uninvited guests. They'd gossip among themselves, but he felt confident they too would keep the matter from Crimpett. And he'd flirt with 'em a little to make sure. A few compliments and smiles had gone a long way toward ensuring him a place in each of their hearts.

With Dicky gone, Alan returned his attention to Jem. "I lost my temper. I apologize for that, but you do see the danger any hint of scandal puts me in should your friends threaten blackmail. And I was wrong not to trust you, but you did try to steal from me."

Jem nodded. "Fair enough. But now things've changed, haven't they? And I promise you I'll not take from you nor allow any of me old mates to rob you. You can trust me now, sir." He looked into Alan's eyes with the long-practiced innocent gaze he'd used when fleecing people. Difference was, this time he meant his promise with all his heart.

Alan studied his eyes before nodding in return. "I will take a gamble and trust you, Jem. Within reason." *Within reason and only a little past it*, that long gaze told Jem.

It seemed time for a change in subject and mood. Jem rubbed the back of his head where it had smashed into the frame of the mirror that miraculously hadn't broken. "What did your solicitor have to say, sir?"

Alan went to the drinks tray. For less than a second, he looked at the used and abandoned glasses. Jem waited for another reproach or perhaps a hard glance. Instead Alan picked up a clean glass and poured himself a half tumbler. He carried it back to a chair and sat heavily.

At the sight, Jem's mouth watered, and it wasn't for the taste of drink. He could tell Sir Alan's leg bothered him, and perhaps he'd allow Jem to have another go at rubbing it and other parts.

Oh, he'd have missed all of the man's parts if he'd been flung out on the street. True enough, he would miss some of the old rum scapegraces like Jerry, but until his master grew bored of him and showed him the door, Jem wouldn't contact them again. The loss of this man Alan would have been a hard blow to endure. Not just the velvet-and-cream life—the man himself. The thought of what he'd nearly thrown away and how much his patron mattered to him made the hairs on the back of his neck prickle. Danger…and excitement.

Alan settled on the sofa and wondered why he felt as if he'd been given a reprieve rather than granted one. He studied Jem, who'd regained that glow of his.

He sipped the brandy and enjoyed the warmth of it coursing down his throat. He breathed in its scent and remembered the taste of brandy in Jem's kisses. That fire was rarer than the brandy itself and worth the risk of keeping the man.

He regarded Jem, who stood arms folded, watching him with a hint of the devil back in those pale eyes. Alan knew that at his core, Jem was an honest soul.

Hell. Despite the danger that the valet had invited into his house—despite his own good sense—he trusted Jem. He almost smiled at the thought. "*Every man has to be a fool on occasion*," his father had told him. He might as well enjoy this foolish sense of well-being he felt in Jem's presence.

Now the man was acting as if the incident with his "mates" hadn't taken place. He'd asked about Alan's meeting with the lawyer. Very well, Alan could let the episode go too, for now.

He stretched out his legs and answered Jem's question. "Gardner told me what I expected, that Mrs. Cutler left her daughter in Schivvers's care, so not much can be legally done to wrest her from him." He paused to sip the brandy and wonder why he'd divulged his business to his valet. Perhaps it was the way Jem listened, alert and interested, more like a friend than an employee.

Alan continued. "But I did learn something of use at the pub where Badgeman's crony Ned Reilly lingers."

He fell silent, and Jem prompted, "What did you learn, sir?"

Alan gave up trying to keep his own counsel. He hadn't realized how much he missed speaking of his concerns to another. His friends had died or drifted away—but never mind that familiar stab of loss. He had to figure out his next move, and just speaking the words could help him think of how to thwart Schivvers.

"I went there to ask the man for more details about the Cutlers' story, and he was able to tell me something he'd learned only this morning from yet another army mate passing through. It seems Mr. Schivvers has returned from Portugal to a place in Sheffield. One assumes with the girl still in tow."

"Bloody ballocks. The badger's hared off to foreign parts for no reason."

"I'll send a message that should intercept him in Lisbon, but in the meantime I feel obliged to take up his quest. I'll leave for Sheffield tomorrow to locate the doctor and see if I can convince him to allow me custody of the girl."

"How'll you do that, sir?"

"My family name carries some weight. As Cutler's superior officer, I can say he once begged me to personally care for his family, and I'd only recently learned of his death." He shrugged. "If that doesn't work, money can go a long way toward smoothing the way to her freedom. Schivvers is a greedy man."

"Will you go on horseback, sir?"

"All the way to Sheffield? It's more than one hundred and fifty miles. Once upon a time, I might have. Now, no." He gave a twisted smile.

"I don't see you taking the mail coach, sir." Jem leaned against the edge of the sofa, far from Alan. At least the man had learned he wasn't supposed to sit in Alan's presence. Except now Alan rather wished he would.

Jem went on. "With the badger off cavorting, you got only that gutless Markham out back. That groom's near as clod-pated as Dicky. And the boy that feeds and mucks out your cattle ain't much more 'n a pup."

Alan could see from that half smile on his valet's face that he had some scheme in mind. "Perhaps I'll hire a postilion," he said, and sure enough, Jem shook his head.

"I got a better idea, sir."

Alan wanted to laugh. Of course he had an idea. And Alan realized he looked forward to hearing the man's no doubt outrageous or amusing plan.

Jem suspected Sir Alan would bing off alone, leave his valet behind and try to forget. His lordship still hated the part of himself that longed for Jem's touch. No mistake, he'd inventory Jem's sins and convince himself he'd be better off without him.

Not if Jem had a say about it. "Perhaps you and me should go. Alone."

"I beg your pardon?"

"I never handled the ribbons, but I'm game to learn, sir. Not that closed-in coach. Your phaeton."

Alan smiled. "That's hardly the proper vehicle for a long journey."

"Why not? Markham showed off how the lid can be raised and lowered for when it pisses rain. It's not one of those high-perch numbers that tips soon as you look at it."

"You're insane. You've never been out of the city, have you?"

Jem shook his head.

"You have no notion what a long journey entails, Jem."

"Bags and trunks. A list of inns. A blanket for when you'd liefer sleep under the stars. A basket of food. We can put some of that at our feet. Rest behind."

"You make it sound a romantic adventure."

Romance is what he had in mind, true enough. Alan, on a blanket in some deserted field under the moon. Or in broad daylight.

"We can move fast on account of the girl you're worrying over."

Sir Alan frowned and was silent for a few moments. "Yes," he said slowly. "There is that. Speed is of the essence, and I cannot think of a faster way to get there. I'd have to stop only to change horses and eat and sleep. That might be the answer. It's not perfect, but perhaps you're right."

"I'll go pack, then." Jem pushed away from the sofa before Alan could change his mind. "Enough for a week?"

"The journey will take days, so better a fortnight's worth. I'll pack for myself, thank you. I had a batman, but I learned how to care for my own gear during my military service." Better than Jem could, he didn't have to say.

"We'll go as soon as may be, yes sir?"

"I don't know about 'we,' Jem. This is business I'd best handle alone."

"But you never know when you'll need help, sir, and with Badger gone, I think I'll suffice. I may not seem like much, but I'm a fine hand in a brawl if it comes to that, or I can be your eyes and ears, for who would look twice at a servant? And come down to it, sir, servants tell other servants all sorts of gossip about their betters. I could be of great use to you."

Had he laid it on too thick with his rambling list of reasons why he should take part in this adventure? Maybe not, because Sir Alan looked at him appraisingly for several moments, and then nodded.

"Very well, Jem. You may attend me on the journey."

After the episode of Jerry and Noah, Jem didn't want to appear too brash and forward, but a man had to take initiative where he could.

So Jem took it upon himself to tell the servants about the master's plans, begged Cook for a huge basket of food, and took off for the stables before Mrs. C., who'd returned early, could corner him and ask more questions. She'd already demanded to know what sort of nonsense he was babbling about. The master never traveled. Never went anywhere anymore. Barely set foot outside the house. And now, a journey? In a phaeton with only a flimsy bellows-folding cover for protection?

"The master's been near death's door for so long, and now he's come up with some foolhardy plan? 'Tis nothing like him. I believe you're behind this, you reckless young fool," was the last thing he heard as he rounded the corner for the stable.

"Right enough," Jem muttered. He'd been excited about the venture, a real journey. Yet her words sobered him. He'd heard how Sir Alan had been ill, plagued by fevers and sweating and raving when he'd been brought home from the war. And then he'd been a slave of the medicines to help with the pain, not to mention barrel fever, the longing for drink.

Jem had no fear of coping with such things should they arise. He'd seen far worse in his day, but the thought of reawakening the master's illness just for the sake of a lark worried him.

Feeling considerably less giddy, he gave the orders to Markham to prepare the phaeton.

He went to find Sir Alan, and found him scribbling on some papers in the study. "Perhaps, sir, you should look into a less rough way to travel."

Alan put down his quill and looked up. "What are you talking about? Your plan is a good one. Four swift horses, a light vehicle."

"Need it be so fast?"

"The faster, the better. I have located Schivvers, and I need to act quickly."

"But you'd sleep sounder at quality inns, and taking your time—"

"Good God. You're turning into Badgeman." Alan got to his feet. "I am a man full grown."

"Oh, I know that well, sir." Jem wanted to wink, but restrained himself. He couldn't help the suggestive tone, though, which Alan ignored.

"If I'd thought the plan a bad one, I would have dismissed it out of hand." Alan crossed his arms over his chest and adopted the straight-backed, head-up attitude Jem thought of as his Lord High Captain Watleigh's posture. "Since you've suddenly taken it into your head I'm again an invalid, let me inform you that the lingering infection is quite gone, and I'm growing stronger daily. And even if I am less strong than I should be to travel, I have decided on this course, and consequences shall be on my head. Should I fall ill or die or grow melancholic or even drink too much again, only one man can carry the blame, and it is not you. Are we clear on this?"

Jem bowed. "As crystal, sir. I'd best be collecting my things together."

Jem raced to his room. He gathered his clothes from the clothespress in the corner and laid them carefully in the middle of his cot. He now possessed several changes of underlinen, day clothes for five days, and two smart uniforms. And no bag to carry it all. He deftly wrapped the counterpane of his bed around the bundle. That worked beautifully. Jem was ready for his first venture out of London.

Chapter Nine

The journey was delayed by two things—Alan sending Jem up to the attics for a proper valise for himself, and then a massive rainstorm. They set out early the next day in the chilly, sweet, rainwashed air of a London morning. Jem's heart pounded fast with anticipation. He'd be leaving the city for the first time. And he had Alan all to himself. No obligations for either of them for several days. Just the open road.

Alan drove well. He was silent and unsmiling, terse when Jem spoke or asked questions about what they passed on their swift start. He fretted over the girl, perhaps, or hadn't had enough sleep, or had regrets about taking Jem. Whatever the reason, Jem ought to have known better than to attempt to jolly him out of the mood, but he couldn't help himself.

"I ain't been on an open carriage like this before. And the animals are something lovely—just about peas-in-a-pod alike. What're their names?"

"The one on the left is Admiral. The other is Rialta."

"How do you tell 'em apart?" He gazed at one broad bay backside, then the other.

"You mean other than the fact that Admiral is a gelding and Rialta a mare?"

"Oh."

"Admiral has a white blaze and stockings. Rialta doesn't."

Jem did manage to stay silent for a time, contenting himself with watching the crowded streets give way to houses separated by expanses of lawns and then even larger expanses of fields.

They stopped at a posting inn and traded the pair for four new horses. Alan went off to arrange for the new, larger team, and Jem watched from the stable yard doorway of the inn, fascinated by the skill and foul language of the hostlers. Every few minutes another horn sounded, and a carriage rolled into the yard.

There was never such a bustling and well-kept establishment in his old haunts, and even if there had been, in his life as a street lad, he couldn't have watched men working. He'd have been chased off. He certainly wouldn't have received the respectful nod from a passing groom. He was still grinning as he climbed up on the phaeton and took his seat next to Alan.

"Four now? I didn't know you could change the number of horses."

"Depends on the style of carriage."

Jem waited for an explanation, but none came.

"How will Rialta and Admiral make their way home? Are they like those birds what find their way back? Will stablelads lead 'em out to the road and point 'em in the right direction?"

"Markham will fetch them." Alan shot him a cool look, as if he did not appreciate silliness. He was still Lord High-and-Haughty.

Fine. Even Jem could get the message eventually. He settled against the bench and stared out over open land and woods, searching out the familiar shape of houses. The sight of so much pale green plant life made him uneasy at first, though he had to admit it was a pretty change of pace.

An hour after they'd left the posting inn, he couldn't restrain himself any longer. "I'd reckon we've lurched along for near three miles without seeing a dwelling or so much as an outbuilding. Who'd have known?"

Alan didn't answer.

"I expect you clap eyes on huge tracts of land without a house in view near every day of your life."

Alan nodded.

"Will you teach me to drive the animals?"

"Eventually."

"Look here," Jem said, prodding just a little more. "When I'm pleased with God and creation, good luck keeping me quiet. But I'll give you a choice. I can sing if you'd rather. Or let my tongue run on wheels. Or if you can't abide either, I might whistle. I could practice a few pig calls since we're heading through the country. Could be a useful skill."

Alan glanced at him. "What if I ordered you to be silent?"

Jem shrugged. "When I feel this happy? I might last a half hour, then burst into song at the top of my lungs."

"What have you to be happy about? It's a long, arduous journey on bad roads."

Jem made a rude noise with his mouth. "What have you got to be sad about? It's a lovely day, you got fine company, though I do say so myself. You're hying off to right a wrong and save an innocent. Cook promised she'd pack some of those mince pasties. Wonder if she lied to me." He twisted on the seat and peered down at the wickerwork basket. "Would break my heart."

"You're rather like a child," Alan said but he didn't sound scornful, and his tight mouth had relaxed.

"I skipped that part o' life. So I decided to try again when I can."

"Poor Jem." He spoke softly.

"No such thing, sir. At this moment, I'd rather be Jem Brown than the Prince Regent himself."

"Why's that?"

He wanted to say *because I'm here with you*, but answered, "Cook's pasties, of course."

At last. Alan's thin face broke into a smile. And Jem couldn't help himself. "Seeing you smile, too. That's worth a king's ransom."

And of course, the smile vanished at once. He even shifted away from Jem, although the need to reposition his body might have been discomfort in his leg.

No, it was another sort of discomfort. Of that Jem grew certain as Alan stared out over the horses' backs, as if they were back driving through the busy streets of London instead the nearly empty road heading north.

Jem figured he'd push the man a little more and clear the air. After all, Sir Alan wouldn't order him down from the carriage and demand he walk back. "About Jerry and Noah," he said.

Alan's brows furrowed. Then his face cleared, remembering. "Your visitors."

"Yah. Them. They're not such cod's heads to dare peach on…um…about what we are."

Sure enough, the broad shoulders went back, and the hard face turned granite. But the baronet didn't deny or protest the phrase "what we are."

That had to be a step in a good direction, perhaps. "Why wouldn't they?" he asked after a long silence.

"Three fine reasons. I know plenty o' secrets about those coves. Because we've known each other donkeys' ages, and loyalty matters. And because they know I'd kill 'em."

"You have a reputation as a bloodthirsty ruffian, do you?"

"Where I come from, a man protects what's vital to him." Jem shut his mouth tight. What an idiot thing to slip. He was a chuckleheaded dolt to say something that might provoke the other's terror of intimacy.

But Sir Alan didn't understand what he'd just accidentally confessed, for he only nodded. "You said as much. You're not likely to get a better job."

For the first time since they set out, Jem's mood grew heavy. "No, sir, that's true enough," he agreed and looked out over the fields. Too much damned green.

Alan must have been crazy to drag his "valet" along on this trip. To sit on that bench with Jem next to him, so close he could feel the warmth from the other's thigh against his—that was a short ride to insanity.

He forgot the lunacy of the idea as they left London, and Jem's eyes widened at the countryside opening up before them. Jem's delight lightened Alan's dark mood slightly. Watching him discover the new world outside London was almost as exciting as the times they'd touched. Almost.

Then the man had shut down, grown quiet. Alan had thought his chatter was annoying; the silence was much worse. He suspected he was being punished for reminding Jem his job was contingent on good behavior.

"Stop sulking," he ordered.

"Sulking?" Jem sounded astonished. "Me, sir? No such thing. Just thinking, is all."

"A thought entered your head that you didn't share?"

Jem smiled, not the usual broad, sunny smile, but close enough. "Near unbelievable, but can happen, sir." He fell silent again.

"Share 'em," Alan said gruffly. "What you're thinking, I mean." He didn't have a high opinion of men who couldn't hold back their own pain or joy. Emotional displays were the sign of an ill-bred mind. But he'd already decided there were worse things than ill breeding.

Jem sighed. "Naw, but I'll tell you another tale if you wish."

"God, no. There is no need for you to act the jester, Jem."

"Comes natural. 'Sides, I like anything that makes you laugh."

Not again. Alan wanted to protest, but he'd asked for the man's confidences, and now he didn't want to scorn them. He had trouble breathing as he tried to think of a way to talk about something that shouldn't exist, which he must deny—the attraction. Lightly, as if he were Jem, he asked, "Didn't your mother ever teach you not to wear your heart on your sleeve?"

The crack of laughter from Jem was loud and entirely without amusement. "She practically taught me naught else, me mum. Ah, Mum. I ever tell you she was a Covent Garden nun—a doxy?"

Alan didn't speak, almost afraid of what he'd hear. He glanced over at Jem and gave a tiny nod to show he was listening.

Jem looked away. "My mum weren't a bad whore. Honest at her work, I mean. No side jobs with smash and grabbers waiting for her to lure customers into dark alleys. Proficient too. She could do two men at once and leave 'em both smiling."

"I'm sorry."

"What for? You ever take her? No, no sorry, sir."

He fell silent, and Alan understood that Jem worried his brief, bitter outburst had offended his master. As calmly as possible, Alan said, "Go on. Please."

Jem pushed a hand through his curling hair and shrugged as if the rest of the story were obvious. "In her world, she could do men, but I couldn't. She discovered my nature, and that meant farewell, Jem. Last time we met up, she spat on me. You'd think one in her line of work would be less prone to casting stones, but I expect everyone wants to feel higher than someone."

"Jem." He tried to think of what he could say. There was nothing.

But the other was shaking his head. "Naw, she weren't bad when I was a babe. Fed me, didn't beat me. I seen far worse than me mum." He laughed, and this time there was a bit of humor. "A stirring declaration of love."

He rubbed his hands on his trousers. "Now your mum, sir? She looked a sweet lady. You miss her, I know."

After Jem had shared his story, it seemed churlish not to reciprocate, so Alan felt he had to answer. "I was lucky to have had her as a mother. To have had such a family. They were good people, my mother and father. They…" But he couldn't speak. For the first time since they'd been wiped out by disease, lost to him, he'd been able to think of his family and remember without searing, bitter pain at losing them. Then, just like that, the ache of their loss filled him again. Unlike the other times in the past, he didn't shut it down at once.

"They died within days of one another. A putrid fever took them, and I didn't know. I was in Spain, and I'd received my injury, and then grew ill as well." To his horror, tears formed in his eyes. He'd been worried about Jem's display of emotion, and now look at this.

He squeezed his hands on the reins hard to pull back control.

He started when Jem put a hand on his thigh. "No," he growled, refusing the comfort or even the acknowledgement of his pain.

Jem tightened his powerful fingers on his leg. "No one can say no to nature when she's calling. I know you don't want to be slowed at all. Do I stand up and let loose into the air, or jump off and run to catch up?"

How many times did Alan have to feel like a bloody fool with this man? He pulled on the reins. "We've been working the horses too hard to stop at once. We must slow for a time." He let the horses walk for a couple of minutes, then drew to a stop.

"Good idea to stop, sir. I'd be liable to fall off while waving me pego in the air. You'd have to lash me corpse to the back."

Alan couldn't help chuckling. He handed the reins to Jem, whose eyes widened. "Just hold them for a minute." He jumped down. "We'll rest for five minutes." Alan grabbed the lead's bridle and led the team off the road and onto a dirt path toward the shade of a few trees.

He considered ordering Jem to work, but instead he pulled the bucket off the back of the phaeton, where he'd ordered Markham to attach it and the man had grumbled that it ruined the lines of the sleek carriage. He filled the bucket with water from a nearby pond and held it up to the horses one by one so they could drink. Alan held up the last bucketful and leaned against the side of the horse. He already knew he missed riding; now he realized he'd missed working with animals and soaking in their stolid, undemanding presence.

Jem must have been lying about his need, for instead of relieving himself, he flopped down on his back on the soft new grass. And almost at once sat up again. "Damp," he announced. "Shoulda spread something first." He went to the cart and pulled out a thick coverlet. "Mrs. C. probably counts the linens every day," he said as he flapped it out before carefully placing it on the grass under a tree. "She'll be waiting for me return with a kitchen knife in her hand. Dull so it'd hurt more as she skinned me."

He lay down again and patted the ground next to him. "Five minutes. In the shade. Rest."

Alan pulled out his watch and flicked it open. "No more than that. We've gone thirty miles. We have more than one hundred to go, and I want to get there in a matter of days, not weeks. We're in luck because the moon is full, but if it's overcast, we won't be able to travel at night. The next inn where I know I can arrange for a fresh, decent team is a good two hours away."

"Two hours and five minutes," Jem said.

"Have I made it plain that I'm in a hurry?" Alan asked, even as he tucked away his watch and sat down on the edge of the blanket. "I'm not here to dally."

"Mm." Jem slid closer. "No long kisses and sighs. Fast and furious."

"No." Alan sprang to his feet—or tried to. His leg started to give out, and he lurched slightly—toward Jem, who laid a strong hand on his hip to steady him.

Jem's eyes widened. "I'm offended, sir. You think I can't manage in five minutes?"

"Manage what?" Then looking into the bottomless sky blue eyes, Alan knew exactly what Jem meant.

"How about a wager, sir? Five minutes or less, and you let me drive when we start out again."

"And if it's longer than five minutes?" Oh blast. His question, meant as a weak jest, was an invitation which Jem wouldn't ignore. The man had already risen to his knees. He was unbuttoning Alan's fly.

Alan needed to break away, move back from the busy hands, but he was frozen with desire, staring down at the top of Jem's sun-warmed head as he pulled out Alan's stiffening cock and rubbed his lips gently over the head. His tongue washed over the top, then along the sensitive underside.

"You decide, sir. Whatever it is, I agree to your terms."

Alan couldn't answer because at that second, Jem turned greedy. A sudden, fierce attack, with so little warning.

He seized Alan's hip, then wrapped an arm around his waist. Without so much as a kiss or a lick, he opened his mouth and set to work on Alan's cock. No gentle caresses or playful licks, he gobbled and sucked, pulling hard.

Alan groaned and pushed forward. The warm mouth surrounded him, and the rush of instantaneous desire flooded him, overriding every other thought and sensation. His whole existence depended on Jem's mouth. Nothing else mattered—not the ache in his leg or the need to be on his way.

A bird indignantly squawked nearby. A breeze touched Alan's face. His thrusts grew more insistent. He treated Jem's mouth roughly, but Jem gave a low sound of approval, and the vibration of his voice added to the driving hunger in Alan's body. So close already.

Alan pushed deeper, and Jem's throat stuttered around him. Too deep, but Alan couldn't help himself—and didn't even try. It felt so good. He looked down and saw why Jem no longer held him. His fingers were wrapped around his own cock, moving hard and fast. Such a sight—a fully dressed man with his cock out, frantically pulling—should have shocked him. Such self-pollution, dirty…and gorgeous. Jem touched himself because he craved Alan.

The sight and realization were too much to bear. Alan almost blacked out as the sudden explosion of a climax hit him. The spasms shook his body, drawn by the unrelenting pull of Jem's mouth.

When Alan could open his eyes, he looked down at Jem, who now licked Alan's cock gently, almost lovingly. The air washed over him, cooling the saliva-dampened skin. Alan couldn't move or he'd fall over. He heard the soft sighing of Jem, who'd also spent, although Alan had no notion when.

Still on his knees, Jem wrapped both arms around Alan, pressing his warm face against his softening cock and trembling legs. Alan touched his hair, the first time he'd reached for him with more than his cock during this interlude.

Jem had moved so quickly, with no kisses or embraces, this episode might have been one of those fumbling, anonymous gropings Alan had indulged in before. Except not quite. None of those releases had held such power. And none of those men had held him close like this afterward.

Jem pressed his face to the sensitive skin of Alan's inner thighs. He gave a gusty sigh against him, kissed him, and muttered something. He climbed to his feet, tucking in his shirt and buttoning his flies.

Alan put a hand on his shoulder and squeezed his silent thanks. Then with unsteady fingers, he reached for his own trousers, which had slid down to his knees. Absurd sight, he thought—for once without caring much.

The horses must have been scandalized.

Come now, when did he suddenly feel so lighthearted about such activity? "What did you say?" he asked Jem, reaching over to take a pale green leaf from his hair.

"I was four minutes, no more. Go on, look."

He pulled out his watch. "More like eight, Jem. You lose. But..." He cleared his throat, which had grown tight. "But I yield to your desire to learn to drive. Come on."

❧

"They look annoyed when you pull 'em up from eating," Jem said nervously.

His mobile mouth had drawn into a tight line, and his hands were tucked into his pockets. Alan understood at last. "You're frightened of horses."

"I near been run over by them bunch of times. And saw a couple go wild. Rearing up and screaming."

"Haven't you ever touched horses?"

Jem shot him a scornful look. "Would you let a dirty street lad pat your cattle, sir? 'Course not—you're sane. Rag-and-bone man had an old nag I patted a few times. Most boys threw stones at it, so no wonder it flinched when I touched its neck."

"A light touch makes a horse flinch. It's how they keep off the flies. How odd you can be surrounded by the animals and not know them well."

"Back where I come from, I was surrounded by banks. Doesn't mean I know money well."

"Lay your hand on his neck."

Jem did. He closed his eyes. "So warm." He stroked and stroked again. "Damper 'n I expected."

"We moved at a good clip long enough earlier, so they broke into a sweat. Come on, then. We'll get you started on the lessons." He thought of how his father had taught him, letting him sit on his lap. Arms around him so they might both hold the reins together. That would not work with Jem.

"Why're you grinning, sir? I haven't even begun to make mistakes."

"You're not the only thing I smile at, Jem." And then he realized that wasn't true. Since they'd met, nearly every smile and laugh had been about Jem. A startling and disturbing thought.

"True enough," Jem said, vaulting up and settling himself on the bench. "The badger is a rollicking jolly lad. And your legions of chums who visit day and—"

"Enough," Alan said. He climbed up more slowly. His leg ached, and he was tired from searing emotion. The sweet peace created by the climax hadn't given way to disgust, and he would not push into dark corners to wake the demons. "The horses are not fresh, so they aren't so mettlesome. But you need to pay attention, Jem. Especially with four in hand."

"Sir, yes sir," he said and did a fair imitation of a salute.

Alan sighed. "I count myself lucky you never followed the drum. I would have had to use the cat o' nines on you every morning and every night if you'd been in my company. Come on. Put out your hands. You don't need to grip 'em like death, but don't let the ribbons slide out of your control."

"Did you beat your men regular-like?"

Alan shook his head. "There were a couple of minor troublemakers—one can't find a large group of men without any such—but no real dangerous influences or criminals."

"No thieves."

Alan didn't bother to answer.

Jem took hold of the lines as directed. Although he looked a little anxious, he still didn't stop prattling.

"This lot is not as pretty as your cattle we left behind."

"I should hope not. The inns don't buy the best horses."

"And you do?"

"I like horses."

The reins were too loose in Jem's hands, and the animals started to slow, more than happy to take another break. Alan reached over and showed him how to gather the lines and apply the right amount of tension. He loved the way Jem's thin, long-fingered hands felt beneath his. He couldn't look at them without thinking of how they felt gliding over his body and the clever things Jem's fingers could do.

"You have to let them know you're in charge," he instructed.

Jem nodded, taking a firmer grip. He slapped the reins against the horses' backs, and they stepped smartly forward.

"You see, there's nothing to it. The important thing is to keep the tension in your arms steady so they know you're guiding them."

Alan glanced at the younger man's face, the furrow of concentration balanced by a slight smile. "So, do you like driving?"

"Aye! Horses are much more pleasant when you're not on the business end of their hooves. I can quite enjoy 'em from up here on the box." He glanced at Alan with a grin, and Alan's heart nearly stopped.

I'm in trouble. He realized it all in a second. Jem's beautiful smile was the proverbial straw that broke the camel's back. Alan could no longer deny his growing emotional attachment to the youth, the feelings that were more than sexual arousal.

He liked Jem. He quite simply liked him very much and could imagine being bathed in that sunny smile every day for the rest of his days. That was a dangerous course on which to let his mind wander.

Alan looked away across the countryside. Tall meadow grass and flowers swayed in the breeze, rippling like ocean waves. Skylarks darted and dived over the wild fields, snapping up insects. The sun bore down on Alan's head, and sweat trickled down his face. He removed his broad-brimmed hat and fanned his face. He'd nearly sunk into a light doze, lulled by the rhythm of the carriage and the hot sun, when Jem's clear tenor voice singing startled him awake.

"'*If you'd get over a maid, tickle and amuse her. Anything she asks, mind you ne'er refuse her. Walk her out each day, o'er the fields romantic. Roll her in the hay, with many a lustful antic.*'"

Jem belted out the "tol de rols" and "fiddle ie dees" like a warbling lark. He glanced at Alan. "You surely know this one. Join in on the next go around.

"'*First her bubbies feel, to raise her hot desire. Next just feel her thigh, then a little higher! If she won't wince at that, put Bob in her grasp then. And depend when it she feels, she'll take a precious rasping!*'" He nodded at Alan to join in the chorus, but he remained mute, shaking his head.

"'*If she simpers 'oh!' embrace her, then caress her. Disrobe her form below, entwine round her and press her. Soon you'll find her yield, for her lust gets stronger. One more close embrace, and she's a maid no longer!*'

"You're not going to make me go it alone this time. Come along, sir." Jem elbowed him, and Alan reluctantly and nearly silently mouthed the "tol de rols."

Jem gave him a stern look, but carried on. "'*But if a widow you'd kiss, you must be much bolder. For as they've sipt the bliss, they don't feel much the colder! If you'd seduce a maid, you must swear, and sigh, and flatter. But if you'd win a widow, you must down with your breeches and at her!*'"

This time Jem roared out the chorus, and Alan tried to join in with a little more heart. They repeated the chorus one last time, ending in loud and ragged dissonance that sent crows cawing up from the field they were passing.

"P'raps it'd be better after a pint or two," Jem said. He glanced at Alan with a sly smirk. "Or if one of us had a few singing lessons."

"I sing adequately," Alan declared. "I don't happen to know that ditty."

"Sing me something then. Fill the hours." Jem slapped the lines again, and the slowing horses resumed their speed.

Alan's first impulse was to deny the request, but Jem was always entertaining him. He should return the favor. Other than the church hymns he'd been raised on, his musical knowledge was limited. In his younger days, he'd been quite an aficionado of opera but couldn't sing anything from memory, which was probably just as well. However, he was a prodigious reader and had memorized some poetry.

"Are you familiar with Lord Byron?" He half closed his eyes as he recalled some of the stanzas of the newly published "Childe Harold's Pilgrimage."

"'*Whilome in Albion's isle there dwelt a youth, Who ne in virtue's ways did take delight; But spent his days in riot most uncouth, And vex'd with mirth the drowsy ear of Night. Oh, me! in sooth he was a shameless wight, Sore given to revel and ungodly glee; Few earthly things found favour in his sight Save concubines and carnal companie, And flaunting wassailers of high and low degree.*'"

"Sounds like my kind of lad, a real bounder. Go on," Jem prompted.

Alan carried on with as many verses as he could remember until he reached, "'*And now I'm in the world alone, Upon the wide, wide sea; But why should I for others groan, When none shall sigh for me? Perchance my dog shall whine in vain Till fed by stranger hands; But long ere I come back again He'd tear me where he stands.*'"

"Gawd, no wonder you were like to throttle yourself the night I met you, if that's the tone of what you been reading in them great books of yours." Jem shook his head. "'Tis a good rhyme, though. Is there more?"

Alan obliged. So caught up was he in the story, which he continued to paraphrase long after he'd run through all the parts he'd memorized, that he was surprised to find it was time to stop for tea.

They watered the horses from a running stream and ate Cook's pasties by the side of the water. Gnats and black flies danced around their heads, detracting from the picturesque setting. They quickly finished their meal and resumed the journey.

After they changed horses, Jem took a turn entertaining by telling one lewd joke after another.

Alan couldn't remember when he'd laughed so hard, less from the hilarity of the stories as from the pure joy of the company he kept.

At last he caught sight of the spires and rooftops of Leicester ahead and pointed them out to Jem. "There's where we'll stop for the night."

"Glad to hear it. Me bum's had enough of rattlin' around in this old cart. Not that the seat ain't plush and all," he quickly amended.

"No, you're right. We've kept up a hectic pace, and the phaeton isn't meant for long journeys. I'll admit my leg's aching. We'll find the best lodging at the Harrier Inn, or so I've been told. I haven't found cause to travel to Leicester before now."

Being in sight wasn't the same as being close, and it took almost another hour for them to reach the town. Alan located the hostelry which had been recommended to him and made arrangement for fresh horses for the morrow, after which he and Jem went inside to procure rooms for the night.

Jem carried Alan's bag upstairs. He hung his clothes, then turned to him. "What now, sir? A bite of supper? I don't know about you, but me spine's clattering against me rib cage, I'm that hungry."

"We shall be obliged to part ways," Alan told him. "You'll take your dinner belowstairs and I in the main dining area. There are separate quarters for servants traveling with their masters. I'll summon you in the morning, but make certain you rise early and are ready."

"Yes, sir. I'll not be a slugabed." Jem gave him a jaunty salute and left the room. It was as if someone had blown out the lamp, leaving Alan to fumble around in the dark.

He ate alone in the public room, not eager to seek out a peer to share the meal even though he spied Sir Henry Blackstone across the room. Alan didn't care to make small talk or answer the inevitable questions about why he was traveling. But solitude left him with plenty of time to think, both about how he would deal with Schivvers and, naturally, about Jem.

The scamp had grown important to him. Life would have been simpler if he'd tossed him out as he'd threatened to after catching him entertaining guests in the parlor. But Alan simply couldn't do it. Besides, the lad hadn't deserved to be tossed back into the gutter for his foolishness. Alan knew how desolate his life there had been, despite Jem's cheerful attitude about it. He couldn't bear the thought of such a bright, clever, joyful young man being ground down by life's harshness, or worse, meeting an untimely death.

So Alan would keep his new valet with him regardless of the danger of his growing attachment to a thief, who may or may not have been plotting with his friends to rob the house. He didn't completely trust him yet, but instinct told him Jem was, at heart, a good man. Likely he'd remain loyal as long as Alan continued to feed and clothe him.

With his plate empty and the last drop of port swallowed, Alan took himself up to his room, limping from the stiffness in his leg. As he slid under the covers, he wished Jem was there to rub his leg and ease his pain. Rub some other parts, too.

He lay, longing for the other man's warm body to be curled up beside his and dreaming about kisses and caresses, until at last he drifted off into an actual dream. The languid, erotic tone of the encounter turned to a nightmare as Jem was snatched away by Mr. Schivvers and Alan searched for him in vain.

Bits of real memory were swirled into the mix—blood, death, violence, and a pervading sense of helplessness. There was nothing he could do to stop what was happening or change the outcome. He was a failure. If he found Jem at all, it would be with his throat cut and perhaps with a leg or arm amputated. He couldn't protect or save him from the evil force that had taken him.

Alan woke, gasping, tangled in sweat-drenched sheets. He sat bolt upright and stared at the gray square of window that signaled the coming dawn. He'd thought the worst of his nightmares were behind him—hadn't had one since Jem had come to stay—but the bone-melting terror was back.

He lay awake, trying not to recall the terror of that dream and how the fear all hinged on the loss of Jem. As soon as he possibly could, he rose, hoping he could leave the uncomfortable thoughts behind in the uncomfortable bed.

Chapter Ten

To save time, they traveled through the next day and long into the moonlit night. They slept outside, each man wrapped in his own blanket, much to Jem's regret, though he'd fallen asleep quickly.

They changed horses at the inns, and Alan kept up the breakneck pace though the roads grew less smooth.

The third day into the journey, and Jem couldn't bear the thought of suffering another bone-jarring foot of road. He wished they'd never left London and planned to never set foot outside the city again if they ever got home safely. He wished Badgeman hadn't heard about the girl in peril or that he'd waited one more day to learn the crucial information that his quest was in England. Then sweet, charming old badger would be the one whose bum felt like it had been beaten by the thickest truncheon ever.

The phaeton jolted into another rut, and Jem gritted his teeth and gripped the armrest of the seat. He'd stopped singing or telling jokes many miles back, sick of his own voice for maybe the first time in his life. Now he slouched in brooding silence. Good God, was he turning into Alan?

He glanced at the other man, who sat with his spine erect and shoulders squared. His military bearing never left him. Jem could imagine him in a smart red coat with shiny brass buttons and those epaulets dangling from his shoulders. The man probably looked right toothsome in uniform. Perhaps someday Sir Alan would put on the scarlet for Jem in the privacy of their bedroom and order him about in that lovely commanding voice that made Jem's hair—and other things—rise.

Hark to himself, thinking of "their" bedroom as if he had some part in it. He must stop considering his master's home as his. Look how easily he'd nearly been sacked. It could be "back to the gutter with ye, Jem" anytime he displeased the man. Important to remember who held all the cards. Important to remember his place. The best Jem could hope for would be to keep Alan happy, and maybe his lordship would continue to keep him around.

He'd no business being melancholy or upset by the knowledge that his happiness depended on his master's whim. The night before last at the inn, for example, he'd grumbled inside at being exiled from Alan's bed and sent to the servants' sleeping chamber. Yet not too long ago, he'd have been perfectly cheery about having a belly full of food and a warm place to sleep at night. Now he was as spoiled as a cat sleeping on a silk cushion with a bowl of cream at hand. Could a cat such as that survive in the alley again? He was giving himself airs, imagining his worth to Sir Alan was much greater than it was.

But he was here to be a jester, so let him earn his keep and remove the strained frown from Alan's face, lightening the last few miles of the journey. Clearly the man's leg was paining him, and he was probably dreading his confrontation with Schivvers. Time to perk up and put Alan at ease with a funny tale.

"Sir," Jem began, "this north country reminds me of Pat's country cousin Danny Bingham and his wife Nancy. A very private conversation between that couple was told to me by Pat over a glass o' gin one night. Seems Danny and Nancy was celebrating thirty long years of wedded bliss by taking a tumble in the hay, as country folk seem fond of doing. Old Danny squeezed his wife's tits and told her, 'Ah, Nance, if these were only a bit bigger and could produce milk, we could get rid of the damned cow.'

"His wife ignored the rude comment, and Danny reached a bit lower, fingering the trap between her legs. 'Sweet, Nancy, you know I love you, but if this were only a wee bit tighter, we could use you as a mousetrap and get rid of the damned cat.'

"A bit riled now, Nancy grabbed her dear husband's tool, squeezed it hard and cried, 'My darlin' husband, if only this were a whole lot bigger, we could get rid of your damned brother!'"

Jem was rewarded with a smile that relieved the grim line of Alan's mouth. That one wee smile did him in. His heart twisted and flipped like a fish caught on a hook and dragged out of the Thames. All in a flash, he realized what he feared most wasn't losing the silk-cushion-and-cream life or being released back into murky, dangerous waters. What he feared losing was this difficult, complicated, dark, and melancholy man. He loved Alan's sweet flashes of tenderness, such as this journey to save an orphan. Not many men of his class would bother about a soldier's daughter. Watleigh had an honorable, upright nature and was dead-loyal to his men, especially trusty old Badgeman. Jem wanted to be worthy of loyalty like that.

Also, Jem had discovered he liked having someone to take care of. He'd be lost without Alan to do for. He didn't want to return to looking out only for himself and letting the devil take all others. He needed Alan to give purpose to his empty life, to warm his spirit as well as his body.

Listening to Alan's warm chuckle, Jem wondered what his master would do if he guessed the way his thoughts lay. Did Alan care for him even a little bit, or was Jem only a bedmate and a temporary amusement to him?

"Speaking of haystacks," Jem said, "there seem to be a lot of 'em hereabouts. Perhaps we should follow the country practice and make use of one." He rested his hand on Alan's thigh and squeezed lightly. "Remember what I done for you? I'd like to try to beat my eight-minute record."

Alan exhaled deeply, not a sigh of annoyance, but a shaky, hungry breath. "You are incorrigible, Jem. There's no time for that now. Sheffield is just up ahead, and I'd like to find an inn and get settled before dark."

Jem noticed that he didn't protest about the idea of sex in a haystack, only about the lack of time. Maybe on the way back... But no, they'd have the girl with them if all went well, and everything would be different.

Alan gently disengaged Jem's hand from his leg.

Subsiding back into his seat, Jem folded his arms across his chest. Annoyance bit him like one of the deerflies that darted from the overhanging tree branches in defense of their territory.

"Ah well, maybe another time." He kept his tone breezy and changed the subject. "You think Danny and Nancy was a pair? You should hear what their rich neighbor Thomas Crowell done to choose a groom for his pretty daughter."

But Jem didn't get to share the tale as they rounded a bend in the road and beheld the town of Sheffield sprawling over the plain before them. It was a great deal bigger than Leicester. Smoke from hundreds of chimneys hung in a pall over the metropolis, which grew on the banks of the River Sheaf.

"It's no London," Jem said with a sniff.

"No," Alan agreed. "No Paris or Rome, either."

"Are you taking the piss, sir?" He glared at his benefactor.

"Maybe a little. Don't be a snob, Jem. Every man believes his home is the center of the world."

They rolled forward over more bumpy, badly rutted road. Jem smelled the familiar sewage scent of river water long before they reached the bridge and crossed over it into the city.

The carriage wheels clattered now over brick and cobblestone. He had to raise his voice to speak to Alan. "Do you have an address for this Mr. Schivvers, sir, or will we need to do some hunting?"

"I shall have to ask the direction, but I have an address in Derwent, not far from here. We'll find an inn on the road and make a plan to find her."

Jem hesitated. "Could it be the girl's fine where she is?"

Alan's brows went up, almost as if he knew Jem hated the idea of adding to their household.

So Jem hastily added, "Even the worst of men can be gentle to their daughters."

"If he thinks of her as such." The grim look on Alan's face would freeze a river on a hot day in August.

Jem nodded. "If he dips his wick with young ones, we got no choice about it."

"None. But you're right. I won't disrupt her life if she's well cared for."

"Could be, sir," Jem said hopefully. "He's got the groats to give her a good upbringing."

But the look on Alan's face remained cold. "I know Schivvers. I don't know his plans for her, but I am certain he wouldn't take on a girl out of charity or kindness." Alan stretched out his legs and wiggled in his seat. "I wish there was a way I might observe her without his awareness of my presence."

"Easy enough. I take a look and report to you." Jem scratched his chin. "Best shave and wash some of the road's dirt off me. Don't want to get run out of the place looking as disreputable as a man who's escaped from the treadmill."

Alan remained silent and staring ahead.

Jem understood and grew impatient. "I swear upon my granny's grave to give a true report. You think I see a whelp being mistreated I'd lie about it?"

"Not exactly." Alan said and fell silent. The horses walked along slowly, and he did nothing to speed them on their way. Alan didn't trust him, still.

Jem wanted to bellow at the man, beg him to forgive his mistakes in the past and swear he wouldn't lie or steal again, but then Alan was explaining his hesitation. "I am not certain that we would have the same notions of what constitutes proper behavior on the part of a child's guardian."

Jem got it now. His master accused him not of being a liar, but of being an ignorant child-beating bastard. Well, true enough, he didn't have the sensibilities of a gentleman. "I'll watch," he said, managing to keep his temper in check, "and tell you all of what I see. No deciding what's important and what's not worth hearing. Agreed? Every word and gesture I see, I tell you."

Alan nodded. "We'll try that first."

They found a small inn with a taciturn landlord and only two rooms. "Ye'll have to share a room."

First good news Jem had heard for a time. He wished he had time for a full bath, but Alan's impatience was palpable even when the man stood in the middle of the room looking about. "I'll wait below," he said, no doubt running from temptation.

Jem hurriedly washed himself in a basin, then put on a fresh shirt, a starched cravat, and a dark, tidy suit that might belong to a servant or a curate on his day off.

Alan met him in the taproom, and they went without another word out to the waiting carriage. The horses had been exchanged for two new ones: a black and a brown. No more need of four for speed and no glossy matching animals in this backwater. Jem examined the horses for a few seconds more, trying to remember all the points Alan had explained.

Alan dropped him at the edge of the little town near the address he'd been given. "I'll meet you back at the inn. I might go into the city."

The house Schivvers rented was set back from the high street, not far from Derwent Hall.

The small green just on the high street offered a public spot where Jem could lean against a tree and keep an eye on the back of the house. He settled on the grass with a chunk of wood and his knife to whittle while he waited for signs of life. The occasional villager passed and slowed to look at him curiously. Derwent was not a hub of activity, and Jem was an object of great curiosity. He nodded and smiled and went back to work on his carving.

After several hours, a barouche rolled from the stable yard behind the house to the front gravel drive. Jem shoved his knife and carving away and trotted toward the road in the front. He whistled a song so anyone watching from the houses near the green would know he wasn't alarmed, merely in a hurry.

The barouche pulled near the front door, and Jem, positioned on the road across from the hedges, watched as a tall man with broad shoulders swept out the front door. He clapped a hat on his flaxen hair. He looked just as Alan had described him once. And his aspect matched his name in that it would give Jem the shivers if he ran into the tall, pale, black-eyed surgeon on a dark night. His expression was as dead and cold as a two-day-old codfish. He had the look of a man who'd stick a knife in your gut without blinking an eye, a lack of affinity to all humankind which Jem recognized from personal experience in the criminal underworld.

The man was closely followed a young girl. The Major—Alan had recalled her real name—Annie Cutler. She was well dressed and looked clean and well cared for. Her hair fell in glossy ringlets down her back. No expense had been spared to dress or shod her, but it wasn't showy wealth. Dainty, with pale skin and a heart-shaped face, she was a naturally attractive child. Jem knew she'd fetch a good price in one of the more shadowy houses of ill repute even if she had been touched. There now, that thought raised a possibility that wouldn't cross a gentleman's mind. Though come to think of it, Alan had mentioned it without wailing or protesting such a thing never occurred. Sir Alan didn't flinch at life's harder realities—except when he thought he was guilty of 'em.

The girl didn't smile or jump about. She only waited, hands clenched at her sides, a dull look in her eyes. Maybe she was tired or perhaps distracted, because she didn't seem to notice how the man waited for her to climb in. Jem could almost hear the surgeon's impatient sigh, though he stood yards away.

Yet the tall, elegantly garbed man didn't seize her or shout. He leaned down and held out his hand so she might grasp it and climb into the low open carriage.

Then she turned her face up to her guardian, and Jem caught full sight of her and knew the emptiness in her face was more than a passing moment of fatigue. She wore a million-miles-away stare, the look of a person trying hard not to exist in that place or moment. Either she was gone in her mind, or she was terrified and longing to be anywhere else. Men on their way to the drop and dangle wore that face. Likely Jem had worn it himself sometimes when with a less-than-choice customer.

The pale, expressionless girl took her place in the open carriage with her back to the horses, and they drove away. Perhaps she had only overindulged in blue ruin, but that would be near as bad, now wouldn't it?

"Oh, shite," Jem whispered.

He considered running after the carriage but instead walked along the dusty road back the way he'd come.

The inn was four miles away, and he broke into a trot to deliver his first report to Alan.

The captain's carriage and team were gone, and the innkeeper, after a barrage of questions, at last admitted that the gentleman had ridden in the direction of Sheffield but had left no word of where he'd gone.

Jem wished he'd stayed put in his position at the entrance to Schivvers's house. He cursed and paced and waited for Alan's return.

After brushing the clothes they'd worn the day before, he pulled out the block of wood he was trying to carve into a horse and wandered outside to the stable yard. Having nothing to do should have been a fine treat for him, but Jem decided he didn't like inactivity. What if the girl and Schivvers returned to the house and he missed a chance to speak to her? He wished he could write a note for Alan and leave.

Well, why not? It wasn't as if his sad excuse for writing would be any great shock to Alan. The man knew he was a street rat.

Almost defiant at his decision, he went to the innkeeper to demand pen, ink, and paper. For once the man moved quickly. Jem sat in a quiet corner of the taproom and stared at the blank sheet of parchment. He wondered if pictures could do the trick, but in the end decided a couple of lines would serve. He wrote and let the ink dry. Once he folded the paper, he flapped it against his hand awhile, then decided to leave it in their room.

Upstairs, he smiled at the bed, imagining Alan sprawled on it, and felt himself stir. No, he had to keep his mind off his cock and on the job at hand. He looked down at the messy note he'd written and left it on the small desk, propped against a vase.

And then, with a sigh, he began the long walk back to Mr. Schivvers's great gray house in Derwent. He rubbed his bum, reflecting that at least he wasn't traveling by carriage.

Back at the house, the barouche had returned and was already in the carriage house. Jem settled to wait for more signs of the surgeon and his charge.

After a long time, a footman in full gear, including wig, came trotting across the gravel path, down the smooth lawn, and then, wonder of wonders, carefully picked his way through the small copse of trees to the public land where Jem sat. The footman was fat. Not just a bit of a pudge, but a sack of grease, as Noah would say. He pulled out a handkerchief and wiped his reddened brow.

"Care to sit?" Jem waved a hand at the ground.

"Naw, thank'ee." He carefully straightened his wig and touched the lace at his throat. "Thing is, Mr. Burton want to know what yer about."

"Sitting on my bum, carving a horse." Jem stood. If his guest wasn't going to rest, he knew he shouldn't. He held up the horse carving. "See?"

The footman squinted and pushed out thick lips thoughtfully. "Nice. Just enjoying the fine day? You've nowt to do wi' the house yonder?"

"Why do you ask?"

"Mr. Burton worrit. Seem you been staring and staring. Know ye the master?"

Jem had trouble understanding the man, who had some sort of broad accent.

"Mr. Schivvers, you mean?"

The footman nodded.

"I don't know much about him."

"Nor do I." The footman's voice dropped, as if the empty green were filled with spies listening to their conversation. "He only recently took the house."

The footman didn't seem eager to return to the house, so perhaps Jem could learn something else from him. Perhaps something about the girl's keepers. "Mr. Burton's the butler? I'll wager a bellowing old tyrant?"

"By bloody half, he is."

The footman shifted away a little so he, unlike Jem, wasn't in direct line of sight from the house. No one would see him lounging against the tree. "Tell me true, lad, were ye watching? Like Mr. Burton thinks?"

"A bit," Jem admitted.

The big man's spaniel eyes bulged as he stared at Jem. "Truly?" He sounded thrilled, like a man trapped in a dull little village, longing for something intriguing to discuss.

"No need for alarm. I'm only a tad curious about your Mr. Schivvers and his little shadow."

"Tha' girl, you mean?"

"The very one." Jem felt his words slow and his tongue slide over the sounds in a new way. He ended up mimicking his elders, his betters, the sinful, and everyone in between. He'd have to be careful about letting himself slip into whatever accent this man had. "She have a nanny or governess or what have you?"

"Nay. Later, he says."

The footman flapped his handkerchief over his face again and pushed away from the tree trunk. The day was warm but hardly steaming. "I'd best be going back," he said without moving.

Jem held out a hand. "Jack Browning," he lied.

"Melvin Lincoln." The footman folded and tucked away the cloth and solemnly shook hands. When he began his slower walk across the green, Jem fell into step next to him. "Why is your Mr. Burton so suspicious of strangers?"

"He's not. Burton's put on airs, but he's from up York way. Not from the south like you and the master, as I can hear from your voices. Burton couldn't care a twist about strangers. More the master. A right cautious man, the master. Burton's following orders, he says." The footman stopped. "Not sure he'd want you walking over with me."

Jem laughed and waved a hand to indicate the softly rolling hills, the puffy clouds. "Hardly the stews of London. He afraid I'll run off with the silver? Just walking you back to the house."

Melvin laughed too. "'Tis nonsense. 'Sides, I got two stone on you at the very least."

More than that, Jem thought, but didn't say. "If I try to make trouble, you'd break me in half I'd guess."

Melvin liked that and practically roared with laughter. Now that he'd completed the embarrassing part of his errand, he was showing himself a jolly lad.

"I suspect you're from London, even?" Melvin asked.

Jem nodded.

"I got a cousin there. In service for a family near Wimbledon. Know that area?"

"Certainly," Jem lied cheerfully. "Pretty place."

"I might go down with Mr. Schivvers when he travels south."

"Is he traveling soon?"

"Sure, sure. Next day or two."

"Ah." Jem studied the side of the house as they approached.

A small face watched from an upper-story window. Melvin walked ahead chattering about everything from the new master who'd only taken a year's lease, to what Melvin wanted to do and see in London.

"No, sir, you don't want to miss Astley's," Jem agreed as he waved at the window. Was it the girl? Just in case it was, he stopped dead, and on impulse, Jem snapped a salute, exactly the way he'd seen Badgeman do. The signals Alan had shown him, might she know them? Feeling like an utter fool, he patted himself on the top of the head, then clenched his fist and moved it quickly up and down between his leg and shoulder. *Join me double time.*

The face in the window vanished.

Melvin, who hadn't seen him making a fool of himself, turned back and held out a soft, sweating hand. "I'll bid ye good day, Jack. Nice though 'tis to see a new face hereabouts, best if ye don't linger."

"Sure enough, Mr. Lincoln. Pleased to make your acquaintance, and perhaps we'll meet again soon." Jem shook hands and wandered back to his spot on the green. For the rest of the afternoon, nothing of note occurred. A few birds pecked around his feet, and he threw them the crumbs of the loaf he'd grabbed for food. His only activity other than whittling consisted of tipping his hat to the pair of girls who paraded first in one direction and then the other, giggling and flashing him hot looks.

The sun sank low, and he set off for the inn. He wasn't sure what he'd expected. The girl to run out of the house and find him? He'd imagined scooping her into his arms, running the miles back to the inn, and presenting her to Alan. More probably if he managed to get near her, she'd commence screaming and kicking.

Chapter Eleven

Alan opened to door to the room and spotted the note at once. It had *Sr* in an uncertain, wobbly hand. Jem? Somehow Alan was shocked that his writing was so tentative, nothing like the man. He stared down at the messy, unsteady letters, blots of ink and a few crude pictures. His first thought was that Jem must have been very upset to have attempted a note. The man had pride and surely knew his writing was shabby. His second thought was, *I'll have to teach him to read and write better.*

Why would he do that? Alan shifted from foot to foot and stared down at the note. Enough with trying to get to the bottom of Jem's soul and improve him. Better to concentrate on trying to understand what he had to say. *Bn der cum bk.* There was a rather crude picture of a dog holding a knife and a beer, and Alan remembered the name of the inn was the Dog and Arms. *grl iz sd. I gu dak ber. Son I km bk. Jem*, followed by a picture of the sun at the horizon and another dog with a knife.

He decided Jem had reversed a couple of b's and d's, and the note read, *Been there and came back. Girl is sad*—or sick? *I'm going back and will return at sunset to the inn.*

Alan traced the letters of the note, wondering how long Jem had taken to write it. He'd wait. After all, he'd had little success in Sheffield, where he'd sought out a lawyer to look into the matter of making the girl at least a ward, with several men acting as guardian instead of simply being under Schivvers's unmonitored control. Alan had convinced the man it was a good idea, but the lawyer warned that the courts might not agree to even hear the matter. They didn't have time for one fortuneless orphan.

Maybe Jem would bring him good news.

The man appeared soon after sundown. Impatient though Alan was to get the news, he could see Jem was thirsty and in need of a rest. He ordered a light supper and they settled in a far corner, away from the fireplace. The taproom was filling with workers, employed by the plating company if their silvery fingernails were any indication. The two men sat across from each other over a small wooden table in a chilly corner.

After downing nearly a pint of some of the inn's decent ale, Jem wiped his mouth on his sleeve and sighed. "Thank you, sir."

Alan nodded. "Go on."

Jem stretched out his legs and winced. "I said I'd report on words I heard, but all I listened to today was a footman. Jolly soul, but of little use to us, at least not for information. I heard nothing from the girl or your friend Schivvers, though I saw 'em not so far away."

He paused. "No. I were to be as a parrot, not telling more 'n I witnessed."

Alan interrupted. "I regret injuring your feelings by saying that I don't trust your judgment."

Jem's blue eyes widened. He burst into a peal of laughter. "God bless it, sir, you make me feel like a spoiled lad on occasion."

"Did I judge wrong?" Alan smiled; Jem's laughter was infectious.

"No, too right, I'd say. My pride was injured, and I was pining away with the pain." He threw back his head, widened his eyes, and clutched at his heart.

"Gudgeon," Alan said. Jem's habit of exaggeration swept the incident into the trivial, but Alan suspected he'd truly been hurt—and perhaps worse, Jem might believe Alan's assessment. "Go on and tell me what you saw, and please tell me what you believe."

The food arrived, and Jem piled thick slices of the ham and spooned the overboiled potatoes onto his plate as if it were the finest fare. He noticed Alan watching him and put some of the potatoes back on the platter.

Alan reached for the plate of ham. "Your note said the girl was, ah, sad?"

Jem beamed around the mouth bulging with food. "You understood the note? Yes. Worse 'n sad, really. She's given up. If a wind came and pushed at her soul, she'd let go."

"She's too thin?"

"No, I said it wrong. Her body looks fine. Trifle scrawny, yes. But it's her heart, I mean. She got no resistance to trouble left in her. Mind you, that's from three minutes of watching. But that look..." He shook his head. "Dazed-like. Opium? Alcohol? Maybe, though she walked without a stumble. No. I think she's pulling away from this world."

"Three minutes of watching told you this?" Alan asked.

Jem had crammed a piece of ham into his mouth. He chewed, swallowed, and said, "Three seconds, more like. I wanted to grab her out of there, sir. Even if she were an unholy bitch." He paused. "Might she be such?"

Alan shrugged. "She was a quiet girl when I knew her, but children must change and grow."

Jem put down the knife and fork he'd been clutching. "You've got to talk to her, sir."

"She hasn't seen me in more than a year. She mightn't know me, but Schivvers will. It might be easier for you to get in to speak to her."

Jem grinned. "Now that's a compliment, sir. You'd trust my report of what she'd say?"

"Cut line, Jem. I already apologized." Had he? He would say more now. "I trust your judgment."

"But I like to hear you got confidence in me. It's sweet music." His grin faded, and he rested his chin in his hand, frowning in concentration. "She'll recall you, I'll wager. Your name if not your face. You got to find a way to talk to her and see if we need to grab her now. Mel the footman claims they're off for London in a few days. Wonder why he's cutting out of this house so quickly. Just took it for a full year's lease, Mel said. Restless soul, is your Mr. Schivvers?"

"He is most certainly not mine, Jem. Perhaps he's moving her around. Not allowing her comfort."

"All that effort for a little mite like her?"

Alan shrugged. "He was hard to distract from a project. A good thing in a field surgeon. He'd start a job and keep going, without looking up even if a cannonball fell nearby."

"Not a coward."

"No, but not brave, either. Bravery requires a man to feel fear and overcome it. I am convinced Schivvers is a little mad. I think he believes himself the center of creation, so of course, he wouldn't die in the war."

Alan leaned back and looked at Jem, who gazed back. Jem's lips parted, but no words came out. Only the promise of that mouth and… *Oh God.* The heat was instantaneous, engulfing Alan, making it impossible for him to draw a deep breath. No one in the taproom paid them any mind beyond initial curious glances, but they mustn't look at one another with any heat. Never in a public place. Nor in private. Not until they had a plan. And then? No tempting thoughts. He had to steady his heart and breath.

So he looked away and tried to concentrate on Schivvers. Now that was a cold bath to chill the warm promise in Jem's eyes.

"Schivvers had a notebook," Alan said, staring down at the congealing undercooked meat on his plate.

"Did he?" Jem sounded distracted. With the way Jem pushed at the food on his plate, Alan didn't have to look up to know Jem's eyes were focused on him, watching his every move. He could feel the gaze.

"Jem." He spoke in a low voice. "No."

Jem made a rude noise and began to eat again. "Right then. What about the notebook?"

"He kept it with him all the time. A small leather-bound book, bloodstained and scuffed. Back before I saw him for what he was, I looked over his shoulder once and saw he had very neat handwriting. He closed the book quickly when I asked him what he was writing. 'Research,' Schivvers told me. 'It's why I'm in Spain.'

"'Medical research?' I asked. I didn't like him much, but I still admired his skill and dedication to improving it. And the man had aspirations beyond mere surgery; I overheard him declare he'd be a physician on Harley Street someday.

"'Of course. And research of the mind. What breaks a man?' he asked me. He wanted to know. He wanted to learn what I'd seen."

"Gawd. What did you say?"

"I think I made a remark like pain could break any living soul. He nodded and told me that was too easy, especially for a medical man. He said, 'I appreciate subtlety.' I remember I laughed, thinking it a joke. He laughed along with me. The man's usually skilled at behaving like a regular person and only makes an occasional slip."

Jem pushed the plate away. "No wonder your badger went off like a shot."

"And why we won't. Better to take a little time and get legal custody of Ann if possible. However, I plan to visit Schivvers tomorrow, check on the girl's condition personally and see if maybe I can convince him to give up his rights without getting the courts involved."

"Sounds like you've thought it out. 'Course, a gent like that wouldn't like his toys being snatched away, so I don't s'pose you'll get too far with him."

Alan thought the same but didn't answer. Inside, his growing sense of anxiety threatened to explode. He wanted nothing more than to go to the man's house right now, break down the door, march in, and seize the young girl before Schivvers could do vile, contemptible things to her. Perhaps it was already too late. While at first Alan had mostly been invested in Ann Cutler's fate on Badger's behalf, his own sense of duty had soon become involved. He felt a debt to Private Cutler and to all the men who'd been under his command—the ones he'd tried to save, the ones he'd failed.

Jem gave an exaggerated yawn and stretch. "Lot o' riding and walking today. I'm that done in. Guess it's off to bed now."

"Yes." The word "bed" sent a shaft of lust stabbing through Alan, straight down to his cock. He was ashamed of his immediate and primitive reaction, as if he were a dog shown a bone and salivating at the mere sight.

He didn't look at Jem as he rose and left the taproom to lead the way upstairs. The bedchamber had been modified by the housekeeping staff in their absence. A small pallet had been prepared on the floor for the master's valet to sleep on. Both men stared at the pallet, at the bed, and then at each other.

Jem smiled. "I can guess which accommodations are mine." He took off his jacket and boots and plopped down on the thin mattress with its stingy single blanket. "Quite comfy, this. But if you care to roll me for it, I've brought my dice along."

Alan had shrugged off his own jacket and stood with his arms folded over his chest. Foolish to continue pretending nothing was going to happen in this room tonight.

"Get up off the floor, Jem," he growled, "and get into bed."

"Aye, Captain Sir. Your command is my wish." The man leaped off the pallet and into the bed faster than a hare. He was already unbuttoning his shirt before Alan could sit to take his boots off.

"You need help with those, sir?" Jem just as quickly abandoned the bed to kneel at Alan's feet and wrestle with his footwear. "Your leg must be bloody throbbing and stiff from riding in a carriage for nigh on three days."

Alan couldn't argue with that. He caught his breath to keep from gasping when Jem finally slid the boot off his heel. He hadn't had this much pain since immediately after the injury, when it had been touch and go whether he'd keep the leg. If Schivvers had had his way, Alan would be walking with a peg today or, more likely, lying under Spanish soil.

Jem helped him undress, easing him out of his stockings, trousers, and linens, while Alan removed his waistcoat and shirt. Alan slid back onto the bed, propping the pillows against the hard wooden headboard, and watched Jem strip off his clothing.

Aware of being watched, the young peacock made a show of it, humming a tune and tantalizing Alan with each bit of flesh he revealed. Slowly his fingers opened buttons, separated hooks from eyes, slid cloth down narrow hips, revealing a scimitar pair of hip bones. The smooth muscles of his chest, the lean sinew of his arms, and the soft down that feathered his lower stomach were attributes displayed like delicacies for Alan's consideration.

To say Alan was aroused was an understatement. He felt as if all the air had been sucked from the room. His body burned as though his fever had returned, and the aching in his cock far outstripped that in his sore leg. He longed to leap from the bed, seize Jem like a predator attacking its prey, and drag him down onto the mattress to ravish him. Or maybe he'd slam him up against the wall and take him there, pumping furiously between peachy globes into that dark, forbidden spot he craved so fiercely.

As he undressed, Jem never took his gaze from Alan's face. His half-lidded eyes burned with promise, and his seductive stripping showed Alan exactly what he could have. When he was finished unveiling his beautiful form, the youth stood with hands resting lightly on his hips, allowing Alan to feast on the sight for a moment. Then he launched his body back onto the bed and burrowed between Alan's legs, reaching for his upright pole.

"Hold, Jem." Alan grabbed the lad's shoulder. "I want something different tonight."

Jem cocked a brow. "How do you want me, sir? I'm up for most anything."

"All taking, no giving isn't fair. Tonight you'll allow me to service you instead. Lie back." He pressed his hand against that solid, smooth chest and pushed him back.

"Truly? But your leg is paining you tonight. It'd be easier for you to lie still an' let me—"

"Don't argue. I know what I want."

It felt good to take control after days of giving Jem the upper hand. Every sexual encounter until now had been initiated by the younger man and had revolved around Alan's pleasure. This time, he'd make sure Jem spent first and hard. He wanted to hear the man groan with delight and see his face transported by ecstasy.

In a trice, they flipped positions. Jem lounged against the pillows like a prince, and Alan wedged his big body awkwardly between the other man's sprawled legs. He was not experienced at this, the only incident being with Jem in his study that first night. Had it only been a few weeks ago? It seemed much longer. The gutter youth was such an incontrovertible fixture in his life now.

Alan glanced up at Jem's face, those heaven blue eyes darkened by lust and fixed on him with avid intensity, moist lips slack. He took hold of Jem's solid penis and glided his hand slowly from base to tip and back again. The foreskin rolled forward then back, revealing the rounded tip already creaming a drop of white.

Alan took a page from Jem's book and made him wait for what he wanted. He leaned to kiss his lightly haired thighs, first one then the other. He lapped delicately with his tongue along his inner thighs, over his hips, and up to his twitching belly, mapping a reconnaissance mission around the target.

Again he flicked a glance at Jem's face. “Do you want more?”

“Don't mind if I do.” His voice cracked, and he swallowed.

“Then ask for it. I want to hear you.” Alan too had to swallow before he could say the erotically charged word “beg.”

“Please, sir. Will you suck me big, fat cock? I'm simply aching for it. I want you to wrap your hot, sweet mouth around me, if you please, sir.”

Even playing submissive, somehow Jem held all the cards. His inflaming words made Alan's rigid cock even harder. He thrust against the bedsheets to relieve the pressure, then lowered his head and took the tip of Jem's cock into his mouth. The loose foreskin moved back, and Alan rolled his tongue over the round head, tasting salt and musk, the essence of Jem.

He swallowed deeper, engulfing more of the long shaft as he grasped the base in his hand and moved his fist up and down. The movement of his hand was well familiar. How many times had he abused his own member that way in the long years of his life? But the sucking was a different matter. It was a strange yet extremely arousing thing to take a man's cock in his mouth. He hoped he was doing it right, thought about how he liked it, and tried to duplicate the moves Jem had performed on him.

Jem seemed to be pleased with what Alan was doing, because it didn't take much pumping or many hard sucks for him to bring Jem to the edge of release. Alan could tell by the increasing raggedness of the other man's breath and the way his hips thrust faster and faster.

He wanted to do something more, something daring, something that would jolt Jem over the edge with a start of surprise. Alan cupped the tight sac of his balls for a moment, then slipped his finger back along the strip of skin that led to Jem's rear opening. He teased his finger around the opening and then, just as Jem was gasping and groaning, he stabbed it inside. The abrupt intrusion sent the man over the wall. He cried out and bucked. If Alan hadn't had both hands busy, he'd have reached up and clapped one over Jem's mouth. The inn's walls weren't built to hold back sound, and he didn't want those in the next room guessing at the intimate relationship between master and servant.

But Jem seemed to gauge this for himself. He flung one forearm over his mouth and muffled his groans of pleasure while he continued to thrust his hips. Alan kept him in a firm grip, milking his cock with rough jerks of his fist and swallowing the creamy emission that jetted onto the back of his tongue.

When Jem at last lay still, Alan released his penis and wiped the back of his hand over his mouth. He remained there another few moments, stroking Jem's quivering leg and gazing at his enraptured face, so entrancingly beautiful he could stare at it for hours. But his leg was hurting and his cock craving release, so Alan crawled up to lie beside Jem and slung his arm across his body.

Jem's eyes flickered open and focused on him. The firelight from the hearth made them glitter like sapphires. "That was lovely, sir. Thank you very much." He glanced down at Alan's massive erection poking into his hip. "But I imagine you'll be craving some relief of your own now. Am I right?"

He slid out from beneath Alan's arm, went to his valise, and returned with the bottle of oil usually kept in Alan's bedside table. "I had hopes we'd make use of this sometime along the road, so I packed it."

Alan smiled. "Good foresight. You'd make an excellent supply sergeant for the army."

"Aye, I could make sure the wheels was greased—and the poles." Jem poured a puddle of oil onto his hand and massaged Alan's cock until it was all Alan could do to hold back.

Alan grabbed his wrist to stop him. "Enough, lad. I'm more than ready."

"Then prepare me, Master." Jem drawled the title so that "master" took on an entirely different connotation that made Alan grit his teeth with desire. The scamp rolled to his side and offered his rear.

Slipping well-lubricated fingers over the taut cheeks and between them, Alan admired the view of shining, oiled skin. He located Jem's tight sphincter and pressed a finger into the ring of muscle. He added another, stretching and widening the passage, and when it could encompass three fingers, he replaced them with the head of his cock.

A grunt and a push, and he was inside, driving up the tight channel. The heat and closeness surrounding him was heavenly—and Jem was an angel. Alan kissed his shoulder and clasped his body tight as he impaled him deeply.

The other man's flesh burned his. Sweat pooled between them as their bodies pushed against one another, struggling like fighters, merging like lovers. Jem's scent was in Alan's nose, his taste in his mouth—the young man filled his senses even as Alan filled him. This union, this joy, was what he'd craved for so long. The act transcended animal sex and became something else, something approaching bliss.

One. Two. Three more hard thrusts, three more clashes of body to body, and Alan released with a shudder. He moaned into Jem's shoulder, bit down on the delicate skin where shoulder met neck.

"Gawd, sir. Right there! Fuck me just like that."

If Alan hadn't already been in the midst of spending, Jem's hoarse voice and coarse words would have driven him there. As it was, they added an extra boost. He thrust hard once more, then shook as wave after wave of pleasure crashed through him.

When it was over, he continued to lay there, his body wrapped around Jem's, his dick buried deep. They were one being at this moment, and he wanted to remain that way for as long as possible. He didn't want to disengage and break the bond they'd forged together.

But then his growing bond with Jem was about much more than their two bodies locked together. Somehow, in a very short space of time, Jem had managed to work his way into Alan's heart. He couldn't be dislodged; he was like a soldier who'd dug into a trench and refused to surrender ground.

"That was right special," Jem murmured, and for once there wasn't a trace of teasing in his voice. He stroked his hand lightly over Alan's arm, which was wrapped around his chest.

"You've undone me, Jem." Alan kissed the spot where he'd bitten the crook of his neck. "You've tricked me, like one of those goblins or leprechauns in your stories."

"Tricked you how, sir?"

"Made me lose my senses. Made me forget reason whenever I'm with you." *No good can come of it, yet I don't even care.* "You've cast a spell over me," he finished.

"Speaking of spells, did I ever tell you about my friend Albert, who—"

Alan covered Jem's mouth before he could go on. "Hush, Jem. No stories right now. Let's just rest here awhile."

He took his hand away, and Jem remained silent. His chest rose and fell with his breathing beneath Alan's arm. A log on the fire fell, sending a shower of sparks crackling up the chimney.

Alan breathed in. And out. His eyes closed.

Chapter Twelve

When Alan opened his eyes, weak sunlight shone through the small, smeary window. He lay flat on his back, his hurt leg stiff as a board. Jem was curled against his side, face burrowed into Alan's shoulder, one slack hand resting on Alan's belly near his flaccid cock. The droopy thing twitched and began to stiffen just from the proximity of Jem's fingers.

They should get up before some servant arrived to poke up the fire for the morning. True, Alan had locked the door, but no sense in taking a chance.

He shook Jem's shoulder. The other man snorted and awoke. "What?"

"Time to rise."

"Right." Jem rolled over and pulled the covers around him.

Alan rose, relieved himself in the chamber pot, washed his face at the bedside table, and took fresh linens from his valise. He dressed, took a moment to rumple Jem's pallet so it would look as though it had been slept in, then stood over the covered lump with the sandy brown hair on his bed.

"Jem, you may sleep in, if you wish. I'm going to eat, then visit Schivvers."

Jem bobbed upright, throwing back the covers. "I'm awake. I'll come with you. I could strike up more conversation with Footman Melvin and learn more about where the girl's kept."

Alan could see he was eager to help, and he'd serve no purpose idling his time away at the inn. "Very well, but be circumspect in what you say."

"Yes, sir." Jem snapped a smart salute, the effect diminished by the fact that he was naked but for a rumpled sheet around his hips.

On impulse, Alan stooped, cupped Jem's jaw, and bestowed a quick kiss on his lips. The daring of that small act sent a thrill through him, and Jem's grin warmed him down to his toes.

"Get dressed. Hurry."

~

After a hearty breakfast in the taproom, they went to the yard where the groom had the phaeton waiting, as Alan had requested. It was a gray day, the sky threatening but not yet delivering rain. They'd almost reached Derwent when the rain broke. It wasn't a deluge, more a light drizzle, not worth stopping to put up the top since they were almost at their destination. But both men were soaked to the skin by the time they'd reached the doctor's house.

Jem held the reins while Alan strode to the front door and lifted the knocker. The door opened almost before he'd let it drop. A stone-faced butler regarded him. Alan's call was unusually early, but he hadn't wanted to give Schivvers the chance to refuse to see him.

He produced his card and offered it to the butler. "Is Mr. Schivvers at home?"

"I will see if Mr. Schivvers is taking callers today." The man ushered him into the parlor before leaving with the card on a silver tray.

Alan studied the parlor but found nothing remarkable about it. Since this was a rented home, Schivvers's personal stamp wasn't apparent in the furnishings or paintings. Alan guessed if he had freedom to explore the entire house, he'd find a more sinister chamber—a library of secret texts, perhaps, or a locked laboratory where the doctor indulged in his experiments. Or his imagination was running wild, and the surgeon wasn't nearly as threatening as Alan had once thought. All sorts of terrible things had happened during the war, on the battlefield and off it. Maybe in civilian life Schivvers was a kinder, better man. Maybe his ward was perfectly safe and the man perfectly sane, despite the flashes of madness Alan had believed he'd glimpsed. And maybe Jem could go an entire day without speaking—none of them bloody likely.

The butler returned, his footsteps almost silent on the plush Turkish carpet. "The master will see you. Please come with me."

"My servant is outside with the horses. Could he wait in the kitchen? The day's turned blustery."

"Certainly, sir." The man led the way toward the back of the house, knocked on a door, and waited permission to enter.

Alan's chest felt tight, and his pulse beat too fast, as if he were about to face an entire enemy squadron rather than one man. He walked into Mr. Schivvers's study and took in the room at a glance before focusing on the doctor himself.

The man turned from the window, where rain pelted against the glass, to face Alan. He was every bit the tall, pale, elegant wraith Alan remembered. His silver blond hair was swept back from a patrician brow, and his facial features were classical. His nose was high-bridged, his jaw prominent, and his mouth a straight line with thin lips. His appearance was more aristocratic than his lineage, and he would not have looked out of place in the drawing rooms of the *haut ton.*

"Sir Alan Watleigh, to what do I owe the honor of your visit?"

Alan had debated with himself how to approach his request, veering back and forth between portraying a manufactured bonhomie and delivering a flat request. In the end, he went for a little of both.

Stepping forward, he shook the man's hand. "It's been some time, Mr. Schivvers. How long have you been back from the war?" He countered the man's question with one of his own.

Schivvers gestured for Alan to sit and took a seat across from him before answering. "I've returned fairly recently. I realize the need for competent battlefield surgeons is ongoing, but after gaining custody of my ward, Ann, I decided it was time to retire from the field and bring the girl somewhere safe at last."

"Ann Cutler? I remember the child, and truth to tell, sir, she is the reason for my visit."

The doctor's brows shot up, yet he didn't seem nearly as surprised as he pretended to be. Of course he would've guessed Alan wanted something from him. It wasn't as if they'd been close friends and Alan would have driven all the way up to Sheffield to reminisce about the old days.

"What do you wish to discuss concerning Miss Cutler?" The man's tone was smooth and calm, but Alan sensed currents and eddies of turbulence underneath.

"As you know, her father, Private Charles Cutler, was under my command."

The butler reentered the room bearing a tea tray, and Alan fell silent until he'd poured and left.

"On his deathbed," he continued, "Cutler entrusted the care of his family to another of my men, Sergeant Badgeman. It was his dying wish that Alice and her daughter's interests were to be looked after by Badgeman—and by proxy, myself."

"You're here to check on Ann's well-being?" Again Schivvers's tone remained calm, but Alan could practically feel the tension vibrating through him. He didn't like being questioned, and why would any man hate it so unless he had something to hide?

"Yes," Alan answered simply.

"If the child is his concern, where is Sergeant Badgeman?"

"He understood you were in Portugal and left to seek you there."

"And you felt compelled to come and talk to me immediately without sending correspondence first or waiting for your man to return? What sort of peril do you imagine the girl in to bring you here in such a hurry?"

Alan shook his head. "I didn't mean to suggest such a thing."

Schivvers cut across him with a voice as sharp as glass. "Why did it take Badgeman so many months to attempt to fulfill his duty to Cutler? If he'd truly wanted to care for the man's family, he should have been there much sooner, offering aid and comfort. He wasn't present at Alice Cutler's deathbed; I was, and the woman entrusted her child to me."

"As you may recall, I was sent home wounded," Alan explained. "So was Badgeman, and when he'd healed, he remained at my side for many months, helping me to recover. It was only recently we learned about Mrs. Cutler's fate. Badgeman was devastated he hadn't been able to fulfill his promise to Charlie. He would like to do so now, and as Cutler's captain, I also feel obligated to step in."

Schivvers sat back in his chair, stretching his long legs before him, feigning an ease Alan doubted he felt. "That is admirable, but there's really no need. As you can see, the girl is well cared for here. She wants for nothing." He waved his hand to indicate the well-appointed study and the house beyond.

"I'm certain you've cared for Ann admirably. But this vow means everything to Badgeman, and I would like to help him in any way I can—legal, financial, whatever means necessary." He dropped a polite hint of threat by suggesting legal avenues and a promise with the mention of possible financial gain.

"Of course I understand about a man's honor and his need to fulfill an oath, but you may tell your man his duty has been discharged. He promised Cutler his family would be looked after, and Ann is most certainly cared for. In the months she has lived as my ward, I've grown extremely fond of the child. I could not imagine giving her up."

"I have looked into the matter of joint guardianship—"

"Entirely foolish for a girl who has no fortune." Schivvers's mouth had grown thin, pressed so tight the skin around his lips was pale. Perhaps the man with ice water in his veins instead of blood had lost the ability to stay cool in the face of any confrontation or danger.

Alan was exhausted already with couching his words in polite terms. He wanted to demand and order, not skirt the issue around like a lawyer, but bluster would get him nowhere. He took a moment to sip from his cup of tea. The brew was strong but already cooling from sitting too long in the thin china cup. It was too soon to offer a bribe of money. That would be a last resort, as he guessed Schivvers would not be inspired to give up his trophy for gold.

"I can see you are committed to caring for Ann, but as I've driven such a long way, might I have a chance to meet the girl and talk with her? I would like to offer my condolences on her parents' deaths and tell her that, as his commanding officer, I can testify her father was a brave soldier."

There was no way Schivvers could deny this basic and quite proper request—unless the child was in such a state that she wasn't fit to be seen.

But Schivvers didn't hesitate. "Certainly. I will send for the dear girl right now."

He rang a bell, summoning the butler, and sent the man to fetch Ann. "Tell her she may appear in her morning dress; there's no need to change her frock for our visitor."

Alan agreed. He didn't want to wait here with Schivvers while the girl prepared for company. The sooner he could meet her and assess her condition, the better.

"How is your leg?" Schivvers changed the subject as they waited in awkward silence for Annie. "Has it healed properly?"

"It was a slow process, but it's completely healed now." *No thanks to you, who would've sawed it off in a blink if I hadn't been conscious to stop you.*

"That's good." The surgeon nodded sagely. "There are too many who've come back from the war with injuries that will never heal. Not only physical, but maladies of the mind and spirit. A battlefield was certainly no place for a child, and I'm glad Ann has recovered somewhat from the horrors she witnessed there."

Alan nodded. There was no way he could disagree. Again the idea shot through his mind that maybe he mistrusted Schivvers for personal reasons—such as nearly losing a leg to him for no good medical reason—when perhaps the man had no evil intentions toward little Major at all.

Then the door opened, the girl walked into the room, and his doubts about the need to get her out of this house fled. Her hair and clothing were impeccably tidy and clean. She looked taller than he remembered her. Thin, but not unnaturally so. Yet as Jem had said, the girl's eyes and posture told another story. Her expression was one Alan had seen on callow soldiers facing their first artillery barrage—tense, drawn, and hopeless. This girl, who had worked beside her mother cleansing wounds and wrapping bandages, had seen plenty of carnage. She'd acted fearless then. She seemed terrified now.

"Ann, come in and greet Captain Watleigh."

When Schivvers addressed her, she flinched. She dropped a careful curtsy and bowed her head. "Good day, Captain Watleigh."

"Do you remember me, Major?" Alan used the fond nickname to try to reach through the sheen of fear and touch the girl. "I was your father's superior officer. Charlie Cutler was a good man."

She lifted her head, and her gaze met his, this time as if she truly saw him. "Yes, Captain Watleigh, I remember you."

"I was so sorry to learn about your mother's death. She was a brave and virtuous woman who did great work for the army. She will be sorely missed."

Ann inclined her head slightly in acknowledgment, but her great gray eyes glanced at Schivvers, checking for his approval. The girl was like a beaten dog living in fear of its master. Did Schivvers beat her, Alan wondered, or were there worse torments he inflicted on her—ones that left no visible marks, but that scarred her soul?

"You were a great help to your mother," Alan continued. "And to all of us. You should be proud of your work."

"Thank you, sir."

He noticed her lower-class accent was gone, replaced by the precise, upper-crust pronunciation Schivvers had taught her.

"Have you a governess, Annie? You must be nearly eleven now, am I correct?"

"Near twelve, sir. We're going—" She cut another glance at Schivvers, and he nodded almost imperceptibly. "We're going to London, sir, where Mr. Schivvers will hire a governess for me. Mr. Schivvers takes great care of me. He provides everything I need."

The last two sentences sounded as if said by rote, like a child reciting catechism she didn't really believe.

"I'm glad to hear that, Annie," Alan said, once again reminding her of her old life by using the less-formal name. "I wonder if Mr. Schivvers could be persuaded to allow you to accompany me for tea at a nearby shop."

"It's raining quite heavily, Sir Alan. I can't have Ann catching her death. Perhaps another time when we're in London it could be arranged. Maybe Sergeant Badgeman would care to see her there as well."

Again, there was no way Alan could argue. It *was* raining, and Schivvers had very graciously given consent to see the girl again. Nothing wrong here at all, except that Major was begging Alan with her eyes, and her body was on the verge of shivering.

"It's nearly time for you to leave, sir. I would not wish to detain you." Schivvers rang the bell, and when the butler appeared, he said, "Send Sir Alan's servant up."

Damn. Alan suddenly felt uneasy.

"Say your good-byes, Ann," Schivvers instructed. "Captain Watleigh must be on his way now. Oh, I forget, we must call him Sir Alan. He left the military life behind."

Once more the girl curtsied with perfect form. "Good-bye, Sir Alan."

Schivvers stood and walked to her. She was absolutely still, and he gently placed a hand on her shoulder. Good God, his fingers tightened so that the skin around his nails went white. The girl didn't flinch. Her back went straighter. Alan wanted to shout, tell him to stop, but he held back in case he'd create more trouble for Ann.

He watched and wondered if he could find physical signs of Schivvers's work on her, because surely such a hold would leave marks. Just as surely, those small signs of disciplinary action would be considered within the rights of a guardian. The surgeon was clever enough to do no more—especially now that he knew Alan was interested. That had to be enough for the moment, Alan thought. Schivvers now knew the girl had friends. If he were truly a monster... Well, at least he'd be less likely to consign the girl to an unmarked grave when he grew tired of her. Could the surgeon have had such a plan? Alan prayed that he was guilty of an overactive imagination.

Without releasing his grip, Schivvers said, "You may go back to your room and your needlework. I shall check on your progress shortly."

"Yes, sir."

Just then, Jem appeared in the study doorway. He glanced at Annie, then at Schivvers, before giving a flawless bow. "Time to go, sir?" he asked Alan, who had also risen from his chair.

Annie's face paled when she saw Jem, and her lips parted. Alan prayed Schivvers didn't notice, although he expected the man missed nothing. The girl continued to walk toward the door, but before she passed Jem—and so quickly her hand was nearly a blur—she made the military sign for *enemy at hand.*

Jem didn't appear to notice. That wasn't one of the signals Alan had taught him, and the girl's action was so hurried, it might have been a series of twitches.

Had Schivvers seen? He studied Jem and probably didn't catch the movement of his ward's hand before she left the room. Schivvers turned and smiled at Alan, a knowing smirk of a man who'd got away with something delicious. Alan's mouth was dry and his heart racing. Instinct told him to leap out of his chair, punch Schivvers's smug face, seize the girl, and run like hell out of this place. His civilized nature told him that was impossible. The constable would come for her, scandal would follow, and when the girl was returned to Schivvers, she'd be in worse danger from him than before.

"You may go too," Alan told Jem. "You can wait for me in the carriage. We'll be leaving soon."

He hoped Jem might get a chance to slip off and talk to the girl. But Schivvers stopped him with a word. "Wait." He walked over to Jem. He didn't touch him but was far too close, towering over him. Alan clenched his fists, wanting to shout at the man to back away and leave Jem alone.

Schivvers's eyes narrowed. "I thought as much. It was you spying on my house just yesterday. Burton noticed you lurking and pointed you out to me."

"Spying, sir? Naw. Wanted to make sure we'd got the right address afore Sir Alan wasted his time." He slid backward a few inches, putting some space between them.

Alan spoke up. "Schivvers, my servant's actions are of no consequence to you."

Neither of them so much as glanced in his direction. Jem smiled vacuously, and Schivvers studied him for a long minute. "You could have knocked on the door and made inquiries like any decent Christian."

Jem's guileless eyes went big. "Oh, so I coulda, sir. But 'twas a pleasant day, and—"

"You saw us, yet when we'd returned from our outing, you were still there." Schivvers's voice trembled. He moved close to Jem again, and his usual calm seemed to slip further, giving Alan a glimpse of the naked aggression beneath that polished, genteel surface. "You were spying, and furthermore, I know you have interrogated my servants."

Alan stood, ready to hurt the man should he lay a hand on Jem. The air was so thick with unspoken hostility, Alan longed to end it with a shout. He'd tell Schivvers of his suspicions and finish this charade of polite behavior.

But then Jem, whose body was relaxed as if he didn't notice anything out of the ordinary, gave a small laugh and spoke."Begging pardon, sir"—Jem still wore a simpleton's ingratiating smile—"but yer Melvin came to talk to me. A good man. I was bored, an' he was company. We talked about London."

Schivvers was silent for several seconds. "This doesn't explain why you spent the better part of yesterday staring at my house."

"Schivvers," Alan spoke stiffly, still wishing he could stop the pretense but willing to go with Jem's lead. "I think you might be imagining threats where there are none."

"Exactly, sir." Jem gave Alan a small bow and turned his attention back to the surgeon. "Begging your pardon, but weren't your house I was interested in, sir. You know on the green, the little cottage a fair ways off at the edge? Well, there're twins what live there." Jem managed a blush. What an actor! Alan wanted to applaud. "Two red-haired lasses. Know 'em?" Jem's smirk was comical, although he spoke less nimbly than usual. He played the role of none-too-bright servant well. "I couldn't sit right outside their door, now could I, sir? Begging your pardon."

Schivvers's aggression abated. He wore a look of disgust now. "Your master pays you to sit outside and ogle girls?"

"'Twas my day off, sir. Got no friends or kin in the area. What was I to do with myself? Those girls are spanking beauties." He grinned but then seemed to recall where he was and to whom he was speaking. The smile vanished, and he stood up straighter.

Schivvers studied him for another long moment. Jem remained still, the perfect servant, with no thought on his mind other than the boots he had to polish. When had he learned how to wear that wooden, bored face?

"Very well. Sir Alan, it appears you employ idiots. And so do I. Melvin is a fool." All affability, he rang for the butler, who had to have stationed himself just outside the door. "Show Sir Alan's servant to the stable yard."

He watched them go before turning back to Alan. "I hope you're satisfied with your inspection of my little Ann?"

"I see your charge is in excellent condition."

"She's a very quiet, obedient little thing. So alone in the world without her parents, and so attached to me." Schivvers seemed to glow with pleasure at the thought. An outsider might think he was merely a proud and devoted guardian to his protégée. Alan knew differently.

Time for him to use a gentleman's solution to a problem—throw money at it. "I appreciate all you've done for the Cutler family, but I wonder if I might, on behalf of my servant Badgeman, offer to take on the financial responsibility for Ann. There is an excellent boarding school in London where I would send her."

The surgeon's eyes narrowed. "I believe the girl just told you I'm hiring a governess to see to her education. Your help is not needed."

Alan wanted to growl with frustration. There was no subtle way to state his proposition. "Mr. Schivvers, you may know that I'm a bachelor, and there are no heirs to my estate. I would like to reward you very generously for your care of Ann Cutler up to this point and relieve you of the necessity of further outlay. In short, I would like to adopt the child as my own."

Schivvers moved closer, and even though Alan outweighed him and had the fighting skills of a soldier, the man was menacing. "I would like you to leave now, sir. Our interview is at an end."

"I can pay you very handsomely, Mr. Schivvers. It would be worth your while to consider—"

"What you are suggesting is unseemly, Sir Alan, and I shudder to think why you're so obsessed with obtaining custody of an innocent young child like Ann. A man of your wealth and position may have become accustomed to indulging his perverse tastes and pleasures with no one the wiser or no one who would dare to tell of your peculiarities. Well, you will not take an innocent lamb like Ann Cutler and twist her to your will. No matter your money or your lawyers, the girl has been legally bound to me in her mother's last will and testament, signed before witnesses. You will never take the girl from me."

His righteous indignation almost made Alan feel guilty...almost, except for the fact that he knew the description Schivvers gave actually applied to himself. Twisting and molding an innocent girl sounded exactly like what the cold-blooded man would do.

"Good day, sir," Schivvers added for emphasis.

The butler had arrived like a shadow to escort Alan from the room, and there was nothing to do but accompany him out the door.

The phaeton waited in front, and Jem jogged up next to him. "What else did he say?"

"We shan't discuss it here," Alan snapped. "Get in."

Only after the carriage had rolled away from the house did the expletives he'd been holding back burst from his mouth.

Jem stared. "I think you blistered me ears. Didn't know you had such vocabulary in you."

Alan gritted his teeth. "It was as you say, Jem; the girl's face was haunted. I have no idea what this man is doing to her, but she looked nearly as if she'd given up."

"What was that thing she did with her fingers? Was I just imagining it?"

"No, it wasn't your imagination. I think she gave the sign for an *enemy sighted*, so I believe there's still some fight left in her. She wants to be rescued. We must find a way to get her away from Schivvers."

Jem remained uncharacteristically silent as the phaeton clattered over cobblestone then splashed through puddles on the muddy, unpaved road back to the inn in Sheffield.

"I can see the lass means a lot to you, sir," he said at last. "I understand a bit about loyalty. Badge made a deathbed promise to help a man's family, so you want to help him keep that promise. Me and my mates had our own code like that—never rat out your mates."

Alan glanced at the younger man. Rainwater had darkened his hair and plastered it to his head. Droplets rolled down his face and bejeweled his eyelashes. Jem blinked them away before he continued.

"That gent is a fearsome, angry man. I understand your concern for Annie. Honest, I do. But where I come from, a poor homeless girl could do a lot worse for herself than take up with a man like that, who houses and feeds her. I know plenty of girls who'd be happy to bed one man rather than turn tricks for half o' London."

Alan glared at him. "Ann is an innocent young girl, not some street doxy."

"All doxies was innocent lasses once, wasn't they?"

"But I can save her from both Schivvers and the streets. I can take her home, give her a good life, make certain she's never harmed again."

Jem's brow furrowed, and a trickle of rainwater slid down the side of his cheek before he brushed it away. "Of course you should do what you can for her. I ain't saying you shouldn't. What I'm askin' is why it's so very important to you? You seem almost desperate to save her, like maybe you're thinking of something else when you see this girl. I wonder what that something might be."

Alan stared straight ahead at the road and pushed his hair back from his face to keep the dripping rain from his eyes. They should've put up the top before they'd started back, but it was too late to bother now.

He looked over at Jem, who still waited for his answer. Alan knew the lad was right. There was more going on inside him than the normal desire to help a child in need. Annie Cutler represented all the innocents he hadn't been able to save at Badajoz. Maybe Jem had earned an explanation at last.

Exhaling a deep breath, he searched for the words to tell the story quickly, succinctly, and with as little emotion as possible. "Perhaps you're right. When I see Annie, I feel like I could finally do some good to outweigh all the evil I've witnessed...and participated in."

"Badajoz again?" Jem asked softly.

Alan nodded. "It was a disaster from start to finish, although technically we won. The losses were outrageous, and the atrocities after the victory obscene. After weeks in the trenches in rain like this, we stormed the city wall. The dead piled up in the breaches, but we clambered over them and kept on going.

"Badgeman fell, and I dragged him to safety and hid him next to a wall. Then I tried to rally what was left of my men. House-to-house combat is nothing like two armies charging at each other on some open plain. It was chaos. But at last the enemy was driven to retreat. They left the city defenseless, and that's when the horror began."

It was Jem's turn to nod, as if he well guessed what had happened.

"These were my men. The few in my company who remained after the bloody battle killed most of them off. Men I thought I knew well, whose sense of honor I thought was unshakable. Men like Rodney Braithwaite, Ned Sanders. Good men. It was as if they were possessed by devils, like hell had come to earth. Outright thievery would have been bad enough, but they were torturing civilians, raping women and even young girls right there on the streets.

"They acted like savages, and I had no control over them. I couldn't stop them. I tried." The thickness in his throat choked his voice, and he swallowed hard lest it break. "I yelled orders, fired off my gun, and was ignored. I pulled a soldier—not one of mine—off a girl, and then a musket ball slammed into my leg and brought me down."

"I thought you said the enemy had run off?"

Alan shrugged. "So they had, but these things are never as clear as civilians believe. There may have been a few enemy soldiers left behind, or it could've been one of our own. Men were shooting off their muskets in celebration. A stray ball could've come from anywhere. At any rate, it laid me flat. When I came to, Schivvers was looming over me, examining my leg and reaching for his saw.

"I heard someone suggest cutting off my leg wasn't necessary. At the time I thought it was his assistant speaking up, but thinking back, I suppose it was my imagination, since the assistant surgeon had learned not to contradict him. I was ready to scramble off that table at once. I told him to leave my leg or I'd have him dismissed from his position.

"Schivvers didn't like being ordered to do anything, of course. 'You don't want my help? I won't give it.' He rolled me onto the ground with the dead and the less-injured, and left me to bleed out or recover. Badgeman found me later. God, he was an utter mess himself, head swathed in bloody bandages. I can't remember how we did it, but we moved to a medical tent and tended to each other until fever took me, and I couldn't lift a finger."

He fell silent, and for once Jem didn't offer a quip or remark. They rode in silence broken only by the sound of rain and the horses sloshing through a puddle.

The sour, sick feeling that always churned in the pit of Alan's stomach when remembering those hellish hours in Badajoz was still there, yet he felt unaccountably lighter. Perhaps it was speaking the words aloud which had unburdened him. He'd never said a word about what he'd seen to anyone, not even Badgeman, who'd experienced enough horror himself.

As the carriage came to a corner, a shaft of sunlight pierced the overcast sky and gleamed on the rain-slicked road. The sudden light was like the odd feeling rising inside Alan, hopeful and new. Despite his fears on Annie's behalf, despite his worries about the future, he felt better than he had in a very long time.

Chapter Thirteen

Jem couldn't bear the thought of Alan pale and near death, bleeding on the ground, dumped there by that bastard Schivvers. The anger settled in his gut, heavy and sour.

He had to think, a change for a lad who'd always responded to the heat of the moment with pure action. That response had kept him alive in his old life. This new one required another style. Jem would come up with a solution to this problem of the girl and stop his master's useless fretting over the past.

He closed his eyes and recalled the visit to the servants' domain of Schivvers's house. No sign of anything havey-cavey, though with the exception of his new chum Melvin, the lot of them struck him as even more full of airs and arrogance than Mrs. C. They'd unbent slightly after they'd seen the phaeton, washed clean by a stableboy at the inn after its long, rough journey. Burton must have decided a wealthy baronet's valet was top of the trees enough to warrant their civility. In fact, the butler had allowed Melvin to give him a tour of some of the house, which had ended only when Jem had been brought before Schivvers. They hadn't toured the bedrooms, of course, or the basement, which Melvin referred to as the master's workspace.

The footman had lowered his voice and glanced up and down the empty hallway with his bulging eyes. "The master's workroom is kept locked at all times. The maids ain't even allowed to go in and clean. We don't even go down the stairs." He raised his eyebrows at Jem as he shared this juicy titbit.

"How're you going to pack it up, then? I thought you lot were heading down to London."

Melvin had heaved a big sigh. "Just learned today the servants are to stay on here, as we're attached to the house. The master travels alone with the girl. He doesn't so much as go out without her."

Poor Melvin, Jem had thought. No big-city adventure for him.

"We expect Mr. Schivvers won't stay long in the south, for he isn't removing all his possessions to London. He don't tell us his plans, but mentioned he would only take his books and such."

"So you do have some work to do packing up."

Melvin had shaken his head. "Not at all. He keeps them locked away down there." He'd pointed dramatically at the stairs leading to the basement and Schivvers's mysterious chamber.

His journals. Of course.

Now, rolling along the rutted country road, Jem opened his eyes and absently pushed the back of his hand at the trickle of rain down his cheek. "Sir. What do you think he'd keep in them notebooks? The servants said he kept a close eye on them. Keeps 'em locked up in a 'workroom.'"

Alan had been staring at something far away over the horses' backs. No doubt looking back at those bad Spanish memories of his. "What are you suggesting, Jem?"

"You need something he cares about to trade for the chit. Or something to hold over him if he comes after her, p'raps. Yeah, that's the way. Tell Schivvers you'll keep mum about what's in those books of his if he gives her up."

Alan straightened. As he did, a rush of cold water washed down from the protective brim of his hat onto his nape, and he grimaced as he rubbed his neck. "I doubt we could wield much power with those books," he said slowly, "but any weapon we can find in this situation might be useful."

We, Jem thought. *That's good.*

"I wonder how we could get such a thing," Alan said thoughtfully.

The rain had finally stopped, and Jem pulled out a handkerchief to wipe the last of the damp from his face and hair. He jammed the wet cloth back into his pocket, determined to speak. Sir Alan wouldn't be surprised to learn of his other talents, so he might as well admit the truth. Still, he kept his eyes focused on Alan as he said, "Now's the time to tell you about my time as a standing budge."

"Pardon?"

"Early on, as a wee chub, I'd scout the lay. I learned to dub the gig of the case."

The corners of Alan's mouth twitched. "English, if you please."

Jem grinned. He positively loved the gleam of amused exasperation Alan shot at him. Jem raised his voice and spoke slowly, as if explaining to a simpleton. "I was a scout for housebreakers. They also taught me how to open the doors of the houses."

"Are you suggesting that you break into Schivvers's house?" The amusement died in Alan's eyes.

"Sure. I'd nab the books and even the kiddie, if I can find her. I'll wager my new shoes I sniff out those books. Easy enough. They'd lie in that workroom of his."

Alan shook his head. “No. Too much of a risk. He is naturally suspicious, and now that I've visited, he'll be far more alert. I'll wait for him to remove to London and take care of the matter then, using legal means. I'm still hopeful I can be named a guardian for the girl.”

Jem made a rude sound with his lips. “Legal be damned if he takes off to save his bacon. You think you'll find the bastard so easy once he flees this small town?”

“I think it's a chance we'll have to take. If you got caught breaking into his house, he wouldn't think twice about killing you, and the law would be on his side. As it is, he surely knows your story about waiting for the twins was a lie.” He frowned at Jem. “Tell me, are there truly twins? Redheaded twins?”

Jem resisted the urge to roll his eyes. “'Course there were. I know a suspicious cove like that would check my story.”

Alan smiled. And then he laughed, a lovely rich sound echoing through the country lane and the still-dripping trees. “You were good, Jem. I'm impressed.”

Despite the chill in the air and from his wet clothes, Jem felt warmth down to his fingers and toes. He was silly to care about the man's approval, but no denying the fact of it. He considered dropping the topic—his gadfly act might annoy Alan. But he was convinced they had to act fast.

“That Mr. Schivvers isn't coming back north, I'd reckon. He don't tell the servants here boo. Maybe he's secretive always, but I'd wager a pony he's planning to disappear into the night. I mean this night, too. Or maybe next. He's got the coin for it.” Jem paused. Maybe that could be point, a way to gain power over the man. Find something dirty as the source of his riches. "Surgeons ain't exactly wealthy—how'd he get his money?"

"I don't know. Perhaps he robbed enough dead soldiers to make his fortune, or perhaps he has inherited money. I know very little about his family except he has no parents or siblings."

No one to notice if the man simply disappeared, Jem couldn't help but think. *That'd be the easiest solution.* The rain had stopped, but now a breeze picked up, and Jem began to shiver.

"Bloody English weather," Alan said. He turned the horses into the inn's stable yard. "We'll change clothes and discuss what to do next."

We'll discuss it. Jem liked hearing that.

Up in their room, Jem built up the fire, and they stripped to their bare skin quickly. Jem jumped under the thick eiderdown and heaved a sigh. "There is nothing better 'n being frozen to the bone."

"What on earth can you mean?"

"Because warming up is bliss." He winked and grinned at his master.

Alan stood naked by the fire, rubbing his hair with a cloth. He spread out his shirt and trousers so they would dry more quickly.

"You're doin' my job for me, sir." Jem heaved up on an elbow and watched. The firelight picked out the muscles of Alan's back and arms. Very nice.

"Don't think I haven't noticed." Alan squatted and picked up a stocking. He grunted as he rose to his feet. The damp weather must have been making his leg hurt like hell. He draped the stocking over the back of a chair. "I should dock your pay."

"Teach me a lesson," Jem agreed. He slid back from the edge of the bed in invitation.

He was almost certain Alan would refuse, likely say something about making plans for travel or the obscenity of such a thing as two men in bed together—particularly in the middle of the day—but he only shook his head and ambled over to the edge of the bed. "A lesson, eh?"

To Jem's great delight, he lifted the covers and climbed in. But instead of lying down, he reached over for Jem and...

"Youch! You got ice instead of hands." Jem bolted upright.

"And your skin is warm. You're quite right. Warming one's self *is* pleasant." Alan continued to run his freezing fingers up Jem's side, ignoring his protests and laughter.

What the hell? Was the man *playing*? The grave and glum Lord Doom was behaving like a child.

Jem could only hope so.

He struggled away and got onto his hands and knees, facing Alan, who'd landed on his side during the brief onslaught. Praying he wasn't overstepping his role in this new game, Jem started to crawl toward him. "My hands aren't so very warm either, sir. Lemme show you."

"Oh, I don't think so." Alan scrambled to his knees, hands outstretched, ready to grab at Jem when he attacked.

The two of them were wrestling, fighting to see who could use the other as a hand warmer. Jem wiggled free and rolled away from Alan. He loomed over Alan, trying to reach his armpits with his own icy hands. Yes, Alan was cursing and laughing as much as Jem, who wanted to crow with joy. Instead he used that burst of pure energy to pin his master and wrap his arms and legs tight around him. Cold fingers had warmed, and now their touches gentled. Horseplay turned into another, even more pleasurable play.

Jem ran his fingers through Alan's still-damp hair and cupped his scalp. He pulled his face close for a long kiss that started easy and light. Alan tilted his head, and the kiss deepened at once.

When Jem pulled back, he wanted to slow things down. Savor the time together and not just fall into the animal lust. Although, God above, the animal lust was perfect too. There were so many things he had longed to do and say to Alan all day, and so few he could. He stroked the man's rough cheek. "You ought to let your valet shave you. He'd do a better job than this."

Alan turned his head to the side and kissed Jem's thumb. "That's not necessary. My valet's fine right where he is, thank you."

"Yah," Jem muttered. "Though truth is, he's better 'n fine at the moment. Truth is, he'd stay right here forever if he could."

Alan's answering smile was faint and maybe a little sad. Jem gave up fighting the heat for a few minutes. They lay side by side, and Jem kissed him on the cheek, the eyes, and moved again to his mouth for hot, thick kisses. His cock, already aching and hard, pushed against Alan's thigh. Alan groaned into his mouth and wrapped his hand around him.

Jem thrust into the circle of his hand. He longed to push Alan onto his back and fuck him, shove hard into his body. Imagining that pleasure made the lust surge and his heart race. He'd grab Sir Alan and demand he open to him and let him sink into that tight bliss.

But he already knew how well they could catch fire. Passion gave Alan an excuse for giving in to desire. It was the other, rarer moments Jem aimed for now. And just as he'd gentled his kiss, now he drew in a deep breath and pulled back from the body he craved. Time to see if Alan would allow a display of the devotion he so longed to show. He kissed his way down Alan's body, stroking his skin, touching the scars and kissing every one—the light tracing of silver on his biceps, the twisted, gnarled flesh on his side, and all the smaller marks and cuts in between.

Alan drew a sharp breath as Jem lightly kissed and then licked his cock. Jem gently cradled his balls, which were already drawn tight. He put his mouth around the other man's cock and looked up into his face. Alan's eyes were shut tight, his jaw clenched. He blindly, roughly stroked Jem's hair and face, silently begging.

Ah damn. Jem couldn't resist the urgent need. He gave up on the soft kisses and softer talk, and drew Alan into his mouth. He sucked and licked hard, concentrating only on the greediest part of Alan—his aroused body—and not the whole man.

It didn't take long before Alan's cock swelled impossibly large. He spent with a quiet, choked sob that might have been a word. He didn't even open his eyes before his breath slowed and his body sank into sleep.

Alan slept as soundly as a well-protected baby. Jem had seen few of those, but he had seen some lulled to unconsciousness by gin in the tavern, put to sleep by their mums so they could do a bit of trade. You could laugh and shout near them, and they wouldn't so much as twitch.

Jem curled himself around the man's back, pressing his erection along the delicious cheeks he longed to thrust between. Alan made a sleepy sound of contentment but didn't move.

Jem would let him sleep. God knew the man needed it. Eventually he rolled onto his back and examined the fine collection of body parts next to him—shoulders, legs, waist, and rear—as he took care of his own need with a bit of what the preachers called self-pollution. He stroked his cock slowly, taking his time until he spent with a grunt and a sigh. He wiped his belly and chest with the edge of the sheet.

Alan never moved, and his slow, easy breathing didn't change. Jem hadn't seen him sleep so soundly before, hadn't known he could.

Maybe the talk of Badajoz had helped to banish some ghosts. Temporarily, of course. Jem knew such memories would haunt a man for a lifetime.

Despite his self-made sweet release, Jem was still restless and soon climbed from the bed. He pulled on his clothes, which were only slightly damp thanks to the roaring fire he'd built. He straightened the room and looked at Alan. The man was still profoundly asleep.

Jem picked up a book and leafed through it, trying to find words he knew. He checked Alan again. Still asleep.

And the day slipped away. Jem sat by the fire, stared at the flames, and thought about what he could do. They were to make plans this afternoon. Time was short now that he knew Schivvers was on his way south—if that was indeed his real destination.

Jem thought of the job at hand. He had no reputation to lose, not like Sir Alan. Best if he went in alone, really.

"Thing is," he whispered so he wouldn't wake his master, "I can't see any other answer. He'll weigh anchor and be vanished forever. You know he will. And if he pokes his pointy nose back in your world eventually, what're the chances he'll be alone? 'Tis true. 'Oh her,' he'll say. 'The girl left me.' She will have too. Left him and her body at the same time."

He found a blank piece of paper and Alan's ink and pen. This time he made an even bigger mess with the ink—his cuff was a blotted wreck when he was done. But he corked up the ink and cleaned the quill as Alan had shown him.

The next bit made him pause and look over at the sleeping form. He knew where Alan kept his purse of gold and silver. He pulled it out from the small trunk, rummaged around inside, and took out a few coppers.

The man slept on. Jem imagined what Alan would say if he woke and caught him in the act of stealing again. Guilt made him feel almost angry. He wasn't taking the money for his own use, for pity's sake. Bribes. A tip for the stablelad.

He walked downstairs through an almost-deserted inn, passing only the landlord who read a paper by the taproom fire. At the stable he ordered the horses harnessed—no way would he attempt this idiot plan on foot.

Though truly he'd picked the right time. Evening was good—not so light that anyone would see and recognize him, not so dark that the world would have settled into slumbering silence.

He wished he could ride on horseback. Maybe someday, if he survived, Alan would teach him. Tonight he'd have to find a place to tie up the phaeton. At last he found a small clearing near a chapel—not far away from the house, but well hidden by a tall hedge. The horses eyed him balefully as he wrapped the reins around a fencepost. "I'll be back," he promised them. He hoped he wasn't lying.

His errand proved easy at first. The kitchen door was open a crack, inviting in all comers. Jem didn't even have to pick a lock. If Schivvers had seen that, he would have had the cook's head.

Jem silently walked in, slid past the kitchen and down the wooden stairs to the basement where the workroom lay. The short hallway in front of the door was deeply shadowed, and he had to feel for the lock in darkness. A few probes with his sharp pick, and it clicked open with surprising ease. The hinges creaked fiercely as he opened the door, and Jem froze. His heart pounding, hair raised like a stray cat facing a snapping pack of curs, he listened for footsteps. Nothing.

Once he'd entered the large, windowless room, there was even less light. Jem couldn't search for anything in pitch blackness, so he dared to light the candle stub he'd brought along with him. His breath caught as he struck the lucifer, feeling as if the tiny spark of sulfur would summon Schivvers like the devil he was.

In the flickering glow, Jem caught glimpses of shelves along one wall with rows of glass jars. Inside the jars were what looked like bits of human body parts floating in murky liquid. He didn't have time to look more closely at them, or at the shadow-shrouded shapes suspended from the ceiling, or at the table in the corner with the straps for wrists and ankles—for operations or for performing intimate examinations?

He swallowed back his growing revulsion and fear, which wouldn't help him accomplish what he'd come for, and concentrated on the books he'd discovered lying neatly stacked in an open wooden crate. Jem didn't look through them, but a few on the top were handwritten rather than printed. And they were small, as Alan had described Schivvers's journal. He crammed several small volumes into his coat pockets and turned to leave.

Footsteps sounded overhead. He quietly closed the door and dived under the desk. Voices came from outside the room, perhaps at the top of the stairs. His heart pounded in his throat. God, Schivvers would find his body here, dead from apoplexy.

The voices faded in the distance. One of them might have been Melvin. Jem crept to the door and laid his ear to it. He heard nothing, not even the creak of a house settling. Nothing stirred as he slipped from the room. He even locked the door, although covering his tracks was useless. It wouldn't take Schivvers long to spot the fact that the books were missing.

Now for the girl.

He hesitated. Alan would be furious enough when he appeared with the books. If he dragged Annie Cutler along to the inn, the man might dismiss him on the spot. Clearly Sir Alan liked planning and making carefully considered decisions. Stealing the girl was about as impulsive as Jem could get and still call himself sane. Naw, he was fooling himself. This would move him firmly into the lunatic camp.

But then he recalled Annie's peaked little face, how she'd trusted him and directed that signal thing at him. He goddamned well wouldn't leave her behind. Taking the books wasn't going to be enough. Not for him, anyway.

So instead of sneaking out the kitchen door again, he made his way up the back stairs and nearly ran into a scullery maid. Jem sucked in and held a panicked breath, then scolded himself for being frightened of a little kitchen maid.

He listened for the sound of people and heard nothing. The barouche was in the carriage house, so he knew they were home.

Why the bloody bowels of hell wouldn't one of them make a noise so he could figure out where everyone was? This felt like a perverse game. He half grinned, thinking of the perverse games he'd indulged in today. Far more to his taste.

The bedrooms upstairs. He'd sneak along there and see if he could find hers.

Two doors down the corridor, he found the spacious, dark-paneled bedchamber that had to be Schivvers's. It even smelled like the man, the sharp scent of pine and alcohol—something too sharp to be good to drink. He couldn't see sure signs that the girl was Schivvers's bed partner. The bed was more than big enough and had more than a single pillow, yes, but that meant nothing. He'd learned that from Alan's decadent bed.

There was a small rug on the floor. The way the rug had been situated, it could be the bed of a favored dog. He knelt and found a hairpin there. Perhaps she'd dropped it. But there were other indications she did more than simply pass this spot—several curling dark strands, long enough to be from her head.

A few seconds later, he found it. A chain anchored to the foot of the heavy bed. The thin chain with pretty decorative loops had a well-polished shackle at the end. Jem understood right then that Alan hadn't exaggerated the man's nature. Only a sick bastard would polish and decorate shackles for a little girl. He prayed he was wrong and that there was some sort of animal about the place that he'd missed.

Heavy footsteps sounded in the hallway, and Jem dived then rolled under the bed, far to the back in the shadows. But if anyone took a notion to peer under, they'd see him.

The door creaked open, and two pairs of feet entered the room—a man's gleaming boots and a girl's bare feet. They didn't speak. Her legs and knees appeared as she sat on the rug. She wore only a shift. Jem saw large hands—a man's hands—and heard the *clink* of a shackle. But it wasn't on her foot. Her wrist? It looked too big for either.

"Lie down," the soft-spoken bastard ordered.

When she lay on the rug, Jem saw the metal band around her neck. Her eyes were closed, so she didn't spot him.

A familiar dull rage filled Jem. Occasionally in his old life he'd felt useless anger at the unkind hand fate dealt some people. Only soon he'd be stepping in and telling fate to go bite itself.

From above came Schivvers's voice. "I might be bathing. I might be eating my supper. Which do you guess it to be?" The toe of his boot nudged her shoulder. Gently. She tensed but didn't answer, and Jem worried at her disobedience, but then the man spoke again. "Ah. You recall my last command to remain silent. Good. Perhaps I'll give you a reward. Yes. You'd like that, wouldn't you?"

She didn't speak.

"Answer."

"Yes, Mr. Schivvers," came her small voice, but she didn't open her eyes. Jem, who'd known a few men who enjoyed cruelty, guessed that was a mistake. Sure enough, there was a jingle and a swish of cloth as the man abruptly hauled her up. No cry from the girl, though. She had been well trained.

"Again."

"Yes, Mr. Schivvers."

"Again."

"Yes, Mr. Schivvers." Over and over went the idiotic exchange. It went on for a few minutes, and then Jem realized at each "again" he spoke, the man shook or pinched or did something to the girl, for her body jounced, and her toes curled. But she didn't cry out.

One of her "Yes, Mr. Schivvers" must have satisfied the arse, or perhaps he only got bored, because at last, without another word, he bade her to lie back down on her mat, and then he left. Jem watched his boots all the way out the door and heard the click of a lock after the door had closed.

He glanced back at Annie. The girl lay on her side, looking under the bed, straight into his eyes. A normal girl would have shrieked, but she'd left normal behind a long time back, Jem guessed. She only blinked, then stared. No smile, no words. He opened his mouth, and she frantically shook her head.

She pointed over her shoulder, stabbing her finger in the direction of the door. Oh. He guessed Mr. Schivvers listened—for the sound of her weeping, maybe.

Jem slid out from under the bed, stood, and dusted himself off. He made a face at the fluff that had collected on his shirt and breeches. Bad servants in this place. Or maybe the master didn't let them in here, either. The girl held the chain that attached her to the bedpost as she slowly pushed herself up until she sat cross-legged on the rug. Likely a jangling chain was another crime in the rule book of her gaoler.

She stared up at Jem, wide-eyed but unmoving. He pulled the tiny files from his pocket and squatted in front of her. Back in his old life, he'd planned to someday get better picklocks and practice more—he wasn't such a perfect hand at the trickier locks. He pointed at her neck. Her face paled, and she shook her head. Did she think he'd stab her with the pointed bits of iron?

He moved closer and mimed opening the collar.

She stared at him with those huge, unnerving eyes. Precious long seconds ticked by. At last she reached up and swiveled the band so that its lock lay at the base of her throat. Such a little neck it was. Schivvers must have taken the exact measure of it, for the band had no room for more than a single adult finger between her skin and the metal.

Jem leaned close and examined the lock. He heard her breaths, fast and with a tiny whimper at the end of each. Or was that a wheeze and there was something wrong with the girl's lungs?

She shook like a whipped dog, and Jem laid a hand on her leg to steady her. It only made the shaking worse. Thickskull thing to do, he scolded himself. No touches the girl didn't invite. He took his hand away at once and shrugged his apology. She simply stared.

The lock was tiny. In the end he filed it enough so he could simply break the collar with his fingers. A grown man could manage such a thing, but not a puny little girl. The sound of metal scraping on metal had made her turn away and watch the door. When it broke, she looked at him again.

With exaggerated care, he lowered the shackle and chain to the rug and smiled encouragingly. *See? No jangling. You can trust me.*

He pointed at the door.

She shook her head frantically and pointed at the window.

Jem walked over and looked out. Two stories up, and the stone building was smooth, with no handholds or convenient drain.

He looked around. Bedsheets? Likely they didn't have time.

He leaned very close and whispered so quietly he could barely hear himself. "No. Gotta be the door. But girl, listen well. I might run into trouble. Could be you'll have to do a big job. A huge one."

She gave a tiny, careful nod, as if the jingling chain were still attached.

"My carriage is just beyond the big hedge at the churchyard. Blue and gold and fancy. If I tell you to run like hel—the blazes, go to the carriage. If I'm not right behind, loose the horses and turn 'em around. Can you?"

She nodded, more easily now.

"Sure. That'll be easy. Get up on the thing. It's a big climb, but you can manage because you're about as brave as they come. The reins. You might have to shake 'em hard and yell at the horses to gee-yup. You've seen that, haven't you? Watched the coachmen?"

A nod.

"Hold tight to the armrest. You're not big enough to control the horses." He recalled something Alan had said about horses' behavior. "I think they'll likely head for home, which is an inn. It's got a picture of a dog with a tankard and knife on the sign out front." The girl could probably read, but he couldn't recall exactly what the place was called. "Got it? It's straight down to the main road and a right toward Sheffield."

She nodded again, and her body trembled so much that he worried she might shake something loose inside.

"When you're there, run and find the captain. You know. Sir Alan Watleigh. He'll protect you and keep you safe."

She looked at the door.

"Likely it won't be a problem. I'll be right with you. In fact, I'm going to carry you."

She cringed again and gave the tiniest of headshakes. *No.*

He gave an encouraging smile and leaned close to her ear again.

"I'm faster than you. You gotta do this. Climb on my back. Pickaback." He shrugged off his coat and held it out for her to stick her arms into. She'd be cold in only her shift when they'd reach the outdoors. Besides, she could cling to his back better if he wasn't wearing the bulky coat. He swiveled and crouched before her. "Come on, then."

Her thin arms went around his neck and suddenly tightened, nearly choking him. She was strong for a slip of a thing. He risked a slightly louder whisper. "Not so tight. It'll look bad if he comes back and finds my body on the floor."

She loosened her hold at once, and a tiny whimper sounded next to his ear.

"Naw, I'm jesting, girl. It would take more to kill me. Ready?"

She might have nodded, or maybe her shudders only grew stronger at that second.

He rose to his feet. She held so tight, he didn't need to support her at all. Her bare legs clasped around his waist as well, grappling him to her as if he were an unexpected life preserver she must cling to or die, which he wagered wasn't too far from the truth.

The girl smelled of piss. She must have wet herself in fear. Jem wasn't afraid of a little dirt and piss, so he wasn't disgusted, but that old, dull ache of anger roiled through him that any child should be so terrified of her master she'd piddle like a whipped pup.

The door was locked, of course, and he squatted, wishing he'd told her to climb on *after* he'd opened the thing. He wasn't about to tell her to get off—not when she held on as if she were a desperate drowning creature.

Lucky for them both, fear made his fingers deft. Jerry once told him he was a contrary lad, because most people in a fright grew clumsy. The lock clicked, and after one frozen moment, when Jem was certain he'd face the devil Schivvers himself, he opened the door a crack and peered out. Miracle of miracles. No one waited in the hall. The servants must have been abed for the night. He moved through the house undiscovered. Her little whimpery breath and the occasional squeak of the floor under his silent feet was all he heard.

This time he found the kitchen door locked, but opening it was an easy job when one was on the inside already. He flipped the lock and was about to open the latch when suddenly the child on his back gripped him tighter than ever, her arms nearly choking him.

"He's here," she whispered. The first words she'd uttered.

At the same moment, Jem registered heels tapping quickly across the floor behind him. He whirled to face Schivvers striding through the darkened kitchen like an avenging demon. The man was almost upon him. Even though Jem was already at the door, there was no time to run. Best he could do was get the girl out and buy her some time.

He dropped to a crouch. "Let go," he ordered.

Annie slipped off his back instantly. Unquestioning and well-trained was just what he wanted at the moment.

Jem pulled open the door and thrust her through. "Run!"

"Ann, stop!" Schivvers's voice thundered from behind him, but his ward didn't hesitate. She ignored the command and tore off like a shot, her feet skimming the ground as she disappeared into the night.

Jem slammed the door shut behind her and drew his whittling knife from his trousers pocket as he turned to face the surgeon. He lunged toward his opponent, driving upward with the blade, aiming for the other man's gut as Jerry had once taught him. He'd never actually been in a knife fight but had no qualms about gutting Schivvers if he could.

Unfortunately Jem was fighting from a weak position, turning back from the door while the other man was already striking at him. And the good surgeon had a blade of his own. The dim hearth light illuminating the room glinted off a long, silver knife.

Schivvers sliced downward and cut through the sleeve of Jem's shirt, sending fire burning up his arm. His blow blocked the momentum of Jem's knife hand, and the little knife slashed through the other man's waistcoat, but no more than that.

He drew his hand back to strike again, but suddenly his opponent grabbed his shoulder and held the sharp blade to his throat. From inches away, Schivvers glared into Jem's eyes. The wild look in his eyes was akin to what Jem had seen in the faces of lunatics dismissed from Bedlam to wander the sewers and slums of London.

"Thief!" The man's spittle spattered his face.

Jem stopped struggling, stopped breathing as he felt the cool metal touch his throat. One little slice, and he'd be gushing red like a fountain. No more Jem.

This is it. This is what the end of my life looks like. The thought was as calm and clear as the spring-fed pool along the road where he and Alan had stopped to water the horses the night they'd slept under the stars. Funny how he was too shocked to be afraid, and all he could think of was Alan's eyes that night and how they'd shone in the moonlight.

But Schivvers didn't kill him. Swift as a whippet, he removed the blade from Jem's throat. Before Jem had a second to react or fight back, his attacker punched the thick knob of the knife's bone handle into Jem's temple.

Stars exploded in his vision, and blackness followed.

Chapter Fourteen

Jem's head throbbed. It felt like someone was thumping his noggin with steady blows of a mallet. And his eyes seemed to be gummed shut, which was fine, since he was afraid to open 'em, afraid of what he'd see and where he was. He listened to the quiet sounds of Schivvers moving around him and felt the flat, hard surface under his naked backside, the restraints around his wrists and ankles. It didn't take the brain power of the Lord Mayor himself to figure out he was lashed to the surgeon's operating table in his private dungeon.

There was something filling his dry mouth—a wadded-up cloth with a bitter tang, bound tight around the back of his head with another strip of cloth. From the smell, Jem realized the awful taste was shoe polish. He was parched, his throat so dry that when he swallowed, it clicked.

His body was stripped bare, and he was naked and vulnerable, his skin twitching and flinching in expectation of pain. His cock rested flat against his belly as if trying to hide itself in the thatch of hair there. Jem envisioned his tackle being cut off and added to the surgeon's collection of floating human bits, and swore he could feel his cock shriveling even smaller, his balls drawing tighter. He wondered if Annie had made it to safety. He hadn't been able to give her much time before Schivvers knocked his lights out. Sweet Jesus, let something good have come from his fool's errand.

"I know you're awake. You may open your eyes." Schivvers was right beside him, his voice hovering over him. Jem would've jumped if he could move at all, but the restraints pinned him flat to the table. As it was, his heart thundered as if it would burst through his breastbone. Was it possible to die from fear? Lucky he hadn't pissed himself like the little girl. At least not yet.

"I'm going to take off your gag so I can ask you some questions." The voice was conversational, almost friendly. "You must promise you won't yell for help. No one would hear you, and even if they did, my staff would not come down here. They've been instructed never to come near my room, no matter what they hear. They are paid very well to remain blind and deaf." His soft chuckle made Jem's skin crawl and his balls try even harder to draw up inside him.

Still, he wouldn't open his eyes. If he could see the room with its horrible jars and hanging things, if he could see Schivvers's face, he would have to accept this as his new reality. But as the man loosened the gag and took the polishing rag from his mouth, Jem could see the glow of light through his eyelids.

"Did your master send you here?" the man asked.

Jem thought fast, calculating the possible consequences of either answer. If he said "yes, and he'll be coming after me soon," he'd be indicting Alan should Schivvers decide to try a legal route to get the girl back. If he said "no, I acted on my own"... Well, the man might still try to implicate Alan, or he might decide Jem was expendable to his master and finish him off. Perhaps he was.

"He doesn't know I'm here. Had nothing to do with it. Sir Alan would never consider anything other than legal means to get custody of the Cutler girl. I thought I could make things easier for him."

"Why does he want the girl so badly?"

Stinging hornets sent a trail of fire up one side of Jem's face from chin to cheekbone. A small, shiny scalpel. He hissed with pain.

"Look at me when I'm speaking to you."

Reluctantly he unsealed his eyes, blinked away the gray fog, and focused on the face floating over him—pale, elegant, a cadaver with an impeccably tied cravat. Schivvers's fair hair was brushed back from his high forehead, which was furrowed in concern but not contorted with rage as it had been when he'd faced him in the kitchen.

Jem glanced past his shoulder, taking in the room at a glance. It was well lit with an oil lamp now, and he could better see the neatly labeled jars of organs and appendages. He could also see the hanging things that had been hidden in shadow before. Mummified cadaver parts, also carefully tagged and cataloged, suspended from the ceiling. Why not? This was a surgeon's study. Nothing amiss here should the law come exploring.

Schivvers held up the scalpel, its blade now rimmed in red, for Jem's consideration. "Answer my question. What does Sir Alan want with Ann?"

Jem's voice was a hoarse croak. "I believe it's just as he said, sir. A matter of loyalty to one of his men. No more than that."

"I want the girl back. Will she run to him? Did you tell her where to go?"

Again Jem considered carefully before answering. On the surface, this was a straight kidnapping. It was entirely within Schivvers's rights to go to the authorities, explain everything, demand the girl be returned to him, and have Jem thrown in gaol. The fact that he was reacting in this furtive manner told him that

Schivvers didn't want the law involved. Maybe he was afraid of what the girl might reveal about him should she be questioned.

"I believe she'll try to go to him." He licked his dry lips, still tasting boot polish. "I also believe if you don't try to get her back, Sir Alan will leave you and your secrets alone. All he cares for is the lass's safety."

"I never hurt her, you know." Schivvers lowered the blade to Jem's chest and trailed it gently from nipple to navel. The stroke felt like the light brush of a feather. It almost tickled. But when Jem glanced down, a thin red line, like a cat scratch, marked the scalpel's path.

The man's mad eyes, shining black as a polished boot, gazed into Jem's. "I'm a scientist. The study of the human body and mind are all that's important to me. Fear and the way that emotion shapes behavior are of utmost interest."

Although the room was quite chilly, perspiration prickled on Jem's chest and slicked his face. His body trembled slightly despite his best efforts to control it.

"Did you know, for example, that words can be as powerful, if not more so, as acts? You'd be surprised at how the threat of pain or torture is as effective as the application in controlling a subject—although physical pain is a strong molder of behavior as well."

"Your studies are in those journals, I wager." Jem was surprised he found enough breath to form the words as the scalpel traced another cold line on the opposite side of his body—nipple to navel, then lower, coming terrifyingly close to the tip of his cock, where it lay against his belly.

Schivvers glanced at the crate full of books. "Yes."

"Your experiments with Annie Cutler, training her to obey your will?"

The man's eyes narrowed. "What are you getting at?"

"Them books is on their way to my master. I gave 'em to the girl to carry." They were still in the pockets of his coat, which Ann was wearing. Would merely the threat of exposure be enough to frighten Schivvers into letting him go? Or would it enrage the madman enough to finish off Jem right here and now?

"You knew I'd been in here, could tell the lock had been tampered with." Jem continued to flirt with death. "See if any are missing."

The man crossed the room in three quick strides and quickly flipped through the top few journals. His face, when he turned back toward Jem, was more terrifying than ever. He flew back across the room like a bird of prey, the scalpel his talon, and loomed over Jem. "What will he do?"

Jem swallowed, making that dry clicking sound again. His head ached badly, and his vision was fuzzy around the edges, whether from the blow to his temple or from sheer terror, he didn't know.

"I think this is what you military coves call a stalemate. My master's got the girl, which is all he wanted. Plus he's got your journals. You drop this fight now, and you can walk away. He don't expose your secrets. You don't accuse him of kidnapping." He decided to press his luck. "You might even consider letting me go so's I can talk to him, help him to see reason."

Schivvers paced around the table, once, twice, three times, every pass making Jem more nervous. He could hear the man thinking, considering his next move, and imagined him making it swiftly by abruptly plunging the scalpel into Jem's throat or heart.

The man stopped walking and stood at Jem's head, just beyond the range of his vision. Having him out of sight, invisible, was extremely unnerving.

"You must think a great deal of your master to dare to come into my house and steal my property for him. I wonder if he has some special...affection for you as well. Perhaps enough that he would not want to let you go, perhaps enough to make him come after you."

He bent low; a hand braced either side of the table beside Jem's head. His whiskey-scented breath puffed into Jem's face as he gazed at him upside down. "Perhaps enough that he'd be willing to trade the girl and the books in exchange for you."

"Don't think so, sir. I ain't that important." Jem wished it wasn't true, but was afraid it was. Sure, he knew Alan enjoyed him, but now that the girl was safe, it was hardly likely Alan would come for him. Especially since it was Jem's own fault he was in this fix. He'd broken into the man's house, got himself caught, and couldn't expect Alan to risk what he'd gained.

"I'm an astute study of human nature," Schivvers proclaimed from above him. "I watch people when they don't even know they're being watched—everyone around me, from gentlemen to rabble like yourself. I can read the fears and needs in them. During the several years I worked in proximity to Watleigh, I perceived his perverse bent by his glances, gestures, his very stance, and I guess now that you are more than his valet. I noted his expression when you entered my study today."

Uncertain how to respond, Jem kept his mouth shut for once. Besides, he was feeling more unsteady by the second, liable to slip back into unconsciousness.

"He has something I need. I have something he needs." Schivvers nodded, and the upside down bobbing of his head made Jem dizzy. "I believe if I send around a little visiting card, a sort of personalized message, he might be inspired to make the trade."

Jem knew better than to believe Schivvers would actually free him. Not after he spilled those unpleasant secrets of his. But he suspected the man wouldn't make it a simple cut across the throat. He'd have to be a mouse to Schivvers's playful cat act for a time. If only he could sink back into oblivion and skip the man's idea of fun.

Schivvers completed his circuit of the table and stopped again by Jem's side, studying his nude body with an intense gaze. "The question is, which part of you will deliver the message most effectively?"

Now would definitely be a good time to pass out, Jem thought.

When Alan woke to find the day had turned to evening, the room empty, and Jem having left him another note, he was enraged.

Sr, Gon to get gril and buks. Be bak son. Below the message was a postscript. It appeared Jem knew enough about letter writing to include the letters *P.S.*

Tuk sum mony and carij. <u>Not</u> to steel. Wil pay bak. He'd tried and crossed out several versions of "carriage" before settling on "carij."

Alan read the cryptic message twice before fully realizing the import. The little fool! He'd gone off half-cocked and with no support. He'd likely end up in gaol—or worse.

He jammed his feet into his boots and hauled on his coat while dashing out the door and down the stairs. Travelers in the taproom glanced up in surprise as he strode through the room, yelling for the innkeeper to have a boy ready a horse for him.

Then he disregarded his own request and went to prepare a mount for himself. He cinched the saddle, adjusted the stirrups, and led the steed from the livery while a gape-mouthed stableboy looked on.

What time had Jem left? How much of a lead did he have? Perhaps it wasn't too late to catch him before he reached his destination, let alone do anything so foolish as break in.

The road between the inn and Schivvers's house was becoming familiar, but it appeared different in the dark of night with no London streetlights to illuminate the way. The horse's hooves pounded over cobblestone then mud from the earlier rainstorm as Alan left Sheffield and approached the sleeping town of Derwent.

A carriage was approaching on the road ahead. He heard the wheels rattling before seeing the hulking black shape of the vehicle and horses looming out of the darkness. A few yards closer, and he identified it as his own phaeton. His spirits buoyed like a skiff on the Thames. *Jem. Safe. Now I'll kill him for scaring me!*

But as his mount drew alongside the rattling carriage and he beheld the figure on the open box, he saw it wasn't Jem. Too short. Too small. The carriage threatened to roll right past him, and Alan held up a hand and shouted, "Whoa!"

The driver hauled on the reins, trying in vain to bring the horses to a halt. Alan wheeled his mount, drew alongside the horses, and reached out to grab the lines. When the vehicle was stopped, he turned to look at the person driving his carriage. "Major? Is that you?"

"Yes, Captain Watleigh." Annie's piping little voice sounded strange coming from the height of the wagon box, their meeting bizarre and dreamlike. Alan wished his eyes would snap open and he'd find himself back in bed at the inn, with Jem lying warm beside him.

"What happened?" he demanded. "Where's Jem?" He eyed the huge coat wrapped around her shoulders—Jem's coat—and his gut began to churn.

A small gulp and swallow came from the shadowy figure of the child. Her pale face gleamed ghostlike in the dark. "Mr. S-schivvers," she stammered.

"Schivvers has him?" The bile in his stomach boiled up into his throat along with his hammering heart. "How did you get out?"

"The man helped me. Told me where to find you and to run. So I ran." Her voice was thick and choked.

"All right. All right. You did the right thing." He soothed her with his tone as he would a nervous horse, but inside his mind raced in aimless, panicked circles. He'd organized attacks and led men into battle, but at this moment, he couldn't think what to do. He could scarcely breathe. *Jem, Jem, Jem.* The name throbbed with every beat of his heart.

The horse beneath him grew restless, sensing his nervousness. He pulled it up sharply, his mind still churning over possibilities. There was no time to get Annie back to the inn. Jem might not have that long. What if, even now, Schivvers had sent for the watchman to take the lad to gaol? Or worse, what if Schivvers was dealing with him in his own horrible way?

"Annie, I'm sorry I don't have time to take you someplace safe. I have to help Jem. You can wait with the horses."

She nodded and responded meekly as trained. "Yes, Captain Watleigh."

He bit his lip and pondered his options, rejecting his initial impulse, which was to march straight through the front door, find Schivvers, and beat him to a bloody pulp. Jem was the goal, the house a fortress to be breached. He must think of it that way in order to operate logically. What would he do in wartime? Reconnaissance. And he had the perfect spy right here with him.

He moved his horse closer to the carriage and leaned toward her to make sure he had her full attention. "Annie, do you believe Schivvers will call the constable to take Jem away?"

She didn't answer at first. Alan fought the impulse to snap at her to give him an answer as he would one of his soldiers. *Gentle. Easy.* She was a nervous child, not a hardened soldier. "Please, Ann. You know Mr. Schivvers well. You know how he thinks. What will he do with Jem?"

There was another long pause. Alan wanted to launch himself onto the carriage, grab her shoulders, and shake an answer from her. But at last she replied, "The Room. He'll take him downstairs to The Room." The hushed gravity of her tone implied a sacred—or profane—place.

He knew instinctively she was right. Schivvers wouldn't want outside help. He'd want to punish Jem himself for stealing his trophy, and he would enjoy doing it in creative, painful ways. Once more his stomach rose, and he felt ready to fly out of his skin, to rush to Jem's rescue. *Patience. Planning.* He must handle this very carefully if Jem was to come out of the situation alive and unharmed.

One step at a time, and right now he must get the carriage off the road and parked somewhere. "Where did Jem have the carriage waiting? Can you show me?"

The girl pointed over her shoulder.

He held tight to his temper as he jumped off his horse and took the length of lead rope from the back of the phaeton. After he'd tied the horse to the phaeton, he'd calmed enough to ask, "Where exactly?" in a friendly manner.

"Churchyard," she whispered.

"We're going to go back, and you'll stay with the horses as I said."

He vaulted up onto the seat beside Ann, took the ribbons from her hands, and drove the vehicle in a loop until the phaeton faced the other direction. After they'd gone only a quarter mile, he saw the chapel with its concealing hedge, and Alan pulled the horses to a standstill.

He tied the team to a post, then climbed into the carriage seat to face the girl shivering beneath Jem's big black coat. As they'd ridden here, an idea had formed in his mind. It wasn't a perfect plan, but it was all he could come up with under the circumstances.

Alan reached for Annie's hand. She started to flinch away, but settled immediately when his hand covered hers, as though conditioned to submitting to unwanted touches. Looking into her face, he met her gaze as best he could in the dark night. He wanted her to see that he meant no harm. He wanted to slowly and carefully present to the girl what he needed her to do, but his pulse was racing, and he was acutely aware of every minute slipping by. Every second Jem was in danger. Visions of Schivvers wielding a bone saw flashed in his mind.

"Ann, you don't know me well, but I hope you can trust me. Do you?"

Her head bobbed once. Her hand was ice-cold beneath his.

"I wouldn't ask you to do this if it weren't absolutely imperative, but you of all people know the danger Jem is in, don't you?"

Another curt nod.

He dipped his head lower, looking steadily into her eyes. "I have to get him out of there before something terrible happens, and you're the key to accomplishing that."

Her hand tightened beneath his, fingers clenching. She didn't like the direction this was going.

Alan took hold of her shoulder, gripping it gently. "I would never force you to face Schivvers again if it weren't absolutely necessary. But you are the one thing he wants and the only"—he hesitated over the words—"way I can rescue Jem." Before Ann could panic, he added, "I will *not* give you back to him, no matter what I might say to Schivvers, but I may have to let him believe I will in order to free Jem. Do you understand?"

Tears shone in the dim starlight as they streaked her cheeks. The first sign of tears he'd seen on her drawn face. His heart clenched. He'd like to tell her she had a choice, that she didn't have to do this unless she felt brave enough, but he desperately needed her help. She was the only tool he had in this rescue mission.

Would she be strong enough to accept the role he despised himself for thrusting upon her?

Her thin shoulder hitched beneath his palm, and Ann nodded once more.

"That's good," he crooned, feeling as slimy as Schivvers for pushing the girl. "I won't let anything bad happen to you. I promise."

Annie opened her mouth and closed it again.

"What? Go on. You may say what you like to me. Don't be afraid to talk."

She gazed at him, eyes dark against her pale face as she spoke in halting phrases. "I know the mission comes first. Mrs. Cutler… I mean, my mum taught me that. I'll help as best I can."

In her eyes he saw a spark of the stalwart little Major who had trotted after her mother among the sick and dying, without ever flinching.

And then she gazed solemnly into his eyes with a look that broke his heart and added, "My father trusted you in battle. I do too."

Chapter Fifteen

The man was humming—a soft, tuneless murmur that unaccountably made Jem's fear grow stronger. He lifted his head off the table, straining to see what Schivvers was doing over there by the sideboard. A drawer opened. There were clinking sounds of metal on metal. Jem pictured an array of sharp, pointed instruments, and his body trembled. He was now drenched in the cold sweat that had popped out all over his skin. Salt stung the razor-thin cuts on his torso and the deeper one on his arm where Schivvers had sliced him in the kitchen. Probably there'd be more cuts before this was over. Likely there'd be body parts missing.

"Sir," he croaked. "Can I beseech you to listen for a moment?"

Schivvers didn't answer, just kept mucking about with his tools. Perhaps he was polishing them.

Jem entreated his shirt-clad back. "I know you want the little girl back. I know she's special to you." He plumbed his mind to find words that might reach the man. "You had her trained up just the way you wanted her—obedient, docile, submissive. But losing her doesn't have to be the end of that. There's others that could serve the same purpose for you."

The surgeon didn't turn, but his hands slowed, and Jem imagined he'd caught his attention.

"Others who might please you even more, who'd be willing to do anything, *everything* you've ever imagined. A person with some experience in giving pleasure."

At last the man turned to him. Jem wished he hadn't. There was some kind of saw in one of his hands, the sharp little scalpel in the other. Schivvers walked toward him. He wore a large white smock that covered his shirt, waistcoat, and trousers, and the expression on his face was utterly blank. Was he hearing Jem at all?

With no other hope, Jem plowed on, hoping to weave a spell of seductive words to protect his body as long as he could. "See, sir, I know what you want. Utter obedience. Another dolly to play with. I can be that. I will do whatever you want. And I can give you pleasure such as you've never imagined. The things I can do... And there won't be any fuss with Sir Alan that way, d'you see? He'll leave you alone. You forget about trying to win back the girl, and use me instead."

Not an ideal plan, but from where Jem was sitting—or rather lying—it was better than most. Once he'd convinced the good surgeon not to cut him up into little pieces, then he could concentrate on finding a way out of here. Be the man's puppet for a while, then murder him in his bed and make an escape.

Schivvers stood over him now, gazing down into Jem's face, and his expression was no longer blank. His lip curled in disgust. "You little animal! Is that what you think I want? Dirty, perverted sex? You disgust me, and you have no idea who I am."

"Why don't you explain to me then, sir," Jem begged. "You're a man of science, I know. Tell me about your studies and what you've learned about human nature. I want to try to understand you."

And because every man deep down wants someone to understand who he truly is, Mr. Schivvers began to talk.

"I love that girl because she is pure. And I want to be there to see the moment of change when her purity is gone forever. But once the moment is past, it can never be recaptured. That is why I spend so much time in preparation. There is much pleasure to be had in games played with the mind, even more so than with the body."

His eyes had the glazed-over look of a man remembering past pleasures, and then they suddenly snapped back to the present and focused on Jem, sharp as scalpels. "Where is the pleasure in corrupting that which is already corrupt, to degrade that which is already degraded?"

"True enough, I imagine, sir." Jem had been testing his restraints the entire time Schivvers's back was to him, without a speck of success. He could no more break loose of this damned table than Anne Boleyn had from the Tower of London—and he was near as likely to lose his head before this was over. His only hope was to somehow talk the man into letting him up, and to do that, he must continue to soften him.

"Must be lonely to have all those deep thoughts and no one to share 'em with but them journals. What kinds of experiments would you work on a young girl to make her more pliant? How'd you break a filly like that?"

Schivvers laid down the saw on the table next to Jem's hip, but trailed the scalpel lovingly up and down his arm. He then began to bisect the deeper cut already on his forearm. Jem held utterly still and gazed at the man with adoration, as if every word that fell from his mouth was a pearl.

"I knew from the moment I saw the little girl that she was special—so brave and bright, helping out with the patients and never flinching no matter how grotesque the injuries. To see her was to want her. I knew that bending then breaking that strong will would be ecstasy, and it was. The first task was to win her mother's confidence and ensure she would entrust the girl to me after her death. The next step, of course, was to engineer that death."

Jem swallowed but continued to stare with rapt interest at the madman.

"And then, step by loving step, I bound Ann to me with chains of trust, then fear, then terror, flaying her down to the bone until only blind obedience was left. I would describe to her all the things that could happen to a little girl alone in the world. I made her see how dependent on me she was and made sure never to leave her side until I was certain her will was broken enough that I could trust her to stay where I'd placed her. Some of this work took place while we were still in Portugal, but I knew in order to really experiment intensively, it was time for me to muster out of the army and bring the girl to the privacy of a home."

Jem would've felt more horror and sympathy on behalf of the girl if his concentration weren't completely centered on the knife carving a lovely pattern of cross-hatching on his forearm. Blood dripped down and pooled beneath his arm on the table.

Schivvers lifted the scalpel long enough to gesture around the room, droplets of red scattering from the blade onto Jem's chest. "It was in this very room that my training began in earnest. Of course, I showed her my collection and told her how easily limbs could be severed"—he indicated the jars and mummified parts—"but I also showed her certain erotic pictures and explained in detail the many things I would do to her by and by. The trick with mind control is to never let the subject fall into a routine. They must be kept off guard, sometimes treated with loving kindness, other times roughly. Awakening a subject at all hours will disrupt her normal sleep patterns and further confuse her mind. She must be made to perform humiliating tasks. Foot licking is good, or crawling naked and whimpering in simulation of a dog—really, anything that makes the subject feel less than human."

Schivvers lowered his voice in a confiding manner and smiled. "I must confess that watching such abased behavior is extremely arousing. You can understand how it is much more exciting than merely taking a girl's virginity. And prolonging this process over months as I have is a pure celebration."

"Absolutely, sir. Being demeaned is my specialty. I've had men ask me to—"

"No!" As if becoming aware of Jem as more than a sympathetic listener, Schivvers glared at him. "I told you. It's the taking of her innocence that matters. *That* is the crux of the game. I would no more be interested in having you at my beck and call than I would a real dog. There are no parts of me I would care for you to lick."

Jem nodded. "Point taken, sir."

"However..." Schivvers resumed his knife play, this time drawing ever-widening concentric circles around Jem's nipple, delicate lines that caused little pain but made Jem's nipple tighten pebble-hard and made his stomach flip over and over. "However, there are other, different experiments I might perform on someone such as you."

"Really? What might those be?" He struggled to maintain his conversational tone, the soothing voice that kept Schivvers talking.

"I've often wondered but haven't had the opportunity to ascertain how long a man could stay alive as small bits of him are cut away. Under ideal conditions, with some laudanum to dull the senses so the patient wouldn't go into shock, how long? Months, I would wager if I were a betting man."

He flicked the scalpel over the tip of Jem's nipple, and pain shot through him.

"I could amputate this bit, for example, and you would hardly miss it. You certainly wouldn't bleed out from it."

And now Jem's eyes closed. He couldn't maintain his frank and friendly gaze at Schivvers's face any longer. He licked his lips and drew a breath, waiting for the bud of his nipple to be cut off.

Instead the surgeon chuckled, a surprisingly warm, deep laughter that would have inspired a smile on Jem's face under any other circumstances.

"Do you see? Anticipation! What a powerful tool," Schivvers crowed. "I may do it, or I may never do it. You don't know, and the fear is practically worse than the pain would be."

"Clever," Jem rasped and pried his eyes open again. "May I ask you, sir, to please loosen the restraints long enough that I might take a piss? I swear to you I'll behave, but it would be a shame to pollute your lovely operating table."

"Vivisection table. And it has been awash in plenty of bodily fluids over the years. I don't think a little urine will matter."

Had to at least try. What the hell will get you to untie me, you insane bastard?

Schivvers laid down the scalpel at last, and Jem heaved a breath—until the man picked up the saw.

"I've allowed you to distract me long enough. It's time to prepare my card for Sir Alan." Before Jem could beg or plead, Schivvers grabbed the polishing cloth and stuffed it back into his mouth.

Jem's teeth clamped down on the acrid-tasting cloth, and he moaned a protest. The fumes from the rag rose to his eyes and made them water.

Schivvers reached for his hand, and Jem knew exactly what he was going to do. As the surgeon tried to pull his fingers straight, Jem clenched them tightly.

"Cooperate. Lay your hand flat, and you'll only lose your little finger. A man can easily live without a pinky. There are other body parts I think you'd regret losing more." Schivvers looked at Jem's cock, which shriveled as if his very gaze were poison.

Still, Jem couldn't bring himself to unfold his fingers. Schivvers delivered a hard rap to the back of his hand with the butt of the bone saw. It hurt like hell, but Jem's fist couldn't unclench. Like an old man who'd had a stroke, his fingers were clawed tight and immovable.

"Castration it is, then," the surgeon said. He laid aside the bone saw and snatched up his scalpel again.

Jem began to scream his anger and fear into his gag. His heart thundered, and he could barely think for the pulse pounding in his ears. Schivvers was right. It was easy to break a person merely with threats.

The surgeon cradled Jem's ball sac almost lovingly in one hand and raised the scalpel.

Jem thumped his fingers on the table to show the man that fine, yes, he could take that little finger instead. Schivvers paused, and Jem thought he'd caught his attention, but no. His feeble noise wasn't why the doctor had stopped. Time had slowed so it seemed to Jem another full minute passed before he understood where the louder knocking originated. Someone was pounding at the door of Schivvers's workroom.

"Mr. Schivvers," Alan called, then pressed an ear to the door. He heard a shuffling sound and a thump. "You are in there, aren't you? Your maid said I could find you here, and she allowed me to come down." The servants were all asleep as far as Alan knew, but perhaps Schivvers would think Alan had roused the whole house.

Alan hoped that wasn't true. He and Annie had entered through a window. Or rather, she had. The thing had been somehow locked open so only a thin child could fit.

The girl, shaking like a tree in a high wind, had been brave enough to return to the scene of her torture, slide through the small opening, and fling open the kitchen door for him. He'd wanted to hug her but suspected she was terrified of physical contact, so he crouched and whispered, "I'll keep you safe. Remember that. Now show me where I must go."

She'd opened the door and pointed down the flagstone stairs, but silently refused to go more than two steps down. She watched from the top, holding the carriage lamp he'd given her. It cast eerie light around the rough subchamber, which looked like a huge wine cellar.

"Mr. Schivvers," Alan called again. "It is Sir Alan. Back again. I apologize for the late hour."

"Ah," came the man's delighted-sounding cry. "Late? No, you are early. I haven't even sent you your invitation."

The man could only sound so pleased when he had a major advantage, and of course, that advantage would be Jem.

It was up to Alan to convince Schivvers he held nothing of any consequence. Alan swallowed hard and spoke. "Mr. Schivvers, what on earth are you talking about? I believe you have misplaced your young charge. I found her. Do you know how she managed to escape your care?" Alan was no actor, but he hoped he'd managed to express gentlemanly interest and not howling panic.

He looked over his shoulder at Annie at the top of the stairs, who watched him with a wide, frightened gaze. He pasted an expression he prayed resembled a reassuring smile on his face, and put a finger to his lips. Then he turned his back and pointed at his other hand so she could see he'd crossed his fingers behind his back. *I'm lying*. Perhaps she'd had a normal enough childhood to understand that particular bit of sign language. She didn't make a sound, so he went back to work with the plan that had come to him as he'd sneaked to the kitchen and made his careful way down the uneven steps.

"Mr. Schivvers," he said again. "I am surprised you allow your charge to run around outside as if she were a Hottentot. Poor girl is barely dressed." He waited for another long time.

He stealthily tried the door, but from the feel of it, it was locked and barricaded too. God, he wished he could slam through, but the door was constructed of sturdy oak and far more strongly reinforced than most ordinary entrances. Schivvers must have something filthy to hide behind such a strong door. Alan wished he had the use of several strong soldiers and a battering ram. But to attack as he wanted to might be to forfeit Jem's life if Schivvers held a knife to his throat. Careful negotiation was the best response right now.

"Are you going to let me in?" he called.

"Your servant is here, Sir Alan. He's admitted it all, your plan to kidnap my girl."

"My servant?" Alan fought the nausea. He wished his voice hadn't cracked. Drawing another deep, long breath, he tried again. Casual, disinterested. "Oh. You must mean Jem. That rascal is here? I had wondered where the man had got to."

"He was trespassing. I think I'm well within my rights to kill him."

Alan wet his suddenly dry lips with his tongue. "He has been a nuisance to you, has he? Again, I can only apologize." He babbled meaningless civilities. Genteel conversation. All he had to do was get the bastard to open the door. He could say anything.

"I'm shockingly sorry he's been a pest. I have worried about young Annie Cutler, it's true, and I suppose he's dull witted enough to have thought he could gain points with me by going behind my back."

"Dull witted? I don't think so, Sir Alan. And I think he's more than a servant to you."

Yes, God Almighty, yes, he was. And if Alan fell quiet now, he'd only confirm Schivvers's belief. "Nonsense," he snapped.

"Sir Alan. You must think me a fool. I know all about you and your depraved desires. That is why I think you would want to trade. My girl for your man."

Alan closed his eyes. Fear shot through him. It couldn't be. He'd been so careful all those years in Spain, so the only way

Schivvers could know the truth would be through Jem's confession. And the only way Jem would do so would be under duress. Under torture. Alan swallowed hard. The bastard of a surgeon would die and soon, he hoped. He raised his voice again and was glad the fury didn't ring through. Only a bit of indignation, which certainly fit the situation. "I think I know what you imply. During all the time you knew me in Spain, did I ever indulge in any sort of depravity?"

"The desire was there. Burning in you."

"Did I do anything even remotely impure? Favor any comely young man or fondle some young new recruit? Of course not. I touched no one," he answered his own questions—truthfully. "So this young idiot. And I don't care how intelligent he is, Jem is an idiot." That sentiment exploded straight from the heart. Jesus God, if Jem died, he'd never forgive him. "This fool is having you on, Schivvers. I admit to these unhealthy predilections—I won't deny it. He must have seen my sick desire, and that formed the basis of his confession. But you know I am celibate. I do not indulge. He is nothing to me. In fact, he is less interesting to me than your ward."

He waited several heartbeats. Was Schivvers considering his words? Killing Jem? Alan raised his voice. "Apparently because you are not opening this door and speaking to me face-to-face, you're speaking the truth about a trade. And if that's true, if you want to take Jem in exchange for Annie, I suppose I must accept."

"No, wait!" Schivvers's voice came from near the door now. "How do I know you've really got the girl? Let me hear her voice. I must speak with her."

Alan looked up the stairs to where Annie waited, snugged flat against the wall, staring down at him with those wide doe eyes.

"She's here. You'll simply have to trust me."

A sharp bark of laughter sounded from the other side of the door. "Ann, if you hear me, answer me now as I taught you."

Her lips parted, but no sound came out. Alan stretched out a hand to her, pleading with his gaze.

"Just give him a word, Major. It's all right," he whispered.

Slowly she set one bare foot on the stairs, then another. Pace by pace she descended until she stood a few steps above Alan. She swallowed, the muscles in her slender neck moving.

"I'm here, sir."

"My sweet Ann." The serpentine slither of Schivvers's voice ghosting through the air made Alan's skin crawl and Ann shudder. "Whose girl are you? Tell me."

"Your girl, sir. Only yours," she whispered.

"Less than a girl. What are you, Ann?"

"Your little dog, sir." She supplied her part of what appeared to be a familiar litany between them.

"That's right. Only a naughty little pup which must obey my every command or be punished."

"Enough!" Alan snapped, breaking the spell the man's voice cast over Ann. She seemed to be visibly shrinking before his eyes. "You've got your proof. I have the girl here, and I'll trade her for Jem if you only open the door. I shall give you until the count of three. Then young Miss Cutler and I will bid you good night, and I will return to London with her. I have no reason to stay here any longer, and my carriage is just outside. One. Two..."

At last there was a sound of bolts drawing back. Alan hurriedly gave the hand signal *retreat* to Annie, and she almost stumbled up the stairs, tripping over Jem's coat in her rush to get away. Good. That would make the next part much easier.

"She's mine. I've made her mine." The door was flung open. For a single heartbeat, Alan stared into the dark eyes and pale face of Mr. Schivvers. Then he stepped forward—and without a word, Alan thrust the knife he'd grabbed in the kitchen into Schivvers's body. He unerringly slid the blade between the ribs.

The man's dark eyes went wide. He blinked once and crumpled, toppling onto his side. Alan nearly stumbled over the still-gasping Schivvers when he saw the horror lying on the table. A naked, bleeding corpse. No, not a corpse. But so much blood. Jem's impossibly blue eyes stared out at him. He wasn't unconscious. Alan yanked the cloth from Jem's mouth.

"You're crying," Jem said.

"Where are the keys?"

"Dunno. Kept my eyes closed when I could." He was a mess. Blood dripping from nearly every part of his body. Lines and curves of blood. His hair was matted with the thick liquid.

Alan went back to Schivvers. He squatted, ran his hands over the blood-soaked clothes, and searched his pockets for keys to the shackles. "You've killed me," the man rasped. A red bubble popped at the corner of his mouth.

Alan didn't answer.

"Damn you, Watleigh. You didn't have to kill me."

Alan found a ring of keys in his waistcoat pocket and pulled it out, surprised to see his fingers slightly shook.

Schivvers was right; Alan hadn't needed to strike a lethal blow to contain the man. Fear and anger had directed his hand, which had been trained to kill.

"You're right," he said at last. "I shouldn't have killed you. I should have made you suffer."

But he wasn't going to lie awake nights and see the surgeon's blood pooling on the floor. He rose to his feet and looked at Jem stretched out before him. That was the image that would haunt him.

Alan tried different keys in the locks. Behind him Schivvers gave a hoarse, rasping cry. He gurgled and fell silent.

The lock on Jem's bleeding left hand clicked open. "Thank you, sir," Jem whispered. "Is he dead?"

Alan didn't turn to look. "You are an idiot. A goddamned driveling idiot." Alan kept his voice low, though inside he still howled and screamed. He went to work on the lock holding the other hand in place. "You are the greatest fucking fool I've ever encountered. I can't understand—I can't begin to imagine—why you would do something so half-cocked. Half-baked."

"Half-cocked?" Jem gave a weak laugh. "Yeah, he was about to make me half-cocked. Half-balled."

"Jem," Alan began. "My God. Jem." He couldn't say more. Perhaps never would, though he knew the truth at last. If Jem had died, every bit of light would have gone out of his life. He needed this man.

Both of them were bloody fools, Jem literally.

"You're still weeping, sir."

He nodded. And for the very briefest of moments, he leaned over the supine figure and kissed an uncut spot on his cheek. "I am indeed," he said.

Chapter Sixteen

Annie waited at the top of the stairs.

"We have to get her out of here," Alan said. "Without waking the servants."

"Melvin said they have strict orders to ignore any sounds from the basement. He did experiments on cats, Schivvers told them. An acceptable practice for a surgeon is how Burton explained it to him, but it made Melvin feel positively shivery, he told me."

Alan found a large roll of sailcloth in the back of the room.

"The man must have wrapped up his victims in this. 'Tis his turn for the winding cloth," said Jem.

"No," said Alan. "We can't hide the evidence; we don't have time to clean up. We must simply go. I need to make sure you're going to be all right."

Jem's clothes were nowhere to be found. Alan cut a length of cloth for Jem, who slowly eased into a sitting position. Alan carefully wrapped it around Jem's naked body. The cloth went red with his blood. Alan felt sick again.

Jem was more worried about Annie. "She shouldn't see me like this," he whispered.

"We can't worry about that now. We must leave."

They crept out of the house, Jem leaning heavily on Alan, Annie running ahead, looking over her shoulder even after they'd left the house behind.

The smell of all that blood made the horses nervous.

They climbed into the carriage carefully, and Annie sat between the men. She shrank away from them both but stared at Jem in the bright moonlight.

"I know I look a fright, Major," Jem said. "But 'tisn't so bad." He hoped not, anyway. He'd begun to shake and felt as if the world were spinning. The pain from all the cuts throbbed with every heartbeat.

Annie nodded solemnly, as if telling him she'd seen worse. She probably had.

"You understand that Mr. Schivvers is gone?" Alan asked. "He'll never be able to harm you again."

They set off at a calm pace. No need to run like the wind and raise suspicion. After a long moment, she nodded again.

"Are you all right, Jem?" Alan asked again over the top of the girl's head.

"Fine, fine," Jem lied. Again. He closed his eyes, but that was worse. When he opened them again, he lurched a little toward Annie, who drew his coat tighter around her.

The devil was gone, but his influence could be felt in all the stinging cuts on Jem's body and in the cringing, silent girl next to him. The cuts would heal, perhaps leaving some interesting scars—he'd be a match for the badger. The girl's wounds might be crippling.

"I might cast up my accounts," Jem warned as the nausea grew. But he didn't, and they made it back to the inn, grim and silent and shocked—and unnoticed.

The innkeeper was there to usher them into the building and cast a suspicious eye at the staggering Jem, but Alan made an excuse concerning too much drink and a tavern fight. He also offered the man a large sum to earn his silence concerning the girl in their company, although he masked the bribe as an apology for disturbing the innkeeper so late at night.

Jem and Annie slowly made their way upstairs while Alan stayed behind to make certain the horses were taken care of by the sleepy hostler.

Up in the room, Annie stood unmoving in the middle of the floor, Jem's heavy coat sleeves reaching past the tips of her fingers. "You can sit down," Jem said as he carefully stretched out on the bed. "Anywhere you like. Forgive me lying down in front of a lady, but I can't stand without falling over."

She dropped to the ground. The poor thing was obviously exhausted. But now he understood. She would do nothing unless told to.

"Annie, you should lie down. On this bed. I won't touch you. On the pallet. Anywhere you wish. And you can take off me coat. Or leave it on, whatever you wish."

She crawled doglike over to the pallet. Christ, as soon as he could, he would coax her out of moving in that fashion. It fair made him ill.

Jem held out his pillow. "You want this?" She shook her head.

When Alan came in, he went straight to the washstand and poured the waiting pitcher-load of water into the basin. "I should wash your cuts," he told Jem.

"Naw. Get the bed all wet? And I'm afraid I ain't standing up again tonight, sir."

Alan started over to the bed with the basin. He stopped and looked down at the floor. "What did you say, Major?"

Had the girl spoken? Jem's ears were buzzing, and he hadn't heard.

"It's all right. You're not in trouble, I promise. Just say it again."

Now Jem heard her whisper. "Spirits. Drink."

Jem gave a weak laugh. "Brandy is perfect. You saying I should drink a glass? I agree."

She shook her head, solemn and scared.

"What should I do with the spirits?" Alan asked softly.

"Alcohol for washing. Mrs. Cutler used to say so. Hurts though," she whispered.

"Very well." Alan put down the basin and fetched the bottle of brandy from the mantelpiece.

As he leaned over Jem with one of his own linen shirts soaked with brandy and dabbed at the slices on his face, arms, and chest, Jem muttered, "I know we're supposed to make the girl more confident, but wasting good drink? And, oh good God—gracious that hurts like a fu—" He clapped a hand over his mouth and let off a series of muffled shouts into it.

Alan worked steadily, pressing the soaked cloth to Jem's cuts. "Mrs. Cutler was a good nurse, and I would be foolish to ignore her advice," he said in a loud voice. He finished the last stinging cut on Jem's leg. He wrapped two long white cloths around his arm and another around his leg. Jem suspected they were Alan's cravats, but he was still feeling fuzzy from the pain of that washing.

"Only a few cuts are still bleeding, Jem. And none are spurting blood. You might need stitches on them. I think we should keep the rest uncovered."

Alan straightened and looked at Annie. "When I knew you in Spain, you called your mother mum. Why do you now call her Mrs. Cutler?"

"He says to." No surprise there—and certainly no need to ask who *he* was.

"Did he tell you why?"

"He is my family. My mother and father and everything I need," she recited and then fell silent. In a nearly inaudible whisper, she added, "But he isn't. He *wasn't*."

And for the first time, Jem felt they had a chance at pulling her back entirely.

"He wasn't," Alan agreed. "He's nothing now. We'll take care of you, and you know he'll never come near you again."

They should just say the bastard's dead. Tell her the entire truth. Likely she heard the commotion and saw the blood. For some reason Alan hadn't said the words yet, and Jem wondered why. Could he seriously believe there was a breath of life left in the surgeon? Jem knew a corpse when he saw one. Mr. Schivvers was no longer among the living. He was cutting off the limbs of the demons in hell.

Alan moved about the room, tidying, doing Jem's job again. Annie lay curled in a tight ball, watching his every move. When Alan came near her, she flinched and seemed to hold her breath.

Jem, who'd been lying on his back, trying to decide what hurt more, his chest or his arm, grew impatient at last. "Annie. If you're not sleepy, lass, might I have a word? Come here."

She crawled over to the bed. He patted the mattress next to him. "Just to sit for a second. And listen." She sat, her hands folded in her lap.

Alan turned his attention to him, frowning. Jem cleared his throat and tried to think of how to say what needed to be said. If someone laid out the rules and kept to them, she'd be better. She needed rules.

He'd use a swell's language. "I expect you won't believe me entirely, and that's all right. But you pay attention, don't you?"

She nodded.

Jem said, "No one is going to hit you." He directed a defiant look at Alan, who stared steadily back. "I swear not to touch you, less it's a matter of danger. I swear on my life not to touch you without your permission. And Captain will make the promise too. Captain?"

Alan nodded.

"Swear," Jem said fiercely.

Thank goodness Alan didn't go into some sort of tirade about being ordered about by his valet. He spoke solemnly. "I swear not to touch Miss Annie Cutler without her permission unless she is in danger."

"No pain of any kind," Jem said, recalling pinches and cuts. "Nothing."

"No pain of any kind," Alan said. And he smiled at Jem.

Annie sat perfectly still, studying each cut up and down Jem's arm. He pulled the sheet up to his neck, wincing as the cloth touched his ravaged skin. He went on. "And yelling at you, Annie? We won't, will we sir?"

"Not unless there's danger," Alan said.

"Eventually we might let loose with a yelp or two. Likely if you do something wrong after being told not to. You remember your mum doing that, aye? Your mum losing her patience? But no yelling for breaking rules you don't know. Nothing you don't expect. But never hitting. No pain ever again. Right, Captain? I swear it."

"We both swear it. Nor will we allow anyone else to hurt you." Again Alan's eyes met Jem's, and something strong passed between them. He was making an oath to her and to him as well. There was the usual intense yearning in that gaze, along with more. So much more. There was a clarity, as if a light shone brightly in the dark depths of his eyes, and all the fears and doubts that had plagued the man were dispelled.

Jem could almost see the change in Alan and was half-afraid he'd imagined it. A trick of candle and firelight along with an acute awareness of all the pain. But just in case, he said, "And I swear it too, Captain. Sir Alan Watleigh. No one will hurt you. Not so long as there's breath in my body."

Alan didn't break their joined gazes for several long heartbeats. Then he leaned down to pick up the basin he'd left on the floor. "Good night, Annie. Er, you might want to lie down again." His voice rasped. As if he held back tears.

She crept back to her pallet. Jem closed his eyes.

"We should all sleep," Alan said, normal again. He took off a coverlet and wrapped it around himself. Holy Christ, he lay on the floor.

"No, sir. You should have the bed, and—"

"Good night, Jem." Now that was right and good. He was back to firm Sir Alan again, brooking no nonsense from his valet. "Sleep well, both of you." And the room soon filled with the soft sound of breathing.

Only, Jem couldn't sleep. The cuts throbbed and stung, and he smiled into the darkness.

~

Alan woke to the sound of the birds squabbling in the eaves. A distant rooster crowed. The room still lay in darkness. Someone in the room gasped, the sound of muffled pain.

"Jem?" Alan said softly.

"Yeah."

"It hurts?"

"Like the devil's piss," Jem whispered. "I'll be better soon, though. And speaking of the devil, he didn't do a thing to my rear, so I can plant it on that carriage seat. If you're ready to go back to London."

Home. With a child he couldn't explain and a man he wouldn't give up. "Do you like the country, Jem?"

There was a long silence. "Depends. Are you talking alone or with you?"

Alan laughed but grew sober at once. He groped for the candle and flint he'd left on the floor near him. He lit the candle. "Later we'll talk of such things." The future he hoped he'd have.

He rose and went to draw the curtains from the window to show the pink and gray of a new day.

He hadn't taken off his clothes and looked a sight. Wearing blood-smeared clothing wasn't the best idea for his plan. After a quick glance at the girl still asleep and breathing evenly on the pallet next to the bed, he pulled out a change of clothes from the valise. He went behind the screen in the corner to change and shave using the cold, slightly bloodied water from the night before.

Just a few things more. At the writing desk he scribbled a quick note. Time to go, but Alan found he had trouble forming the words to explain his next step. He moved about the room, keeping an eye on the Major as he laid out the bloody clothes.

"I reckon I should take care of those," said Jem.

Alan pulled on his braces and stepped closer to look him over. The man was in obvious pain. "You said you could travel. Were you telling the truth?"

Jem nodded gingerly. "Certainly."

"Good. Because I might need you to take care of the Major and get back to the city alone. Just the two of you. You know where my money bag is, I know."

Jem's steady gaze made him uncomfortable. This plan was as harebrained as Jem's had been, but Alan couldn't think of any way to avoid it.

"Jem." His throat was thick with longing. "I trust you. I know you can take care of the Major now. I'd trust you with anything of mine, including my life."

Jem's smile was a thing of beauty. "Yes, you can."

"But I must go. And I might not be coming back. If you need help, if you grow ill, I left the name of the solicitor in Sheffield. He should be able to act as my man of business. I've written out directions for him."

Jem sat up, wincing. One of his cuts had opened, and the cloth around his arm was scarlet.

"Is your arm all right?"

"Bugger my arm. Where are you off to?"

"I murdered a man. I can't go until I know that no innocent has taken the blame. And if I find I must confess, I don't want you or Annie anywhere near here. I want her gone where the law can't take her from your care. You and Badgeman will keep her safe."

Jem swore, but then Annie gave a soft moan, and he stopped abruptly. Both men stared down at her in dismay until she rolled onto her side and her breath steadied. She still slept. Jem rubbed his hand over his hair, making the curls even wilder.

He whispered, "When they see that devil's room… If they see what he did to me, 'course they'll let you go."

Alan caught sight of himself in the small mirror on the wall. He rejected the idea of getting a fresh cravat since all were either wrinkled or binding Jem's wounds. He buttoned his waistcoat and reached for his dark blue jacket.

He turned to face Jem again. "Yes. If I'm arrested, I'll send for you. You can leave the Major with Badgeman. But that little girl…" He held Jem's gaze steadily, no need to look away. "She should get away from here and not have to enter that house again."

"Badgeman can bloody well bring his colossal bloody self up here and bloody well watch over her. I'll not be leaving if there's a chance you end up in prison. Don't worry yourself. I'll find a good story for the girl's presence." His fast grin lit his face. "And from now on I'll be calling her Miss Badgeman, since he's the softhearted damber that launched us arsy-varsy into this affair."

Alan opened his mouth to issue an order, to command Jem to follow his direction, but he understood that some sort of line had been crossed. What had happened last night, the vow that was deeper than mere words spoken, had changed them both, and he wasn't sure what Jem was to him anymore—other than essential. Maybe that was it. He couldn't afford to lose the man. Except, no, he didn't think he could do or say anything that would drive him away. The strange little oath they'd taken in the dark bedchamber of a second-rate inn seemed to hold mystical power that gripped them both.

So he nodded. "All right. But the two of you shan't come with me today. You're still in pain, and Annie shan't go back there."

"Absolutely never."

"Oh, good," Alan said drily. "So you'll pay attention to my orders when you agree with them?"

Jem's smile turned wicked. "About sums it up, eh?" The grin dissolved, and his brow puckered. "'Tis a pity you were brought up with such a complete set of upright morals, sir. I'd say we pack up and get away fast as we can."

"I can't."

Jem pushed his hands at his hair, still stiff with blood, and made a face. "I expect I do know why. If you tried such a thing, you'd have more ghosts at your heels. A reckoning of some sort, eh?"

"Ah. You understand."

"I do, and I'm glad of you and your nuisance decency. Most of the time. When that streak of nobility doesn't mean you're begging to be led to the scaffold." He cleared his throat and gave a quick glance down at the slumbering girl. "One request before you go?"

Alan waited.

Jem whispered, "A kiss."

Alan walked to the bed and looked into blue eyes, serious yet still bright with unquenchable cheerfulness. "Jem," he said, and again words failed him, so he put his mouth on Jem's—a light, careful touch, for those lips were still dry and cracked from the gag.

Jem groaned under the soft brush of Alan's mouth, and just as Alan would have moved away, Jem's hand caught the back of his neck and held him in place. Jem moved his mouth and opened it so Alan could taste the familiar flavor. The kiss remained sweet, never falling into the mindless heat of sex, though that tension lay close to the surface. A promise.

Alan broke away, his chest so tight he could barely draw breath.

Jem searched his face, unsmiling. "I do dearly love you, Sir Alan Watleigh," he whispered.

Alan grew dizzy. He opened his mouth.

Jem touched his cheek. "Naw, don't have an apoplectic fit, sir. Just wanted to let you know, but I don't expect you to fall on my neck with your own declarations of undying devotion." He clasped his hands at his neck and fluttered his thick lashes, the parody of a lovesick girl. "Oh, Jem my angel," he said in a high mockery of a woman's voice. In his own voice, he added, "Ow. My arm hurts. Best not to fall on any part of my body."

He'd turned it into a joking matter again, Jem's way to cope with strong emotion. Alan couldn't speak and only nodded.

"I'll see you," he said. "Take care of the Major and yourself. Please, Jem." He tried to put his meaning in those last words and turned and walked out without looking back. He might lose his heart for this task if he did.

Chapter Seventeen

Alan ate breakfast at the inn. Before departing, he paid for a tray of food to be sent to his room, telling the taciturn landlord that his valet was ill and possibly contagious. "I thought he merely had too much to drink last night. But now I think it's more. He's got a fever."

The landlord's peevish scowl deepened. "I'm not going nowhere near him, then. And I won't let the maid clean that room."

Perfect. "Just knock on the door and tell him the food is there. He's not so ill he can't take care of himself." He laid an extra couple of coins in the man's palm, and the landlord's expression returned to his normal merely sour instead of curdled.

Alan ordered a hack from the stable and, in no great hurry, rode toward Schivvers's house. He didn't notice the slight ache in his thigh or the lush green countryside as he rode. He didn't even think about the trouble he might face at the end of the ride. Jem's face, his smile, those words. Alan smiled back at the imaginary Jem in his mind. Even when he realized he was as much a moonling calf as any young swain in the first throes of love, he couldn't stop smiling. Depravity be damned. No one would be able to resist Jem, the young dunderhead.

He grew sober as he drew near the gray house. The front door lay open, and several men stood on the steps, talking in an agitated manner. Neighbors gathered on the green to gape. Alan had wondered how he could make his approach seem natural, but it was a simple thing to act the part of an acquaintance of the man stopping to find out what the trouble was.

Alan swung down from the saddle and tied the horse to a young tree in the front.

He didn't expect the matter to be simple. He'd approach the main investigator of the crime and delicately discover the names of potential suspects. The servants seemed likely.

"Sir. There has been a most unfortunate... But no, you'd best follow me." Burton bowed solemnly, his barely suppressed excitement evident in his quick step as he led Alan to the same study he'd seen on his first visit and left him standing by the window. Alan gazed out at the dozen onlookers on the green. He thought he saw two redheaded females there. Jem's twins.

"Sir Alan?"

He turned and saw a vaguely familiar face with thinning gray hair and a drooping jaw atop a large stomach, with very little neck or chest to separate them. Alan smiled before he realized that might not fit the circumstances.

"I see you recall me," said the man who held out his hand. "Wilkins. I knew your father in London. Terrible thing, your family's passing. I sent a note round, but I expect...you..."

"Of course, thank you," murmured Alan. "How do you do, my lord."

"I'm the JP, and there's been a terrible, terrible...er..." The man's face reddened. Alan wondered if the man would ever finish a sentence. "How well did you know Mr....?" He waved a pudgy hand around the room.

Alan was determined not to lie. "We served in Spain. I was under his care when I was injured."

Lord Wilkins seemed to relax slightly. "So not best of friends, which one might say… Terrible things have happened."

"My lord? Since you are the justice of the peace, I know you must keep some matters private. What can you tell me?"

Lord Wilkins indicated a chair, and Alan sat. With a deep sigh, Wilkins sat across from him. "Terrible things," Alan prompted.

"I'm sorry to say that Mr. Schivvers is dead. But that is not the worst of it, if you can believe it."

Alan could, but he remained silent.

Lord Wilkins looked down at his hands. He wasn't watching Alan as he went on. "From what the borough constable has pieced together, it is a sad story of murder and worse. His description of the scene was so dire, I came to witness for myself that the fellow did not exaggerate. I am afraid he did not."

"Go on," Alan said.

"Mr. Schivvers had a little girl. A bastard child, we believe."

Alan began to say, "Er, not really," but Wilkins didn't notice and plowed on. "We believe that she died, murdered by Mr. Schivvers. Because though he might have been a good surgeon to you…"

Alan didn't even try to clear up that misconception.

"I'm afraid, my dear sir, that he was a bad man." Now Lord Wilkins looked up, as if waiting for a response.

"I must say I suspected as much," Alan said. "Even over in Spain."

That must have melted the last of Lord Wilkins's discretion. The story poured out now—the grisly discovery of the body, the hideous room set up for torture.

"And what does your investigation reveal?" asked Alan. "You mentioned murder."

"Yes, yes. The little girl. He killed her and disposed of the body—bloody evidence of torture, perhaps dismemberment, is all over a table in the room. And then in a fit of remorse, drove a knife into his own black heart."

Alan gazed at him. Even he, an untrained observer, knew the angle of the wound was entirely wrong for suicide. He'd learned that much from seeing men die in war—not to mention from driving a knife into the surgeon's body.

"Suicide?" he asked.

The man nodded.

"That's your official finding?"

Lord Wilkins drew another heavy sigh. "I'm afraid I must give that ruling. It's most distressing."

Alan had to ask. He felt like a fool, but one more prod, and he'd leave it alone. "You don't suspect, say, the girl of stabbing him and running away? Or any of the servants?"

"It's patently obvious what happened here," Lord Wilkins said, almost indignantly. "If you'd care to examine the crime scene, a most distressing sight. Blood on the table. Her blood, sir."

No doubt the old man had spent a long time in that room—and next time he visited his London club, he'd be able to gain every member's attention with the grisly details.

"Oh, no. No, of course not, Lord Wilkins. I wondered if you'd examined all possibilities."

"In some cases there is no need." Lord Wilkins gave him a solemn look. "I have heard criminal cases for many years and count myself among the country's experts at discerning simple truth."

"Will you look for the girl's body?"

"I expect we must, although I shan't put much effort into the matter. He was a devilish, clever man. A true fiend who knew how to dispose of his victims." Lord Wilkins's voice dropped. "We think we've already found part of her in his horrible collection of souvenirs."

"Ah," said Alan. Now was the moment to speak. Yet no matter how hard he tried to work the story in his head, he couldn't come up with a version that would allow Annie to ride away from here under his protection. To stay out of prison he would have to lie, and he wasn't even certain which lies might suffice. If Jem were here, he'd have a version that might work.

Instead of lying or telling the truth, Alan simply didn't speak. He didn't need to because Lord Wilkins filled the silence with platitudes about how one never knows, how the mildest of men can have the blackest hearts.

"The servants are shocked, I can tell you," Lord Wilkins said. "Burton, the butler, discovered the body. The one named Melvin, a local boy, fainted dead away when he saw that room for the first time. Naturally it is horrible, yet I expect they will be dining out on this horror for the rest of their days."

Alan half listened as he wondered if he did Annie Cutler or her dead parents a disservice by allowing her identity to die. His silence meant her name would only be recalled as that of a victim in a horrific murder. The moment he walked away from here, she'd be reinvented.

"*Annie Badgeman*," Jem had said. It might work.

He suspected she wouldn't mind the loss of her name as the price paid to put Mr. Schivvers into the past and to never return to this house. What would Alan tell her later on? The truth, because he expected Badgeman and Jem wouldn't allow him to do otherwise. Perhaps when she was old enough, they'd tell her what happened together.

For a brief moment, he saw himself and Jem in a few years. Together. He put a hand over his mouth to hide the smile.

Lord Wilkins interrupted himself to ask, "Are you well, Sir Alan?"

"Yes. It's a shocking story, my lord. And I'm sorry to hear it."

That was the first lie he'd told because, of course, the JP's story neatly tied up every sort of loose end. Alan reminded himself that he didn't want to allow any suffering to occur as a result of his actions, so who was he to ruin a perfectly good explanation of events just because the account wasn't true?

It took some effort to hide his relief under a mask of stunned sorrow. Alan wished he'd managed acting as well as Jem did.

At last he stood and shook Wilkins's hand again and thanked him for his explanation, his condolences, and his kind words. When Burton came to show him out, Alan pressed a large tip into the butler's hand; he felt he must give something to the poor man who stumbled over the mess he'd made. "My condolences. I hope you and the others find new employment soon."

Alan walked to his horse. It took some concentration not to burst into song.

~

Since the drive to his estate near Shrewsbury would take only a short day, as opposed to the grueling two-day trip to London, Alan decided to head for Shropshire. Jem should probably remain in bed a few days, but Alan was anxious to quit Sheffield before one of Schivvers's servants recalled something incriminating and the JP changed his mind about his verdict of murder-suicide.

On his way back to the inn, he purchased a suit of boy's clothes for Ann to wear. No need to tempt fate by having some shopkeeper read the news of Ann's murder and later remember the odd gentleman who'd bought a little girl's dress.

When he returned to the room, Jem was sleeping and Ann sitting on the pallet with her arms around her knees, rocking slightly. Alan was not too familiar with children but knew how to calm a frightened horse, so he crouched at the girl's side, though not too close, and spoke to her quietly.

"Mr. Schivvers is dead. Gone forever. You don't need to fear him any longer, nor do you need to fear anything from me or Jem. Do you understand?" Although they'd promised her the same thing the night before, she would need to not only hear it, but see the proof in their behavior before she would believe. He'd worked with enough badly broken horses to know how long it took to gentle the fear out of them.

The girl looked at him without blinking and nodded slightly.

"But because of how he died and how we took you from him, we will have to change your name, your identity." Pain throbbed in his leg, folded as it was in an awkward squat. He shifted and massaged his thigh with one hand. "You can still be Annie, but from now on we'll introduce you as Mr. Badgeman's niece."

When her eyes widened in recognition, he added, "You remember Sergeant Badgeman, don't you? I know your parents were fond of him."

Again she nodded.

"You will be in his care as well as mine, and together we'll make certain you have everything you need." He heaved himself to his feet with a grunt. "Now we have to leave here as soon as possible. I must get Jem prepared to travel. You know a lot about nursing. Will you help me to care for him?"

"Yes, sir." The girl sprang to her feet.

Alan handed her the parcel with the newly purchased clothing and shoes in it. "First, here are some clothes for you to change into. Boy's attire for now, I'm afraid. When we reach my home in Shrewsbury, I'll have a seamstress come and sew a wardrobe for you." He gestured to a corner of the room where the screen stood. "You may change behind that. I'll be over here rousing this slugabed."

Without waiting to see if she obeyed—he knew she would whether or not it made her uncomfortable—he turned to the patient in the bed. Jem was usually a light sleeper, so the fact he'd remained unconscious during Alan's conversation with Ann was a little alarming. Alan gazed at the white bandages against the almost equally pale skin and the red lines that marred Jem's body here and there. His beautiful blue eyes were closed, and without their animated expressiveness, Jem appeared a different lad altogether—younger, more vulnerable, and far more innocent than he actually was.

Alan couldn't resist brushing a hand through the riot of light brown curls. He pressed his palm against Jem's forehead and felt heat—too much heat. The man had a fever. A wearing journey was the last thing Jem needed. Alan wished he could allow him the time to recover here at the inn, but the longer he remained in Sheffield with Ann, the more danger he put her—and all of them—in.

As his hand lingered on Jem's face, the man opened his eyes and blinked. "Morning, is it?"

"Yes. I've been back to Schivvers's house, where the authorities are examining the crime scene. Everything has turned out much better than expected. They believe the case to be a murder-suicide since Ann is missing."

The arched brows shot even higher. "Murder? Of Ann? Well, that is some fine detecting. How did the authorities come up with that?"

"Schivvers's chamber and notebooks told much about the man's character."

Alan recalled the notebooks in Jem's pockets and decided they'd burn those before leaving the inn. No need for anyone to find them in his possession. No need for anymore evidence of the surgeon's true character. He'd left more than enough behind.

"The logic is flawed, but before anyone figures it out, we need to be on the road to my house in Shropshire." He rested his hand on Jem's shoulder. "How are you feeling today? I hate to have you travel, but it's unavoidable."

"I'm feeling like someone mistook me for a fine Christmas goose and decided to carve me up. But you know how I love to travel. I'm game to go." He started to sit up, and his face went even whiter.

Alan had to help him sit upright and piled pillows behind him. He stripped the soiled bandages, sponged the wounds clean, then replaced the bandages with new strips of torn cloth. He'd have to order new cravats and linens along with Ann's new wardrobe.

To distract Jem from the pain of daubing at the wounds, Alan told him a bit about the Shropshire estate. "It's lovely, rolling country. As soon as you're well, I'll teach you to ride, and we'll canter across the countryside. You'll love it."

Another lift of that eloquent brow. "D'you think? I've only just grown comfortable riding behind horses. Can't imagine being atop them will suit me."

Alan chuckled as he eased Jem's shirt onto his arms and buttoned it. "Aren't you the one always encouraging me not to fear new things? A good ride is *exactly* what you need." He grinned and winked as he delivered the double entendre.

Jem laughed. "My word, if he hasn't discovered a sense of humor!"

Next, Alan carefully fed the notebooks into the fire before he served the breakfast which had waited all this time outside the door. It was cold by now, but both Jem and Ann gobbled it down.

Alan had already ordered the carriage prepared before coming up to the room. Now it was simply a matter of carrying down the baggage and trying to shield from prying eyes his injured valet and the sudden addition of a boy to their party. Annie's disguise included her hair braided and stuffed up under a cap. She made a presentable boy, but her fine features didn't bear too much scrutiny.

Jem walked gamely and mounted the wagon box before slumping, exhausted. Since the seat was only comfortably wide enough for two on a long journey, poor Annie rode behind, wedged in with the luggage. She didn't seem to mind and was probably happier not to have to sit hip to hip with the two men.

"One more stop, and we'll be on our way out of town," Alan informed Jem.

He sent a message to Mrs. Crimpett, telling her he wouldn't be returning to the London house for some time. She could reduce the staff and close some of the rooms. Thinking of Jem's fondness for Dicky and Mrs. Crimpett's treatment of him, he told her to send the footman along with Badgeman to the country. Then he included a sealed message to Badgeman for him to read on his return, informing him of the developments and instructing him to go to Shrewsbury. The lady would be indignant about paying the postman almost two shillings from the household funds to be informed of something she had no wish to learn.

It was past noon before they were finally on the road from Sheffield, but Alan believed they could make it to their destination by nightfall. Unfortunately the staff there would not be expecting them. There would be no fires laid or dinner warming on the stove. The bedding and rooms would not have been aired for quite some time, and the house would be short-staffed. Unavoidable, and probably for the better. The fewer servants who witnessed his arrival with Jem and Annie in tow, the better.

The road east was not as well maintained as the highway down to London. The phaeton rattled and jolted over ruts and rocks. Alan glanced at Jem's face, noting his clenched jaw and his frown. "Are you doing all right?"

A single nod was his reply and a clear sign that Jem was *not* all right, since he was never so silent.

"Have I told you yet about my Uncle Edward?" Alan asked. "He was as wealthy as Croesus, but a singularly stingy man. During their married life, he never allowed his wife, my Aunt, uh, Abigail to spend a penny of his vast fortune on renovating their dilapidated house. The draperies were moth-eaten, the upholstery worn, and the masonry crumbling around their ears."

Jem cast a sideways glance at him.

“On his deathbed, my uncle the miser insisted that his money be buried with him. Of course my aunt agreed with his dying request, and when the day of the funeral came, she placed a box in the coffin with Uncle Edward's body.

“After the last shovelful of dirt covered his grave and the family was walking away, I had to ask my aunt if she'd actually honored the man's request and buried his money with him.

“'Absolutely,' she replied. 'What kind of woman do you think I am that I would not honor my dying husband's request?'

“'You mean to tell me you put every ha'penny of his fortune into the casket with him?'

“'I certainly did. I wrote him a bill of exchange for the exact amount of our estate, signed it and everything. I'll be waiting for him to present it.'”

Alan waited a beat before glancing from the reins in his hands to Jem's face.

A weak smile curved the man's lips, and abruptly Alan longed to lean over and seize their softness in a hard kiss. But although the country road was empty—nothing but singing birds and thudding hooves disturbing the silence—the Major sat right behind them. He had to content himself with returning Jem's smile while letting his gaze linger on the other man's mouth. His intense look was a promise for later.

“You could work on your timing, but not a bad effort,” Jem teased.

“Come now. It was better than that.”

He shrugged. “I'm not sure. Tell me another.”

"Afraid that's the only one I know. But I can tell you a true story"—Alan paused—"about my family—my brother Jonathan and my parents."

This was the wrong time. Jem didn't need to hear a sad tale when he was so uncomfortable and exhausted, but Alan was suddenly ready to tell him about what had happened to his family. He wanted to share everything with him.

"When Badgeman and I returned from the war, both of us wounded, it was to find that a fever had taken my brother Jonathan and both my parents. The missive informing me of their passing must have gone astray on the way to the front or passed me as I was transported home. I was out of my head with fever, and after that, addicted to laudanum. I could only bear to view my life through a haze. If it weren't for Badgeman, I'd be wandering in that fog still. But he forcibly removed the drug from me and helped me through the worst afterward."

He thought of how sharp and hard and painful the world had been without the soft cushion of the opium to dull his senses. "After that, I did what I had to in regards to my father's estate. There were decisions to make, tenants I was responsible for, land agents and lawyers to confer with. But I haven't yet traveled to either of our country properties, hidden away as I was in London. It's long past time I visited the house near Shrewsbury."

Alan paused and looked at Jem again. "And I have you to thank for forcing me out of my useless, brooding state. Badgeman may have helped me overcome an addiction, but you single-handedly saved my life."

"Single-handed? That's a lot to lay on a fellow." Jem smiled, but a frown furrowed his brow. "I don't think I did much of anything. Just provided some diversion, gave you a laugh or two and a little pleasure."

Heedless of their silent passenger, Alan reached out and grasped Jem's hand. "No. You did much, much more than that. You've given me hope and joy and a reason to live." Remembering Annie, he lowered his voice. "I just wanted you to know that."

Jem's eyes caught the azure sky and reflected it in shimmering pools. Tears? He blinked them away. "Well, Sir Alan, that's a fine declaration. I'm honored. But it reminds me of a wedding proposal my sister once almost received. Would you like to hear about it?"

"Rest your tongue, Jem. You don't have to entertain me." Alan patted Jem's hand before pulling his own away.

"Yes, sir." Jem leaned against him, arm to arm, and it wasn't long before his head nodded sideways to rest on Alan's shoulder too.

Alan glanced behind him. Annie, snuggled between the pair of valises and wrapped in a blanket, was sound asleep. He slipped his arm around Jem's waist and held him steady as the carriage jolted along.

After a stop for a change of horses and a meal at a wayside inn, it was late afternoon by the time they finally reached the county of Shropshire, nearly dusk before they arrived at the house. As Alan had expected, the place was shuttered and dark.

He stopped the carriage, set the brake, and helped Jem then Annie climb down. "I'll have to rouse the groom. You two stay here."

It took him several minutes to locate Brumbridge, whose flushed face and sour smell indicated he was well into a bottle of gin. When the man opened the door of his room at the back of the stable, his eyes widened with shock on seeing his long-absent master. Alan ignored both his surprise and his drunken state—one could hardly expect a man to be completely sober late on a Saturday night—and told him to tend the horses or send the boy to do so.

"Young Wallace from the village has been helping out, sir. He comes in days. I'll put up the team myself, sir. 'Tis good to see you back. Will you be staying on for a time?"

"Yes, I believe so. I'm currently driving a hired team and will need you take this pair to The Green Man. That's the local posting inn if I recall correctly."

"Yes, sir." The man bobbed his head, pulled up his braces, and followed Alan from the stable into the yard. He cast an interested glance at Jem and Annie, but of course didn't say a word as he led the team away.

Well, there was one who'd seen Badgeman's "niece" dressed as a boy. Alan hoped he could keep the others who would witness her transformation to a minimum.

The dark bulk of the Watleigh mansion sprawled like a sleeping giant against the darkening sky. Alan faced the front door with some trepidation. A thousand memories flitted through his mind of a childhood spent rambling the grounds and the countryside beyond, of summer holidays engaged in fierce fighting and competitive riding with his brother, of family outings, parties, foxhunts, and balls. More of their life had centered on this country home rather than the house in London. He would feel the absence of his family far more acutely here.

"Sure you got the right place? You look like you have some doubts." Jem prompted him to move.

Alan lifted and dropped the knocker. "I haven't been back here in several years. Can't say I'm prepared with the key."

It took some hard and repeated rapping with the knocker before he heard a flurry of footsteps and the door was pulled open. Mrs. Hanover, carrying a lamp in her hand, stood in the doorway. She was dressed in a white wrapper over a nightgown, her iron gray curls hidden beneath a puffy nightcap.

"Master Alan! I mean, sir. What a surprise. We weren't expecting you, Sir Alan. Cavanaugh has gone to town. If we'd known you were coming, he'd have been on hand to greet you. Welcome home, sir."

"Good to be home, Mrs. Hanover. We've had a long, hard day's drive. I hope it's not too much trouble for you to put together a tray of cold meat and cheese."

"Right away, sir. But first let me prepare some rooms for you and your"—she looked past him at Jem and Annie—"guests."

"This is my valet, Jem, who was most unfortunately beaten and robbed in the city recently. You may place him in the room adjacent to mine. And this is Mr. Badgeman's niece, Ann, who has also been through a harrowing ordeal. You may prepare one of the guest rooms for her."

He'd given some consideration as to how to explain Annie's odd attire and had decided the best course was to say little. It wasn't a servant's place to question.

"Yes, Master Alan… I mean, Sir Alan." She smiled, and the corners of her eyes crinkled in the friendly way he well remembered. “Hard to get used to your title, sir. 'Twasn't so long ago you were underfoot in the kitchen, begging Cook for sweeties.”

He smiled back. “Those are fond memories for me too, Mrs. Hanover.”

“I'll hurry as fast as may be, sir. There's only one girl on hand right now. The rest are day hires. I'll set her to laying fires in the bedrooms while I prepare your food.” She frowned. “Ach, but you'll want a fire in the parlor too.”

“It's all right. I can manage to start a fire myself. I understand the place is short-staffed, and you were given no notice of my arrival.”

Mrs. Hanover bobbed a curtsy and hurried away, still clucking like an anxious hen whose feathers had been ruffled.

“I like that one,” Jem remarked. “Much nicer than Mrs. C.”

“Yes, she is.” Alan turned to Annie, who stood silently by the door as if ready to bolt through it at the slightest provocation. “You must be hungry, my dear, and chilly. Why don't you come help me light the fire? I'm certain you have experience with that.”

Alan reached out his hand, held it steady, and waited. After a long hesitation, the Major reached out and took it. Progress made. He exchanged a quick glance with Jem over the top of her head.

Together they walked into the parlor off the main hall. Alan urged Jem to sit, and the exhausted lad dropped without protest onto the hard striped sofa.

What would Mother say? The brief thought flitted through Alan's mind, but he was past caring about what his dead mother, Mrs. Hanover, or anyone else thought about the oddity of a servant sitting while the master of the house laid the fire.

Luckily kindling waited on the grate, while several logs were piled nearby on the hearth. How long ago had some servant prepared the fireplace for the return of a family which would never come home? Alan drew flint from the holder on the mantel, but handed it to Annie. "Show me how it's done."

She nodded and crouched on the hearth to strike sparks from the flint, then fanned the flame with the bellows hanging nearby. Alan stayed back, letting her work, guessing that doing something constructive would allay some of her fears at being in yet another new place.

He went to the sideboard and poured a glass of brandy for Jem, crouched by his side, and offered it. "Here. This will drive the chill away."

One eye opened, and Jem reached out to take the glass. "You spoil me, sir. I'm not certain who's the master an' who's the servant any longer."

Instinctively Alan opened his mouth to reprimand such insolence, but Jem's face was so pale, he didn't have the heart to scold him. "Better keep such thoughts to yourself in front of Mrs. Hanover," he said mildly. No use in pretending he still thought of Jem as an underling, a lesser man. Their bond was now too strong to deny and too deep for him to consider Jem as anything less than a partner, no matter what their roles might be in society's eyes.

Jem sipped the brandy, then rested the glass on his leg and watched Ann work with the fire. Warmth was already taking the damp chill from the room and eradicating the slight mustiness in the parlor. "You're good with the little girl, making her feel at ease. I think she's stronger than she looks, and she'll overcome what's been done to her."

Alan nodded agreement. “Fresh air and exercise will go a long way toward healing her spirit. I should've remembered that for myself when I was hiding in London this past winter.”

“'Twas a hard time for you,” Jem said. “At any rate, you're here now.”

Alan gazed around the familiar room, his mother's taste in decorating contrasting with his father's insistence on displaying some ugly family heirlooms, such as the painting of Commodore Avery Watleigh over the fireplace. The firelight glowed on Ann Cutler's sober face and cast shadows on Jem's. Alan felt a strong swell of affection for the vulnerable pair, the unexpected daughter and lover which he'd never have imagined he would have. This was his boyhood home, rife with memories, but it was also a place for new beginnings and a new sort of family.

Chapter Eighteen

The day was hot, but Annie wouldn't complain as she sat on an upturned bucket out in the sun, watching Jem learn to ride. The horse walked then trotted in endless circles in the pasture near the house. Of course Annie wouldn't complain. Fear still held her. Now her fear was she'd be banished from their presence.

Usually she followed Jem everywhere. And if she couldn't find him, she'd follow Alan.

They allowed her to be in their company all day after Mrs. Hanover told Alan that the girl trembled when they were out of sight. Either Jem or Alan would sit in a chair in her room as she fell asleep at night. Jem wondered if they'd still be doing that when she was a grown woman. At least Annie slept through the night and didn't come looking for them if she did wake up.

Both of them in the master's bed would be a difficult thing to explain to the girl.

Jem had stopped paying attention, and the horse did something to dislodge him. When Jem landed on his rear, he longed to curse, but he'd learned to curb his saltier language in Annie's presence. He didn't even feel he could complain. The quiet example of Miss Cutler—no, they called her Badgeman now—made him feel like a whiny child instead of a grown man.

The second time he fell off, he stood and rubbed his rear with an exaggerated groan anyway, because maybe, just maybe, that had been a little giggle from the bucket when he'd hit the ground this time. Worth the indignity.

He showed a rolling limp for her benefit as he walked back to the horse.

"It balked," Jem said to Alan, who'd come over to give him a leg up. Purely unnecessary, but Jem wasn't complaining about the chance to be near him and maybe even touch him.

"Yes, he did," Alan said unperturbed. He didn't try to defend the big hairy beast or offer to kiss the aching parts of Jem's anatomy. "Hold on with your thighs," he added for the thousandth time. He cupped his hands so Jem could mount, and that impersonal too-brief contact—his hand on Jem's boot, Jem's hand on his shoulder—made Jem long to twist around and kiss him instead of letting him push him onto the horse.

After a few minutes of Jem's least favorite exercise so far—sitting on a horse as it trotted in circles—Alan called, "Good. You're learning to sit up straight and move with the animal." That bit of praise helped. Alan had adjusted his usual manner as well nowadays. No roaring Lord High-and-Mighty or barking captain. Not with Annie nearby.

Alan, who held the lead rope, soon drew the horse to stop. "And now we'll put a saddle on him and you'll try again, Jem. The groom who taught me claimed riding bareback first helped you understand the horse better."

Jem held back his opinion of the likely canine parentage of that groom. He slid off the horse's back and muttered, "Sounds like rubbish to me."

It was true that with saddle and stirrups, riding seemed a much easier thing. He could swing up and onto the animal alone using a stirrup, no trouble. When Jem could hold the reins and control the horse on his own, suddenly the world was a much more interesting place. He could go anywhere now, and fast. True, the ground was still too far away below, but he was getting used to that. Speed and the thrill of controlling the huge animal under him meant he at long last understood the thrill of riding.

"Annie's turn," Alan said. This hadn't been part of the plan, but she clearly longed to ride. She'd touched the horses without any hesitation, watching them instead of Alan or Jem. And Jem noticed her moving while he rode, as if she was trying to copy the motion he felt.

Still on horseback, Jem turned his mount to watch Alan, knowing the man wanted to reach out and touch Annie, to help her onto the placid horse he had ordered for her lesson.

Sure enough. "May I help?" Alan gave up on waiting for her to speak.

Jem was surprised when Annie shook her head. She silently climbed onto the horse, using a block. She sprawled over the animal as she clambered onto its blanket-covered back, but she showed no fear, and once perched on the broad back, she sat with perfect form. Even Jem, the sack of grain on a horse's back, could recognize that. He guessed she must have ridden before, probably in Portugal, and hadn't bothered to inform Alan of the fact. She still rarely spoke unless spoken to.

Alan laughed and unhooked the lead line. "Never mind the lesson," he said and pulled her off the horse. She didn't protest but she did fold her arms and push out her lower lip. A good sign of anger, Jem thought.

"We're not done riding," Alan told her. He reached for the saddle that rested on a post.

After Alan put the saddle over the blanket on Annie's horse and adjusted her stirrups, he allowed her to remount. The three of them rode through the meadow down to the stand of trees where they could be in shade. Annie had no interest in a walk or even a trot. She directed her horse to canter along the edge of the meadow.

"Damn," Alan said as he watched her take off across the field.

Jem twisted in his saddle. Sir Alan frowned, his mouth pressed tight.

"What's the trouble?" Jem asked. "The day is blooming perfect. And look at us; we have a moment without the mouse. Better still, see her charging across the field with a smile on her face, by all that's holy."

"That's the very problem. I should have taught her to ride with a sidesaddle. She'll have to learn to adjust."

Jem nearly fell off his horse again, laughing. "Adjust? I should say so. Riding 'tis the least of her worries. First she needs to learn to say a word without her voice trembling."

"She'll never have a normal life," Alan said, his voice and body tight. "Not just Schivvers. Being here. With me. Us. It's not normal."

That again? Jem nudged his horse in the direction of an interesting narrow path through the trees. Better to ride off ahead than scare the horses—which he would when he shouted at the daft Alan to remind him she wouldn't even be alive if it weren't for Alan's concern.

God, he'd have given anything to have had a man like Alan Watleigh in his life when he was a child. Not just for his ability to provide shelter, food, and clothes. The man's patience was a marvel and a blessing for any child. Who'd have known he could be so calm?

Jem sucked in a long breath and decided he could keep his temper too. He'd skip reading Alan a lecture and attempt a normal conversation. "True enough that the chit's got her fits and starts. But other things too have formed her into something unusual. Look at the way she loves to be out of doors. Even if Schivvers hadn't snagged her, she would have had a strange life for a female. Easy to see she's ridden a horse in this manner before. And I'd say all those years with her mum and dad turned her into someone who hates four walls."

Alan smiled as he saw her cantering back across the field. "And today she's shown herself to be a centaur."

And just like that, his worry seemed to ease away. He still rode straight with shoulders back, but the stiffness seemed gone from his form and mouth.

Even better, when they announced it was time to return to the house, the girl acted like a child. A stubborn, normal child with a temper.

They'd gone exploring down the path into the woods. For a time, they'd dismounted and rested by a stream. Annie had been dropping sticks into it, watching them float away, carried by the swift current.

When Alan made the announcement, she paused and shook her head. Instead of going to her horse, she very deliberately bent to pick up another stick. Alan and Jem got on their horses. Annie dropped the stick into the water. Then went in search of another stick.

"We're going," Alan repeated.

She paused and shook her head, again.

"Hark this, sir," Jem said in a low voice. "She's disobeying us. 'Tis a miracle."

Alan flashed him a fast grin and turned his horse back in the direction of the house.

"You're leaving? Going?" she called after, sounding panicked.

"Back home. It's time," said Alan. "My leg hurts."

"Oh." She gave a little cry. "I'm so sorry. I'm sorry. Oh, I'm sorry. Don't leave me." She rushed to her horse, which had been tied to a small tree.

There was a stump she could have used as a block to remount, but with a sigh, Alan slid from his horse. He handed Jem the reins and walked over to where she stood. Jem couldn't hear what they talked about, but she soon calmed. Alan helped her back into the saddle—he actually picked her up, and she didn't appear to mind his hands on her waist.

"There now," he called back to her as he strode to where Jem waited. "I would never abandon you. Jem would kill me."

"I would indeed," Jem said in a hearty voice.

Alan rolled his eyes at Jem and grimaced only a bit as he swung back onto the saddle.

~

Later that day, Jem walked into the library, a dark room mostly because the damask curtains were kept drawn to protect the expensive carpet and books from direct sunlight. He found Alan pulled up to his desk, flipping through some account books, frowning down at the neat figures entered by the steward. Annie lay flat on her stomach, propped on her elbows, reading a book.

Jem knew better than to bother Alan when he wore that fierce expression of concentration, so he asked, "What's that you're looking at, Annie?"

"A history of ancient Greece," she said. "But I do hope to go outside soon."

Jem beamed at her. Not only had she offered an unsolicited opinion, that sounded almost like a whine. Excellent progress.

"Annie's a good reader," Alan said. Apparently the numbers were failing to hold his attention, for he suddenly pushed back his chair and came at Jem. For a moment Jem wondered if by some miracle the man would hug and kiss him right there. Instead he leaned close and, his breath warm on Jem's ear, he whispered. "I have a wonderful idea. Ask Annie to teach you to read. It will make her feel competent."

Jem motioned for him to go out to the hall. Annie followed but stopped in the doorway to watch. The distance she'd allowed them to go away from her was growing. That was some way to gain some privacy.

Jem turned his back and in a low voice muttered, "And I'll feel like a great addle-pated fool, being taught by a slip of a girl."

Alan paid no attention to the weak protest. He put a hand on Jem's shoulder. "She'll have to sit close to you, and she won't feel threatened. And she'll feel important helping you. She likes that."

"Oh, bugger," grumbled Jem. "I'll give it a go." He'd much rather have Sir Alan teach him.

Alan was right. The girl did like the idea of being able to do something a grown-up man couldn't manage—and she did have to sit close to him. She was too polite to mock Jem too, a nice change from Noah, who'd attempted to teach him some letters.

❧

The next day, Alan left to speak to the vicar about repairs to the church's bell tower. It rained, and Jem talked Annie out of taking a walk in the downpour. He had his second reading lesson and sat on the sofa with Annie next to him. She was so close, her leg pressed to his, but she didn't seem to mind at all. Jem wanted to point it out so she could see how far she'd come, but instead he concentrated on the lesson, deciding if she was going to be so dedicated to the effort, he should put in some work too.

A book lay open in her lap. She read aloud in a low, hesitant voice. Jem thought he could recognize some of the words she ran her finger over.

A large man appeared in the doorway. Jem noticed only because Annie had stopped reading and looked up. No visitors had been announced, and this ragged figure looked more like a beggar than a respectable caller. It took Jem a moment to recognize the man, but even as he rose to his feet to greet Badgeman, Annie was off the sofa, the book was on the floor, and she was running across the room. Toward the man, not away.

"Sergeant," she cried. Amazing that she knew the man when Jem had trouble, but perhaps he'd worn that poor excuse for a beard in Spain.

The badger went down on one knee, his arms open. She pelted into him and wrapped her arms around him.

The mistake he made was returning her embrace. Suddenly she was a fighting animal, struggling to break free.

He let go at once, and she burst into gusty tears. "I'm sorry," she whispered and ran to the door, red with mortification. But Jem stood there, blocking her way.

"Here now, Major, no need to run away," he said cheerily. When he saw her anguish, he quickly added, "You can go if you want, but I wanna say congratulations on that. On what you just did."

Damn, he hoped he was doing the right thing. She looked up at him, and the tears now streamed down her face. "What do you mean?" she asked, sounding like an almost-normal, exasperated girl.

"I don't wanna remind you of the bad days, Annie. Really, I don't. I know how you feel. I have nightmares of Schivvers's workroom meself. But think what would have happened a week ago if someone had hugged you and it made you unhappy."

She wiped her eyes with the back of her hand. She didn't answer, but he knew she listened. They had a bond, both having suffered at the surgeon's hands. Although Annie's mental torture had lasted for months and Jem's for mere hours, the scare had been enough to scar him for life. If he'd been a different sort of man. As it was, Jem had learned young to be a duck—to let everything roll of his back like water. There was no black mood or terror a joke couldn't fix.

He continued. "You'd have flinched, but you would have held yourself still and put up with a touch you hated. Now you've learned to fight when you feel scared. Mr. Badgeman, Sergeant Badgeman, I mean, is cheering for you. I know he is. Hollering and shouting huzzah. I promise you. After all, he is a fighting man. No, don't look daggers at me, girl. I'm not making a jest of it. Well done, Major!"

Alan must have mentioned something of the girl's problems in his correspondence with the badger, because instead of directing a look at him that might have incinerated him, Badgeman only nodded at Jem and said, "Of course, Major. I'm that glad to see you again, I forgot I should keep my hands to myself. Won't happen again, I promise."

She fiercely wiped at her eyes again and, still standing near Jem, turned to face the badger. "But I don't want to be scared of you, Sergeant."

"You're not—not truly scared. See, you're still here in the room. That other part will go away later," Badgeman said. He sounded stern yet kindly, like a sergeant addressing a fresh recruit soon before battle, giving a speech he'd given a thousand times before. "You know when you're ailing, getting better 'tis slow. And you still ache even if the illness is gone. The aches'll go in time too. Same thing."

She smiled, and it almost looked like a real expression.

Who'd have guessed the big lout would be so good at soothing the skittish girl? Jem wished Alan had been there to hear his ex-sergeant. He flashed a sign of approval at the man, who simply raised his one mobile brow.

Badgeman reached for his bag and swung it up onto his shoulder. He spoke to Annie again, still casual as can be, but with that note of authority. "It's like riding, Major. Has Captain Watleigh let you go on horseback yet? He wrote he planned to."

She nodded. Jem wondered about the letters Alan had written to his ex-batman. He felt a twinge of jealousy only because he'd love to be able to read those words, straight from Alan's hand.

Badgeman went on. "He must have taught you not to rush your fences."

She nodded again, then added, "But I'm not jumping yet. Alan says soon."

Drat, another mistake they'd made. Badgeman flashed a look at Jem; no anger, yet clearly showing a touch of surprise to hear the girl's inappropriate use of a first name.

All he said, however, was, "Exactly. Everything in its time. Let me stash my kit, and we'll have tea, and you'll tell me about riding. Good to see you, Major, Mr. Jem." *Mr.* Jem? What had Alan written to him?

After he left the room, Annie asked Jem, "His face looked different. Did Mr. Schivvers get him like he did you?"

Of course she hadn't seen him after Bajadoz. Jem shook his head. "No, he got the marks in the war."

She went back to the couch and picked up the book. "I miss my mum and dad. But I won't miss that part. Not at all." She sat with him on the couch but kept looking toward the door. And when the badger reappeared, clean and shaved, she stood up again at once.

"Why don't you give Mr. Badgeman a tour, Annie?" Jem suggested. "I'm sure he's mad to see the place."

For the first time, Badgeman gave him a direct look and a real smile. "That's a right fine idea, Mr. Jem. Come on, Major. Forward march." They disappeared down the hall, the big shambling bear of a man and the young girl.

She turned into Badgeman's shadow.

Jem didn't expect to miss having the girl follow him, but now he had to go and find her if he wanted her company, and he discovered he often did. Badgeman looked almost relieved when

Jem took her away for a reading lesson—but equally relieved when he brought her back.

She would never be boisterous, but her piping voice could almost sound normal, and she would follow the badger and ask questions.

Jem and Alan were crossing the hall one morning when they heard Badgeman say in his slow, amused voice, "Major, I told you I got to add these figures. That means you need to be quiet two seconds in a row."

"Hallelujah," Jem said in a low voice. "If she's driven *him* to saying that, our Major musta been gabbling enough, making up for all those months of staying mute."

Alan gave him a beaming smile. That made him want to crow with joy too. "Do you know the expression 'my cup runneth over'?" Alan asked.

Sure he did, but Jem said, "A waste of good beer?"

"It's from the Bible. It means I have more than enough for my needs. It can be an expression of extreme happiness." *My happiness*, he didn't say, but it was there in his face.

"More than enough? Naw. There's no such thing as too much happiness."

"You're right, of course."

"I always am. Ain't you used to that by now?"

Alan only laughed. Just the way Jem hoped he would.

Chapter Nineteen

Jem rolled over in bed and stretched out a beseeching hand. "I need you, Sir Alan. Don't deny me."

The suggestive tone coupled with that half-lidded, sleepy-eyed look and bed-tousled hair—not to mention the fact that the boy was stark naked—drew Alan to him like a moth to flame. And oh, what a lovely burn it was.

He stood, arms folded, beside the bed, just out of reach of those grasping hands. "I have obligations. I can't simply loll around in bed with you all day. The servants would notice and start to talk."

"Ach, the servants. A bloody busybody lot if ever there was one. Wish they'd all disappear and leave us in peace."

"And who would cook the meals you're so fond of and keep you in clean clothing? Who'd make your bed and draw your baths? Are you prepared to take over those tasks for yourself?"

Jem stretched and yawned, raising his arms above his head, which lifted the tight little buds of his nipples and sent a wave of heat rushing through Alan. "Mmm. I'm too accustomed to sittin' in the lap of luxury now. Couldn't really do without the servants."

"Me either. Especially my valet."

Alan surrendered, as he'd known he would, and lay down beside Jem on the bed. He slid a hand across the smoothly muscled chest and stomach, curved it around his waist, and drew the man close before plucking at his mouth with little nibbling kisses. The tender kisses quickly grew fierier, as they always did, and soon he was plundering Jem's mouth and thrusting his straining cock against his hip. The heat and friction felt so good, they made him want more—much more.

Jem's fingers threaded through his hair, cradling Alan's head and pulling him even closer. Their mouths clashed together in a demanding duel until at last Jem pulled away with a gasp. "La, sir, you can kiss. Enough to steal a man's breath."

Alan loved the compliment. He'd never imagined simply kissing could be such a pleasure, but he'd grown to crave it and wanted to do it every time he so much as glimpsed Jem across a room. Now he nuzzled Jem's morning-stubbled jaw and nipped his neck, making the man squirm.

Pulling back, Alan regarded him. "How do you feel about taking a ride later today? There are some tenants I should check on. Might as well turn the duty into an outing."

Jem caressed the side of his face, then let his hand trail down Alan's neck and chest in a slow glide. "I like you in the country like this. You're much more at ease. As for a cross-country ride, me bum's just beggin' for more torture, especially after my ridin' lesson the other day."

"You'll only get better the more you try. At least you don't sit in the saddle like a sack of meal any longer." He smacked Jem's hip. "Come with me. You'll enjoy it."

"Ah, sir, I can't refuse the offer of a ride with you. The only thing I'd like more is a ride *on* you, with me holding the reins this time." He paused and quirked a brow at Alan. "Is that something you'd ever consider, Lord Bumbuggerer?"

Alan hadn't believed anything Jem could say would shock him any longer, he'd grown so used to the lad's irreverent comments. But the teasing title Jem bestowed on him, coupled with the suggestion he might like to be the one doing the driving for a change, stole Alan's capability for speech for a moment.

Jem waited, watching him with those dancing, devilish blue eyes. "Tell me you've never thought about being buggered, never wanted to surrender control and find out what that's like."

When he could breathe again, Alan replied, "I honestly never considered it." Which wasn't strictly true. In the deepest recesses of his imagination, the parts he'd barely acknowledged to himself, he had wondered what it would be like to play the female role in a coupling. What different kind of pleasure was to be gained that way?

"You should," Jem replied. "You might like it. I'd be more than willing to help you find out."

Alan noted his tone, amused and teasing, yet serious underneath. This was something Jem wanted, something he was requesting for himself. Until now their relationship had been weighted in Alan's favor, with Jem working for his pleasure and deferring to his decisions—more or less. Now he was letting Alan know he would enjoy trying a different role in their relationship. After everything Jem had done for him, the joy he had brought into his life, the least Alan could do was agree and submit.

Submit. The word sent a surprising shiver of excitement through him. His cock, which had flagged somewhat during this exchange, hardened once more. As he'd learned to do on the battlefield, Alan made an instant decision.

"Very well. No time like the present. What shall I do?"

Both of Jem's brows shot up, and his eyes widened. "Good gracious. You needn't sound like I'm marching you to the gallows.

This will be a pleasure for both of us. But I hardly expected you to decide in a moment. 'Twas merely something to think about."

"I've thought. I'm ready. Tell me what you want, and I'll do it." To prove his commitment, Alan reached out and took Jem's cock in hand. Solid, rigid, the blood pulsing beneath the smooth, warm skin. He supposed the way to begin was to suck Jem's cock for a bit. Well, that was something he liked to do, an easy way to start.

Alan slid down in the bed and fondled Jem's balls in one hand while taking his penis in a firm grip. He drew the tip into his mouth. A swirl of the tongue around the shaft, and then he sucked it deep. Jem's quiet gasp and thrusting hips were his reward.

This is all for you. Your pleasure, what you desire. The thought sent a glow of warmth through him and another surge of lust to his cock. Surprising how the idea of giving pleasure could cause great pleasure.

Alan labored lovingly on bringing Jem to the brink of orgasm, sucking until he tasted musky juices on his tongue and massaging with even strokes until Jem thrust rhythmically into his hand.

"Lord, sir, I'm going to spend if you keep that up."

Releasing Jem's erection, he crawled up beside him, taking a moment to retrieve the bottle of oil from the bedside table. "Shall I anoint you with this?"

"Give me a second. One touch and I may spill." Jem smiled. "Kiss me first."

Alan obliged, slipping his tongue between soft lips and rubbing it sinuously against Jem's tongue. After he'd kissed him breathless, he pulled away and moved his lips all over Jem's face—kissing his forehead, his eyelids, his cheeks and jaw, and then his neck. He kissed across the hard plane of his chest and nibbled on the tight buds of his nipples, first one then the other. The salty taste of his lover's warm skin, the sight of his face tense with pleasure, and the sound of Jem's quiet groans and sighs made a heady aphrodisiac for Alan. His pulse pounded, and his cock ached like his wounded leg on a rainy day. But he ignored his desire to bury himself balls-deep in Jem's tight bum. This was Jem's turn, and he would make sure it was everything his lover wanted it to be.

Alan uncapped the bottle of oil and poured a little in his hand before setting the bottle on the table. He warmed the oil between his palms, then wrapped his hand once more around Jem's shaft and massaged it from base to tip and back again several times. The thick length glistened with oil and shone a dull red, it was so suffused with blood. Jem's cock was beautiful.

He glanced up to see his lover's avid gaze fixed on Alan's fist around his cock. Jem licked his lips and swallowed. They remained parted and moist, inviting more kisses—or an eager cock thrust between them.

“Now, my lad, I've got you ready. Will you do the same for me?” Alan made his voice a throaty whisper as he moved up to lie beside Jem. His buttocks clenched in anticipation of Jem's entry. Nervous excitement pulsed through him, and he realized he was looking forward to this.

What had begun as an attempt to please Jem seemed likely to open doors to all sorts of new pleasure for himself as well. And while God might be looking down on him with disfavor for engaging in the act of sodomy, Alan thanked Him nevertheless for bringing Jem into his life. His world had been turned upside down over the past few months, and surprisingly, for a man who'd always insisted on control, he liked it that way.

Jem stared at his own cock jutting erect and proud from his tawny tangle of pubic hair. It was shining from the oil Alan had massaged it with, slick and ready to push into Alan's tight rear. Jem wanted that with all his heart, but he was a bit nervous too. There hadn't been many occasions in his life when he'd had the opportunity to be the man in control, so to speak. Because of the nature of most of the men who came trolling for street boys like him, he'd been more apt to receive a good rogering than give one.

For that matter, much of his trade had been limited to hand or mouth work. Somehow those poor benighted gents who craved a man's touch but denied their own natures had been able to justify a tug or a suck, but actual sodomy was a step too far for many of them.

And so, Jem's experience at fucking rather than being fucked was limited.

He wanted to do this right. Make sure Alan enjoyed it and not lose control and release too soon. But the way he felt right now, he was about ready to fly out of his skin with excitement. He wanted to mount the other man, give him the banging of his life and howl to the rafters while he did it. One of these days they must ride somewhere far out into the country, where no one could hear them, and do just that.

For now, Jem would settle for a quieter coupling. He reached out to push a lock of Alan's dark hair back from his forehead, then leaned to kiss him softly.

"Are you ready for this? I promise to go slow." He trailed a hand down Alan's chest, brushing his fingers through the smattering of crisp hair that covered hard muscles. For a moment he let his palm rest flat, feeling the fast beating of the other man's heart. It's beating for me, the whimsical thought came to him, and he smiled.

"Best you lie on your stomach, sir," he suggested. "Face-to-face is more loverly like, but 'tis easier from behind."

"Jem."

"Yes, sir?"

"I think you can stop calling me sir when we're alone like this."

"Yes, s—Alan. I'll make a note o' that."

Alan rolled onto his stomach, his face in profile against the white pillow. For a moment, Jem simply admired him. He was beautiful like this. The hard planes and angles of his face and body were relaxed—although the muscles in his rear flexed. The warm yellow glow of the light sneaking between drawn curtains limned his every curve in gold. Appeared it was going to be a fine, sunny day out, but for now they'd let the night linger in their room a little longer. No one would come to disturb them. The servants had strict instructions not to rouse Alan in the mornings or even come near his room until after he'd risen and come downstairs. This gave Jem time to return at leisure to his own chamber every morning.

It was a necessary fiction which sometimes grated. One would think a man as rich and powerful as Sir Alan could do as he liked in the privacy of his own home, but it seemed to Jem the nobility were nearly as shackled as the prisoners in Newgate.

But now, right now in the bar of early morning sunlight that splashed across the bed, he and Alan were free to do as they pleased. And what pleased Jem was to reach out and stroke both hands the length of Alan's body, from those strong, broad shoulders, down his long back, to his narrow waist and hips. The taut buttocks rippled again, quivering from the tension in the man.

Jem slapped his bum lightly. “Ease up. Squeezing tight will do neither of us any good.”

He stretched full length on top of Alan, groin to buttocks, belly and chest to back, and pressed kisses to his shoulder. “Relax yourself. Trust me.”

“I do.” The reply was muffled, as Alan's mouth was half-buried in the pillow. He glanced at Jem over his shoulder. “I'm merely…aroused.”

Jem rocked his hips, gliding the throbbing length of his cock in the groove between those glorious buttocks. It felt heavenly. “That's good,” he murmured.

He sat up and straddled Alan's hips, then massaged his shoulders and back. The tense muscles relaxed beneath his kneading hands. Jem moved lower, between Alan's legs, which he pushed apart. Time to concentrate on his backside. He stroked his hands lightly down the sides of Alan's hips and up the slope of his buttocks.

The firm cheeks filled his hands nicely as he squeezed and massaged, moving ever closer to his goal. Alan moaned and shifted when, at last, Jem slid the edge of his thumb whisper-light down the crack between. He reached for Alan's balls, tickled them with his fingertips until the man squirmed, then rolled the soft sac in his hand. Alan lifted his bottom, a sign of offering that made Jem's cock throb even harder. He was desperate to drive himself balls-deep between those luscious cheeks.

Jem reached for the oil on the bedside table and poured a little in his hand. Once more he slid his fingers between Alan's tensed buttocks, but deeper this time. He found the tight aperture there and rimmed it with one finger, a gentle, teasing demand for entry. The ring of muscle clenched then released, and he dipped his finger inside.

Alan made a quiet sound in his throat and lifted his hips again. Jem added a second well-oiled finger, stretching the tiny opening while he took hold of his cock and stroked it. When he could move two fingers freely, he added a third, slathering oil in and out of the ring of muscle.

Alan tilted even higher, and Jem guided his cock to his entrance. The tip breached the portal, and he pushed against the initial resistance, which seemed impossibly tight at first. Jem sucked in a breath and drove harder, his excitement mounting at the sensation. Alan's hot channel surrounded him, and instead of rejecting his cock, it now seemed to be pulling it in deeper. With a groan, Jem thrust and filled the other man deeply.

"Good Christ, sir," he muttered, forgetting he was to call his lover by name now. Sir he'd been for so long, and sir he probably always would be to Jem.

His belly rubbed against Alan's lower back as he rocked against him. The nape of Alan's neck and the softly curling hair there filled Jem's vision. He wanted to bite that vulnerable curve of flesh and not let go while he ravaged the other man with hard thrusts of his cock. The animalistic urge took him by surprise.

He pulled out and thrust again, still slowly and carefully. "Is this all right?"

Alan nodded, his dark head moving against the pillow. "More," he grunted. "Harder."

"You like it, then?" Jem was pleased.

"Burns," was the terse reply. "It's good."

Smiling, Jem set a faster pace. His cock receded from and filled the tight channel over and over—a little less carefully now, a little faster and deeper. He knew when he hit Alan's sweet spot inside, because the man grunted and jerked. Ah yes, right there.

Jem drove deeply, reveling in the heat and pressure surrounding his cock and in the hard body beneath him. He gripped Alan's shoulder with one hand and his hip with the other, and fucked him hard. It was a different feeling up here, on top, and Jem enjoyed the sense of mastery. And because he was Jem, his pleasure came out in words.

"Like it rough, do you? Tell me."

"Yes." Alan gasped as he thrust back onto Jem's impaling cock. "I like it."

Jem pummeled him with rapid jerks of his hips. "More. Tell me how it feels to be fucked."

"Good."

The man was absolutely no use at dirty talk. Jem sighed and gave up. This was a lesson they could work on another time. Warmth unrelated to his rising climax rushed through him at the thought of all the future times they would have together. Alan had assured him of a home for the rest of his life. They would be a pair, as devoted to each other as any married couple. Jem had a home at last with an odd, makeshift family that included Annie and a crusty old badger.

Somehow the warmth of that knowledge mingled with the baser pleasures of the body and became a powerful force. Waves of bliss rolled through Jem, caught hold of his cock and brought it along for the ride. He pushed deep one last time, burying himself inside Alan, and he spent and spent.

He shuddered and shook against the big, strong body beneath him. When he finally opened his eyes and came back to himself, Jem blinked and focused on the back of Alan's neck again. He was draped over the other man like a blanket, fused to him by sweat, and happy to be melted together that way. Alan's back rose and fell with his breathing, giving Jem a gentle ride.

Reluctantly Jem disengaged from the other man and rolled to his side. "Let me finish you off too." He urged Alan onto his back and scooted down to take his massively swollen cock into his mouth.

In less than two minutes, Alan was groaning and releasing. Ripples pulsing through his penis. Jem swallowed, released the man's cock from his mouth, and moved up to lie facing him again.

"All better?" he asked with a grin.

"Perfect." Alan paused, then added, "It was good. All of it."

"Not so bad being fucked, is it?"

"Not bad at all." And if ingrained guilt still lingered in Alan, Jem didn't see it on his face or hear it in his voice.

They lay in contented silence for some time, while the golden bar of light from the window moved an inch across the bed.

At last, Alan sighed and sat up. "I suppose I must start my day. Too much to be done to lie abed."

"Me too," Jem agreed. "Cravats to fold. Boots to polish. A valet's work is never done. Besides, I promised Miss Annie I'd teach her to cast dice, and then there's our ride to look forward to later this afternoon."

"Dice? Do you really think that's appropriate? Do you think Badgeman will approve?" Alan slipped on his linens and stockings and picked up his breeches from the chair where Jem had laid them out the night before.

"The girl must have a bit of fun along with her lessons, and what old Badge don't know won't hurt him." Jem wrapped his arms around his knees and watched Alan dress.

Alan shook his head as he fastened his breeches. "Incorrigible, Jem. What am I to do with you?"

"Keep me right close by your side so you can keep an eye on me, I reckon."

The big man moved to the side of the bed, his torso gloriously naked and his lower half encased in tight riding breeches.

He reached a hand out and touched the side of Jem's face. "That I can do. That I'll be happy to do."

Again that unaccountable swell of warmth flooded through Jem, bubbling up like a pot ready to boil over and filling him completely. Too much emotion, too powerful for him to cope with. His eyes itched, and he blinked away the prickling as he cleared his throat.

"Have I ever told you about the young lady from Southwark who owned a goose that could lay golden eggs?"

Alan grinned. His habitually grim expression, caused by frown lines that would never completely fade, lighted like the sun breaking through an overcast sky. “Really? That's a remarkable thing. Do tell me all about it.”

“That I will, sir.” Jem stopped the happy smile that threatened to curve his lips and maintained an impassive, stony expression as he began his tale. “You see, sir, it all started with a simple wish, as these things so often do…”

The End

Other Titles by Bonnie Dee & Summer Devon

Seducing Stephen

The Nobleman and the Spy

House of Mirrors

The Psychic and the Sleuth

The Gentleman's Keeper

Serious Play

Fugitive Heart

About the authors

Bonnie Dee

Whether you're a fan of contemporary, paranormal or historical romance, you'll find something to enjoy among my books. My style is down to earth and my characters feel like well-known friends by the time you've finished reading. I'm interested in flawed, often damaged, people who find the fulfillment they seek in one another. For more information on my back list go to http://bonniedee.com

Summer Devon

Summer Devon is the alter ego of Kate Rothwell. Kate invented Summer's name in the middle of a nasty blizzard At the time she was talking to her sister, who longed to visit some friends in Devon, England—so the name Summer Devon is all about desire. Kate/Summer lives in Connecticut, USA, and also writes books, usually gaslight historicals, as Kate. For more information about Summer and Kate go to

http://katerothwell.com http://summerdevon.com. Summer can also be found at https://www.facebook.com/S.DevonAuthor

If you enjoyed *The Gentleman and the Rogue*, you might also like *The Psychic and the Sleuth*, available at Samhain Publishing and other booksellers.

Trusting a psychic flash might solve a mystery…and lead to love.

Inspector Robert Court should have felt a sense of justice when a rag-and-bones man went to the gallows for murdering his cousin. Yet something has never felt right about the investigation. Robert's relentless quest for the truth has annoyed his superintendent, landing him lowly assignments such as foiling a false medium who's fleecing the wives of the elite.

Oliver Marsh plays the confidence game of spiritualism, though his flashes of insight often offer his clients some comfort. Despite the presence of an attractive, if sneering, non-believer at a séance, he carries on—and experiences a horrifying psychic episode in which he experiences a murder as the victim.

There's only one way for Court to learn if the young, dangerously attractive Marsh is his cousin's killer or a real psychic: spend as much time with him as possible. Despite his resolve to focus on his job, Marsh somehow manages to weave a seductive spell around the inspector's straight-laced heart.

Gradually, undeniable attraction overcomes caution. The two men are on the case, and on each other, as they race to stop a murderer before he kills again.

Excerpt:

London, 1892

"I'm getting a name. I believe it starts with a W." The young man in the checked jacket spoke in the sepulchral tone one expected from a Spiritualistic medium. Lush, dark lashes fluttered against his cheeks, and full lips parted as his eyebrows drew together in a frown.

He might sound the part, but his appearance was wrong, Court decided. His clothes, for one thing. Most mediums he'd observed wore dark, dignified clothing, as if to lend gravity to their incredible claims. Oliver Marsh's scarlet waistcoat and checked jacket were too flashy by far for the role he was playing. Made him appear more like a fly-by-night salesman than a portal to the other world.

"Wilma? No. Winifred." Marsh's head cocked as though hearing an unseen voice whisper the name in his ear.

Court forced his eyes not to roll at the act. The young lady beside him gasped, and her limp, clammy hand gripped his tighter. "I have an aunt named Winifred. She died two years ago."

The spiritualist inclined his head. "I'm getting the sense of her presence, a sense of great love and peace. She's content on the other side, but she has a message she needs to deliver."

Miss Abigail Fontaine leaned forward, eyes wide. "What does she want to tell me?"

Mr. Marsh's frown deepened, and he moved his head slowly from side to side as though searching for a sound that came in intermittent bursts. "She says…" A long pause. "Don't. There is something you are about to do, a big decision. She's warning you against making the wrong choice."

The redhead gasped again, and her grip on Court's hand became almost painful. "Rodney? Aunt Winifred doesn't approve of my fiancé, Mr. Pepperidge? But that's impossible. Why not? Ask her why not?"

Court's jaw tightened as he watched the medium play the young woman like an angler taking his time reeling in a fish. He didn't know how Marsh had secured the details of the Fontaine woman's engagement or why he would interfere. Perhaps her family or the Pepperidges didn't approve the match and had paid Marsh to encourage Miss Fontaine to end it. Any scenario was feasible except for the possibility that Miss Fontaine's aunt was actually transmitting a message from beyond the grave.

It was Court's job to expose Marsh as a charlatan to stop him from taking money from gullible people. Posing as a believer, he'd observe the man until he was able to prove he'd fleeced a customer or coerced money from someone. Because he'd been too damned persistent on a case that hadn't been assigned to him, Court no longer hunted murderers. It was some consolation to reflect that he would be stopping a predator. A man who gave false hope to the desperate was the lowest sort of scum.

He would maintain his cover so he could continue to interact with the spiritualist. Soon enough the false medium would be arrested, ending another shameful career.

Marsh paused and frowned some more, belaboring the effort it took to reach through the mists of time and space to reach the dead. "This spirit seems to feel your young man is not all he has represented himself to be. I'm getting two messages from her, a sense of deep love for you and a clear warning, but nothing more specific."

Court had tracked another medium a few years earlier—that one had stolen works of art during weekend parties—and he'd been to enough séances now to know the routine. At this point, the medium usually snapped out of his or her trance, making a great show of weariness, and would leave the table. The excited guests would break for refreshments as they pondered his great spiritual gift and discussed the messages. In Court's opinion, there was more thrill-seeking than actual spiritual resonance about these affairs.

But tonight the medium didn't immediately open those long-lashed eyes. Instead, he held very still, and his face turned markedly pale. He caught his breath before he spoke again, and when he did, his voice was low and rasping, scraping up Court's spine like a file. "There is another presence."

Their hostess and fervent spiritualist, Lady Markham, was beside herself with excitement at the prospect of more messages from beyond. "Are you all right, Mr. Marsh?"

"Oh God." Marsh grimaced as though in pain. "She is… She needs…" he stammered.

"Who? Do you have a name?" Lady Markham murmured, anxious not to break the medium's concentration at this delicate moment.

"A flower. White. Not a daisy. She's"—Marsh caught his breath and exhaled a name—"Lily."

Court felt like someone had driven a fist into his stomach. Lily. The image of his cousin's face came to him. God, he wished he could see a picture of Lily laughing, but no, he saw the moment of her death. Every detail from the blood oozing from the back of her head, to the anguish in her eyes just before they closed for the last time—he bit down on the inside of his cheek to stop himself seeing the rest. God damn Marsh.

"The man scared her. He said she'll join the others." Marsh's voice was anguished and his expression contorted. It was quite a performance, and Court was having a hard time keeping his dyspeptic stomach from lurching. The medium must know he was a police inspector and his true purpose in attending the séance. But how had Marsh found out about Lily?

Marsh choked on a sob. "She's looking at Robert."

"Robert Littleton?" Lady Markham looked at the white-haired gentleman seated across the table from her.

"Not I, madam." Littleton's handlebar moustache twitched as he spoke. "There's never been a woman named Lily in my life."

Robert Court stirred uneasily. He hadn't given his first name when he'd contacted Lady Markham about her interesting new protégé; he'd simply called himself Mr. Peeler, the name he often used for this sort of work.

What was Marsh's goal? What did he hope to achieve by baiting him? Court wanted to let go of the sweaty palm of the man named Abernathy on his left and Miss Fontaine's slender hand on his right to jump up and walk away from the table, but he mustn't react to Marsh's words. He couldn't let any of them know who he truly was, and they *would* interrogate him if they thought the pronouncement from beyond held meaning for him.

"He said there were others," the medium's desolate voice continued. "Murder. Murder."

"Oh my goodness." The elderly woman beside Miss Fontaine broke the circle and reached for her handkerchief to dab at her forehead. "This is too much, Lady Markham. Entirely too much. I don't wish to participate any longer."

"Shh, Marjorie," their hostess said. "A murderer's identity may be revealed here tonight.

What greater purpose could there be for these gatherings than to bring about truth and justice?" Diamonds flashed in Lady Markham's ears, matching the sparkle in her eyes. Her ladyship was the type of woman who wore jewels even for an informal gathering with friends, overdressed and with too much time on her idle hands, but a caring person at heart, Court believed. She'd be appalled to learn she was the reason her good friend Mr. Marsh had come under the gaze of the authorities.

The relatively minor case of a spiritual medium had been handed to the serious-crimes officer because Marsh had begun to bilk the wealthy. Lord Markham disliked having his wife throw money at Marsh and had complained to Sir Bradford, the commissioner.

"Carry on, Mr. Marsh," Lady Markham said. "What else does Lily say?"

Court studied the medium's face, noting how his eyes darted back and forth beneath the lids. He was quite an actor, with a full arsenal of emotions in his quiver. Tears leaked from the corners of his closed eyes and rolled down his cheeks. Court watched in fascination as they dripped off that smooth-shaven jaw onto his crisp white shirt collar and felt a ridiculous urge to lean forward and wipe away the tears.

It's all a sham, he reminded himself. *Bits of facts stitched together with fancy.* A swindler was adept at learning everything about the people he planned to cheat and then striking them at their Achilles' heel. How Marsh had learned about the Lily Bailey case was all that mattered.

"He was stronger than I imagined. I didn't listen to you about being careful, dear. I should have listened to you. Oh, Phillip," Marsh whispered the words.

Court felt another blow to his gut, for only he had heard those words after he'd been summoned to the scene by the constable. She'd returned to consciousness for a few heartbeats, whispered the few garbled phrases, just as roughly as Marsh had, and no one else had been within hearing distance. Another thought came to him—there might be a simple explanation why Marsh might have been lurking so close. He could be the murderer.

Printed in Great Britain
by Amazon